PRIMAL SIN

ARIANA NASH

Primal Sin

Ariana Nash - *Dark Fantasy Author*

Subscribe to Ariana's mailing list & get the exclusive story 'Sealed with a Kiss' free.

Join the Ariana Nash Facebook group for all the news, as it happens.

Copyright © 2020 Ariana Nash

Cover Design by Covers by Combs

Edited by Rascon Revisions

ANTI-PIRACY WARNING

Long ago, a demon stole an angel's heart. He did not think the angel would miss his heart, because angels do not feel. But the demon was wrong. Without his heart, the angel became a monster. Where before, there had been compassion and trust in the angel, now he was hollow and hungry for vengeance.

The story of the demon who stole an angel's heart does not have a happy ending. If you steal ebooks, neither will you.

Warning: The unauthorized reproduction or distribution of this copyrighted work is illegal. Criminal copyright infringement, including infringement without monetary gain, is investigated by the FBI and is punishable by up to five years in federal prison and a fine of $250,000.

CHAPTER 1

*S*evern

ONE OF THE few remaining guardian angels in all of Aerie stood at the end of the long glass table speaking of war, of sacrifice, and of duty. These things were the pillars upon which the vast city of Aerie stood. The guardian, Mikhail, went on addressing his eager audience of angels, their faces turned toward him, doe-eyed in awe. They'd all conveniently forgotten how their city was built on a foundation of bone.

Severn, seated to Mikhail's right, hadn't forgotten. Although, some days and nights, he wished he could.

He only half listened to the rallying words, pretending to contemplate the battle to come. In truth, he contemplated only one thing: how he would take Mikhail's wings, cutting them clean off with two great arcs of his blade. The first strike would be quick, the second more difficult.

Severn would keep those severed appendages and hang them on the wall somewhere once all this was over. Of course, Mikhail would fight to his last breath, and Severn would take that from him too—take *everything*.

Mikhail held his silvery gray wings loosely clamped, their arches towering above his already impressive height. Long, dark hair lay like black silk over his shoulders and down his bare chest. The ends gently curled, licking against defined abdominal muscles. He appeared to be no older than a few decades, like most angels around the table, but appearances in Aerie were deceiving, and angels didn't wear their age on their skin.

Mikhail's lethal beauty was also a weapon. He was so fucking pretty even his enemies would do him, then try and kill him afterward. What did angel taste like?

"...I'll expect of you, Severn."

Mikhail's rumbling tone summoned Severn back from his blood-soaked fantasy into the too-bright war chambers. Sunlight glanced off toughened glass and immovable steel, making the room and the angels within dazzle.

He straightened beneath the weight of a dozen gazes, each expecting a response. "Of course, Your Grace." He bowed his head. "My information is faultless. We cannot fail." The answer was the typical reassurance Mikhail always sought from him. Severn delivered it with smooth perfection.

Mikhail's hand landed on Severn's shoulder. His thick fingers dug in and squeezed, and the angel's smile grew. Modern myths told of how Mikhail's smile had brought a demon army to its knees, each soldier weeping tears of love. Severn knew the truth of the day that spawned that story. The demons had wept, but not from love. They'd all perished, watching their wings twist and crumble to ash on countless pyres.

The angel's grip on his shoulder delivered a sharp snap of invasive power, forcing him to grit his teeth.

"It all hinges on you, my friend."

Maybe Mikhail's smile was genuine. Severn could only hope. If the angel was capable of feeling anything at all, it would make what was to come so much more satisfying. Severn returned a well-practiced example of his own smile, and Mikhail released his iron grip.

"Prepare for battle," Mikhail commanded, freeing the angels from their seats. Severn stood with the others and thumped a fist to his chest in unison with them. He turned to leave when Mikhail's fingers snagged his wrist.

The touch sizzled, sparking a strange array of sensations through Severn, the prominent one being the urge to shake the angel off and draw his sword. His heart stuttered, falling into a faster rhythm, his body fighting to remain calm outwardly. Touch was dangerous, especially from Mikhail.

"A moment?" the guardian asked.

Severn nodded, relieved when Mikhail freed his wrist. He watched the others leave the chamber, envious of their escape. Although they had their wings illusioned away, they each carried that same air of power and arrogance in their stride. Severn appeared the same to them, perhaps more so because of his position at Mikhail's side. He'd worked to make it so, to make them believe his lies. They didn't even know he'd lost his wings to the vicious male standing behind him. Nobody here knew Severn. And the time had almost come for the deception to pay off.

The tall door—built high to accommodate wings—

clunked closed, sealing Severn alone with Mikhail. The silence was a hungry void, one demanding Severn shatter it. His fingers twitched at his sides. Power writhed beneath his skin, like a thing alive with its own mind, and it wanted out of this room, away from his enemy.

His heart thumped too loudly. So loudly, Mikhail must have heard, but the angel turned away, presenting Severn with a wall of pristine feathers.

A sudden memory launched itself through Severn's mind. Barely more than a pup, decades ago now, his friend Samiel had dared him to steal an angel's feather. A joke. Such things were impossible in those times. Samiel had laughed, taken Severn's hand, and they'd run together through London's old streets, over cobblestones and through the ruins of previous wars, but Severn had never forgotten Samiel's request. Then, when they were both grown, the war claimed their service, like it did so many. After one brutal battle, in the killing field strewn with dead, Severn had found an angel's feather among the cawing rayverns pecking at the carcasses. He'd plucked it from the quagmire, finding it almost perfectly clean. His smile had cracked the mud and blood caked on his face, and he'd taken his prize back to Samiel, just like he'd joked all those years ago. But Samiel hadn't returned after that battle, and none thereafter. His bones, like so many others, forever lay buried in mud.

Severn had kept that feather, so very like Mikhail's. Still had it today.

"We have a spy among our forces," Mikhail said.

Severn's fingers twitched again, this time itching to grab at the blade resting against his back and swing it with the full force of his vengeance.

"Her name is Cassandra." Mikhail lifted his head, sending his gaze far out the balcony doors into the sun-drenched blue skies. "She has quietly picked apart my bonds and threaded herself within my ranks. I am... I regret I did not see it sooner." He looked over, and for the briefest of moments, regret did soften the angel's gaze before his frown corrected it. He straightened, his face determined again. "Remove her from our ranks, Severn."

"Do you have evidence of her betrayal?" His voice showed no sign of his internal wrangling. His lies remained faultless.

He knew of Cassandra, had seen her among the warrior ranks but not in battle. Nothing about her had seemed remarkable, which likely meant she was good at subversion, if that was indeed her role.

"A trusted source informed me," Mikhail said. "It is evidence enough."

Severn nodded and vowed to discover who his trusted source was so he could avoid them. "I'll see it dealt with." He turned on his heels and retreated toward the door, pulling his twitching fingers in against his chest to keep Mikhail from seeing. The touches had cost him. He'd waited too long between feasts. This meeting was unscheduled, and the days and nights leading up to these final moments had been long and arduous. No time to feast, to sate himself, to recharge—

"Severn..."

"Yes, Your Grace?" So close. The door was only a few strides away. But now, as he turned back, Mikhail approached, bringing with him the suffocating weight of his power. He seemed impossible, this world-ending angel, like a creature made from dreams and nightmares crafted into his final male form, framed by velvet, storm-touched wings. Every stride had purpose. The cut of his unblinking gaze landed deeply, like it stripped Severn of all the lies and saw everything he fought day and night to hide. Severn's heart raced again. None were immune to Mikhail, although many tried to be. They all paid with their wings.

Mikhail stopped close. Seconds felt like hours. Too long a gaze would issue a challenge but too short made Severn appear weak, and he'd never been that. Not now, not then, not ever. Slowly, he closed his eyes and dropped his head.

Mikhail's touch suddenly stroking down his jawline crackled with yet more power. "I can trust you in this?" the angel asked.

The touch warmed like it had around Severn's wrist and sparked awake other sensations. Sensations that had been grossly neglected for too long. This was what happened when Severn forgot who and what he was, and it had been happening more of late. He could not afford such mistakes now.

"Keep it... between us," Mikhail said, his voice a soft, intimate whisper. "The others need not know."

Severn's blank expression twitched. Oh how he despised this monster and dreamed night after night of killing him in all ways, but he too was not immune to Mikhail's power or the starved reach of Severn's own ability.

Keeping his eyes closed and his head down, he funneled his thoughts away from how Mikhail stroked his jaw and of how that simple touch felt like something he could pull inside him and devour and poured it all into maintaining his illusion. An illusion built on lies, built on bones, and made stronger with every battle won.

"Look at me." Mikhail's voice smoldered and crept around Severn's defenses.

He could do this.

He'd been doing this for what felt like forever. Sometimes it felt as though he'd lived a lie longer than he'd lived the truth.

Lifting his head, the full weight of Mikhail's powerful gaze fell over him in a wave of pleasure and heat, making him want to fall into the male's arms and confess all his terrible truths. Locking his jaw, he smiled at the angel trying to drown him in righteousness. He didn't look like a mass murderer, but having fought beside him for almost a decade, Severn knew a killer was exactly what he was.

"Will you serve me forever, Severn?" Mikhail asked as though doubting Severn, but it was himself he doubted. Few saw these moments of vulnerability. To see such moments now was a testament to how far Severn had come.

"Always," Severn breathed. Mikhail would read the shudder as one of respect, not exhaustion.

Mikhail stroked his fingers down Severn's cheek and traced their tips across Severn's lips. "Soon, they'll all be dead, and we can rest."

"Soon," Severn whispered, afraid the strain of anything more would wreck his voice.

"Find Cassandra." Mikhail tore himself away, moving so swiftly that Severn rocked on his feet. "We leave for the frontline at dawn."

Severn stumbled against the door but hid the misstep by pulling it open and falling into a march away from the chamber and from Mikhail. Breathing too hard, he passed others, all watching and wondering why Mikhail had singled him out. They knew Severn was trusted, they'd seen him in battle, seen him protect their leader with his own life. None doubted him; he'd made damn sure of it.

But making lies true took great power, and as Severn walked the upper hallways, weaving his way through glass corridors toward his own chambers, every step felt a little heavier, and every beat of his heart thudded harder. Those last moments beneath Mikhail's scrutiny had cost him. Maybe too much. He could not fail now. He just needed... space. He needed to get out of Aerie, to get away from the light.

One misstep would be forgiven, but two, three? No. He was Mikhail's most revered soldier. The most powerful angel in Aerie besides Mikhail himself. He did not make mistakes.

The glass walls blurred, and the door ahead spawned copies of itself. Severn blindly reached out and shoved through, stumbling inside his chamber. The door swung closed, and he fell against it, holding the lies behind him. *Too close.* The tremors migrated from his fingers, up his arms, and traveled down his back. He just needed... something he couldn't have. Not here. Later... Yes, later. He'd don a cloak and descend through the bowels of Aerie to the cauldron, and there, he'd get his fix. He looked to the open balcony, checking dusk's progress. Once darkness fell, he could prepare...

A breeze stirred the balcony drapes around a female figure. Had she always been there? He rubbed at his eyes, hoping to sweep her visage away, but instead of vanishing, she started forward, taking shape inside Severn's shifting focus.

Blue eyes scorched his soul. Blond hair blazed. An angel.

Cassandra.

Destiny had delivered her to him.

She smiled and lifted her steel angelblade, a broadsword almost as long as she was tall.

"Severn." Cassandra's dark-feathered wings peeled open, framing her warrior's physique and filling Severn's chamber lounge area nearly from wall to wall. Her sword caught the reddish dusklight, slicing that light across Severn's face. "I am here to cut the wings from your back and present them to Mikhail as evidence of your treachery." She delivered the lines with absolute conviction, showing no signs of fear—and why would she fear him? She had righteousness on her side.

Severn hid the surprise of her words behind a sigh. "You're too late." He was weak, but not weak enough to be bested by yet another angel with a hero complex.

He stepped forward. "Mikhail already took my wings." Confusion muddied her striking face. Why would an angel take another angel's wings? They wouldn't. Then something solidified in her mind, and a new determination lent her stance more strength.

"It's true then?" she asked. "You are a traitor?"

Clearly, she knew enough that she could not be left alive. Severn drew his sword from its sheath. "He took my wings, but I'll gladly line my bed with yours."

CHAPTER 2

Whoever had fed Mikhail the information that Cassandra was a spy had lied. Cassandra was no more a traitor than Severn was an angel. It seemed there was a person of interest among Mikhail's ranks, someone Severn would root out later, after this inconvenience was dealt with.

Cassandra used both hands to grip her sword and circled, one step crossing the other, keeping Severn firmly in front of her. She was angel through and through. Severn saw it in her eyes, her stance, and of course, her shimmering wings. She was devout and a damn good soldier. It was almost a shame to kill her.

"Lay down your sword and die with dignity," she said.

Chuckling, he rolled his shoulders, shaking out the dregs of exhaustion and pulling on his dangerously low power reserves. "Dignity?" She spoke of dignity as though she were its judge. The dead didn't get to demand dignity. "Fly away, angel, and live another day to fight for your beloved Mikhail." The moment she turned her back, he'd slice through it. Her glare said she knew as much.

True power drove strength through Severn's veins. If he'd had wings, he'd have flared them wide, scars and all. But now all he had was his wits and his blade, and both were sharper than Cassandra's. Because while she thought she knew the real him beneath his angel-skin, she still didn't believe it. Not really.

"Why do you visit the cambions?"

Severn snorted a dry laugh and kept circling with his blade pointed downward. Angels. So naïve. "Clearly, you have never tasted cambion flesh. So sweet and warm beneath the tongue." Severn hadn't, not recently. But the words had their desired effect.

Disgust made her wings shimmer. She retracted them, so his debased suggestion couldn't touch her exquisite perfection. *"You are no angel!"*

Now she was catching on.

"What *are* you?"

Even now, she refused to see the truth. Severn strengthened his two-handed grip on his sword. It was a true angelblade, stolen from a dying angel. It had fit perfectly in his hand the moment he'd pulled it from the mud of the killing fields, and he'd known then that destiny had another path for him.

They'd circled around so that Severn blocked Cassandra's easiest flight-route off the balcony. Her glance over his shoulder told him she knew, but she wasn't concerned. She should have been. He hadn't risen to Mikhail's side by lies alone. He'd have killed every last angel to get to the top. It just so happened lies were easier.

"How could you betray him?" she demanded.

The irony of the question stole his breath in a broken laugh, and then he lunged.

Her blade came up, blocking his with a teeth-jarring crash of metal on metal, but he'd already seen her broadcast the move and had angled his sword's edge to slide down hers, striking the guard and bouncing off. She whirled, shying away from the attack, yanking her wings back, using their great weight to counterbalance the heaviness of the blade. She was a story of violence in motion. As a pup, when he'd watched the battles rage in the skies, he'd once thought the angels beautiful, until he'd grown enough to know that when angels shone, demons died.

Her blade sang, coming at him in a thrust he narrowly avoided. The edge whispered past his shoulder. He jerked his sword's pummel up under her chin, slamming her head back. She reeled. And he kept on swinging, crashing into her every parry, driving her back.

Blades rang. She danced lightly on her feet, but in the confines of his chamber, she had nowhere to go, and that was her mistake. Her wings touched the walls. She thrust her sword at him and roared, pouring all of her power and strength into a lunge Severn saw coming the moment this battle began. He twisted to the side, unhindered by wings. Cassandra overbalanced, stumbled forward—

Severn pivoted. The edge of his angelblade cut through sinew, muscle, and bone, slicing her right wing off in one savage strike. Grief made her wail. It was only now, fallen to her knees, she understood her enemy.

The severed wing thumped to the floor, twitching and useless. Blood soaked down her back, and a snarl pulled at Severn's gritted smile to see that blood, so bright. He kicked her in the back and pinned his boot against her spine, holding her against the floor.

The second blow severed her remaining wing. Her scream shattered, her voice breaking apart, just like the rest of her. She saw her detached appendages and grasped at the feathers, as though she could somehow collect the pieces and put herself back together again.

Severn kicked the wings from her reach and circled around to face her tear-stained face. Agony made her ugly. Without her wings, she was nothing, just a feeble thing kneeling in a pool of blood.

"*Why?*" Her nails dug into the polished marble floor.

He caught her chin in his left hand and leaned close. The sparkle of her eyes had snuffed out. She'd die a slow, painful death without her wings. Long ago, Mikhail had assumed the same of Severn, and that mistake would eventually cost the angels everything.

"Why are you doing this?" she whispered. "Why do you hate us?"

A smile crawled across Severn's lips. A real smile, part of his true self leaking through, but still Cassandra refused to see. Maybe she wasn't capable. He breathed in her sparkling scent, tasting the crackle of fear, and brushed his jaw against her feather-soft cheek, then whispered the truth into her ear. His name. A name he'd dared not speak in ten years. It was freeing really, to speak the truth he'd so long clung to, keeping it chained inside himself.

"*No...*" she gasped, and the last bright spark of hope faded from her eyes.

He let her look into his eyes, really look, and finally, she saw him beneath the lies. And she understood it all.

"I will be the end of all of you." Sinking his hand into

her hair, he heaved her toward the balcony's edge. She twisted and kicked and grabbed at his grip. He'd killed many before, but those kills were quick, brutal. Necessary. This was... This tasted like vengeance. Anticipation whispered around him, arousing all the parts he kept hidden.

At the balcony's edge, the wind tossed his golden hair and cooled his face. He'd always avoided the edge, knowing his end was just beyond it. But he'd risk it now, for this, for her. She looked up at him, her hands clasped at his wrists, her eyes begging, pleading. She'd been a good soldier. Faithful. True.

"Don't..." she whispered.

She'd likely lived a dozen human lifetimes, seen the rise of Aerie above London's dark streets, but she would not be alive to see Aerie's fall.

He yanked her to her feet, his own muscles burning from the strain he'd already placed on his body. Just one last act and he could feed. Breathing in sweet air, he admired the red-tinged dusklight in the angel's golden hair and listened to the wind. It had been so long since he'd answered its call.

Aerie was built high above the clouds, where the air was thin and the view a never-ending wash of blue or red or black, taunting him with its inviting expanse. For so long, he'd hated it, like he hated everything else, but here, on its edge, he saw the beauty in that endless nothing.

Thrusting his arm out, he held Cassandra aloft, dangling over nothing. She didn't fight. They were beyond that.

"Please... Do not hurt him." Tears sparkled on her cheeks.

He let go.

She didn't scream. He'd thought she might. Leaning over the edge, he watched her fall, her arms spread. Even in death, angels were self-righteous. The red-touched clouds swallowed her, and she was gone. He waited, counting down the seconds until enough time had passed for him to be sure she'd met her end. London's horizon of jagged spires invited a quick death to any who fell from Aerie. That was all the mercy he cared to give.

Retreating from the edge, he made it inside moments before exhaustion racked him, dropping him to his knees. The angel's severed wings lay discarded on the floor around him. Two gruesome trophies. He'd present them to Mikhail, and maybe the guardian would let him see the others in his collection. But all of that must come later. He was too weak for this, for anything, and savagely vulnerable.

He stumbled about his chambers, set the sword down, and dug out a dark, hooded cloak, tossing it around his shoulders. His tingling fingers fumbled the neck button once, twice. He'd waited too long. If any of the angels saw him, if Mikhail saw him... They wouldn't. The night before battle they were all preoccupied. Besides, if any saw him, they'd assume he had everything perfectly under control, like always.

Dusklight crept through the windows, drawing long shadows across the floor, chasing daylight from the motionless wings. He brushed off his strange sense of grief and left.

~

WHILE AERIE SAT POISED GRACEFULLY above the clouds,

its series of disks supporting an entire city of angels, its enormous pillar foundations were firmly rooted in what had once been London's square mile—the great city's bustling commercial center. Angels considered Aerie to be their pinnacle, a story in glass and steel of how they had broken free from the filth at their feet and risen above it all.

Severn hunched in the corner of one of Aerie's vast service elevators, hidden among the crates, mostly unnoticed. Those who did see him were paid to look the other way. A dangerous ruse, but necessary. Aerie's thousands of nephilim—half human, half angel—staff were easily swayed with small, gifted angel trinkets or tokens. Like rayverns, they loved anything that sparkled, and Aerie was full of shiny shit.

Severn's heart thumped a countdown to his fix.

The dry mouth and fuzzy thoughts were the least of his concerns. If he drew too much attention by stumbling about, he'd soon find himself spirited away to a correction facility. He'd rather throw himself off a balcony than end up behind those bars.

The doors rumbled open, and he stumbled out, clinging to a crate for the first few steps before peeling off into the shadows. The air smelled hot and sweet, like rot and too many bodies, which was no surprise, as these old London streets, in the area known as the *cauldron,* were crammed with refugees. Their shanty homes all huddled close to Aerie's vast foundations. It was dark too. So dark, sometimes he tasted its kiss. The sun didn't shine beneath Aerie.

His boots splashed through oily puddles, making reflected neon lights ripple. The crowd enveloped him in movement and touch and smell and sight. His senses buzzed awake, suddenly stimulated after too long in the clean brightness of Aerie. Another time he might have appreciated it more. He'd always fucking loved the cauldron for its chaos, but not tonight.

All the bright, flashing signs taunted. Streets down here ran vertical as well as horizontal. Footbridges spanned the narrow gaps above, like silken webs in forgotten crevices. The mess to Aerie's order. Naturally, Mikhail hated it, and so, of course, all angels hated it. They didn't know what they were missing.

He veered down a familiar side street, hoping it was the correct one, looking for the blinking red light that would guide him to oblivion.

An old crone loomed from the dark, a bowl in her liver-spotted, gnarled hands. "A token for pleasures... Just a token, and I'll make your dreams come true..."

In his eagerness to avoid her, he fell against the wall and grabbed at his hood, hiding his face.

"A token, and I'll make you *come*." She thrust the bowl under his nose and grabbed his balls with her free hand, her strength twice that of the withered old crone she appeared to be. The sudden physical contact sent a lightning strike of lust up his spine, tearing down all the barriers he'd erected.

"Fuck off," he grunted, slapping the hand on his balls away, keeping his hood down and face hidden.

She laughed, and in the space of a few blinks, her withered old hands smoothed to perfectly clear, young skin. Her face tightened, making all her age-lines disappear. Thick dark hair ate her mop of silvery tendrils and fell over her shoulders. She smiled glossy, scarlet lips. Her tongue poked out, its forked tips flicking, tasting. A cambion—half human, half demon.

"Hmm..." she purred, thrusting her artificial face in his and breathing deeply, "Ah, don't like this one either, eh?" Her jaw squared off, the twisting illusion making Severn's head throb. Her hair shortened, and her lips thinned, and now she was gorgeously male. Their forked tongue licked up Severn's cheek, warm and wet and strong, an advertisement for the pleasures their tongue could twist from him. "Hmm, now he's hungry, yes?"

A dangerous shudder awoke parts the earlier fight had already aroused. The cambion's scent tingled Severn's nose and laced his throat, trying to convince him he really did want to fuck them against the wall, and if he let that scent work its magic long enough, there'd be no fighting it, not in his weakened state. Mistakes like this were exactly why he couldn't afford to abstain. He should have known better, should have *been* better.

He grabbed their face in one hand and shoved hard, throwing them backward. They flailed and toppled into their flimsy hut, spilling a verbal tirade of cambion, loosely translated as, *"I hope your dick shrivels and you die unsatisfied!"*

"Yeah, yeah... You and me both." He staggered on, looking for the illuminated Infinity sign. If he didn't find the club soon, he might even have to return to the crone and pay them to perform for him. It wouldn't be enough, but it would top him up, allowing him to keep his wits.

He could just rest a while, just lean against the wall and close his eyes. Nothing would change. The weight of destiny wasn't going to forget him. He couldn't stop. Couldn't go back. There was only moving forward. Until tomorrow. Until he was free.

A flicker of red caught his eye, and there, the Infinity logo buzzed and blinked. Already painfully aroused, his skin sizzled with the thought of what was to come. The straining erection would prove more difficult to ignore, but that would soon pass. Physical gratification was off-limits, but mental... oh, he could drink that down until dawn. The thought alone had him salivating.

"Good evening, Anon." A gentle hand, skin tinged purple, found his and led him through the doorway, soaking both him and the demon known as the madam in red from the sign above. "We did wonder when or even if you might return." Her smooth voice stroked against his primal needs. He knew the voice. He was safe... mostly. "It has been some time, no?"

He spared a grunt in reply, aware deep inside that he was a fucking disgrace to his race but far beyond expressing much of anything on the outside.

"Take a seat." The hands gently eased him into a large armchair, cradling his tired body. The same hands roamed back up both arms and down his chest, rising and falling with each ragged breath. He'd been so long without physical touch, it hurt, but he ached for more. The firm, warm hands took liberties by sliding over his thighs. Glossy black nails, so like claws, dug in. His cock jumped in response, desperately needy, like the rest of him, and the hand found its straining length through his trouser fabric. Pleasure was a sudden, blinding force, threatening to pull on his thin thread of control and utterly unravel him.

He had her neck in both hands before realizing he'd moved. A little more pressure and her smooth neck would snap.

Lust rode him hard, making everything bright and

sharp, overstimulating his starved brain and body. "Don't fucking touch me. Ever." He shoved her back, like he'd shoved the wretched crone away.

She straightened, but instead of taking offense, she stroked her long fingers down her neck and tilted her head back. Light traced the curve of her two black horns. Severn's foggy gaze tracked the movement of her hands, snagging on how curls of hazy smoke peeled off her skin. That smoke, invisible to most, was the elixir every cell in his body craved. Seeing it after starving himself for so long almost doubled him over in pain.

"Fuck..." He slumped forward, folding around the agony. "Get on with it." He threw himself back in the armchair, tugging the hood back down to shadow his face as his body raged.

He wasn't meant to be like this, and that was the problem.

"Hm," the madam purred, seeing too much with her yellow eyes. She raised her hand and clicked her fingers. Two males entered the room, one blond, one with copper hair and a splash of freckles. Both ridiculously attractive thanks to their angel heritage. Some part of him registered their rumbling voices but didn't care enough to decipher the words. They spoke nephilim, a language halfway to angel and half in the gutter, like him.

The trio wasted no time in embracing, the madam pressed between the two males. Tongues tasted and explored, hands stroked, fingers peeled off thin layers of clothing, and Severn's sharpening gaze tracked it all. Smokey tendrils lifted off the madam's glistening skin, soaking the air around them, mingling with the same haze seeping from the males.

He could almost taste it, feel it setting ablaze his every nerve ending like fireworks.

The three writhed. The blond's erection, trapped behind his thin pant fabric, had found the valley of the madam's ass, and as he mouthed a wet trail of kisses down her neck, his hips rocked, driving his cock against the tightness between her ass cheeks. The ether around him swelled, scenting the air. Severn parted his lips, inviting it over his tongue, aching to taste the nephilim's sweet arousal.

When the ether hit, Severn's spine locked. His fingers hooked into the chair's arms. If he could have crawled from his own skin and drank the desire from its source, he would have. But the chair was his sanctuary, there could be no moving from it, no engaging in their act.

All good things come to those who wait...

The redheaded male reached beyond the female demon, stroked the blond's arm, alerting him to his position, and pulled him into a hungry kiss. Their ether beat outward in waves. All three pulsed with smoke, filling the room with its intoxicating spell.

Severn dropped his head back, slowly opening his senses to all of it. Too fast and he'd black out. Power poured under his skin, lifting him up, filling him. He gorged on their pleasure, feasting on their mindless ecstasy, and as they lost themselves in the frenzy, he fell with them, drinking down their primal desires. He barely registered how they fucked—whose cock entered whose hole—just that they did, and they *wanted* it. That was key. Forced pleasure was almost worthless. The freely given kind was the difference between cold starlight and the blazing sun. Lust was easier to harvest, but joy and violence also worked. Joy was in short supply these days, but sex in the cauldron was abundant.

The trio climbed to their peak, mindlessly thrusting and grunting in their pursuit of that cresting break, and when they came in unison, spilling their seed, nerves twitching, pleasure rode Severn so hard he barely contained his own cry, keeping it caged behind gritted teeth.

Momentarily sated, the trio parted. The two males paired off and crawled onto a bed Severn had been too lost to notice when he'd arrived. He saw everything now. The peeling paint, the claw marks above the bedstead, the rivulet of cum dribbling down the demon's thigh. She stroked the wetness onto her fingers and licked it clean. "Enough for you, Anon?"

"Nowhere near." The words came out harsher than they should have. Their fucking had taken the edge off his needs, but his reserves had been too low to begin with. "More." Jerking his chin at the males, he added, "Only them."

"Of course," the madam purred, moving to his side. "But now you're more coherent, there's the matter of payment to discuss. More will cost more."

"You know I'm good for it."

"Not tokens. Not from you," she leaned in, whispering, "*angel.*"

He tore his eyes off the pair of males and lifted his gaze. The madam loomed over him. He hadn't wasted much time studying her before, he'd always been half starved on arrival, and she'd never failed to be more than eager in satisfying his needs, but he looked at her now— really looked. Her age was difficult to determine. After reaching maturity, sometime in their twentieth cycle, any outward aging ceased in pure demons, unless they wanted to appear ragged, as some did. Her purple skin was smooth, her jaw square enough to pass for male at a glance, but female on closer inspection. The clothing, if straps of cloth could be called clothing, wrapped around her torso, beneath her breasts, crossed her back, and looped around each thigh. Short black horns spiraled from her head. The fact she wasn't attempting to hide her demon heritage in the cauldron—so close to Aerie—said a great deal about the madam. She was either ridiculously reckless or insanely brave or both.

The madam arched a brow and flicked her long fingers. "Did you really believe a cloak would hide what you are?"

He hadn't, not really, but in the beginning, they'd all needed the cloak to pretend what was happening was perfectly legal.

Seeing the concern on his face, she added, keeping her voice low, "Don't worry, you're not the first angel to seek my services. If I'd wanted to alert the correctioners, I'd have done so after your first visit, no?" Reaching up with her hand, she almost touched his face but pulled her fingers back before making contact. A moment stretched between them. She tilted her head, examining the invisible line he'd drawn and whether it was worth crossing. "I've always wondered what angel cock tastes like."

Then she'd be sorely disappointed in his. "Keep wondering."

Chuckling, she finally straightened and draped herself over the corner of his chair. "You have our discretion, at great risk to our operation. So, I must ask for something in return."

The fact other angels had been serviced among the cambion was interesting. Angels didn't experience many emotions, didn't feel much at all, and none were supposed to be sexually active, making Aerie a desert to the likes of Severn. He'd revisit her interesting fact later. If he had a later. In a decade, he hadn't thought much beyond tomorrow's battle.

His gaze found its way back to the pair on the bed, their limbs now as tangled as their tongues, ether rising off their damp skin, drenching the air. His mouth watered. It wasn't just sex for the pair of nephilim. They were deeply attracted to each other. Emotions like theirs were rare and fucking delicious. "Name your price."

She watched them too, although she'd seen the pair perform time and time again. Still, the glint in her eye told him she could appreciate the art in their coupling. "A feather. Easy enough for you. One from your own wings will suffice."

Easier said than done when his wings were lost. Besides, his had never had feathers. "Fine." He had access to a single feather. One close to his heart, the same one he'd hoped to give to Samiel. What had he saved it for if not the night before the final battle? This feast would make him strong, and tomorrow he'd make Mikhail pay. "Why do you want it?"

She smiled, revealing jagged, triangular teeth. "Do you really want to know?"

Want to, yes. Need to? No. It was just a feather, and in paying for this, it could serve him like the memory of plucking it off the battlefield never had.

He flicked open his shirt buttons, drawing the madam's gaze to his chest. Demons and angels getting up close and personal was exactly the kind of behavior that would get them both thrown in the correctional. She wasn't his type, but from her erect nipples and dilated pupils, he was certainly hers. "Don't get excited," he purred, feeling his lips tick into a small smile. After Aerie, all desire put a smile on his face, even the misplaced kind. "These goods are off-limits."

"You've made that perfectly clear."

The feather, when he produced it, had grayed with age and long ago lost its glittering sheen. The fronds drooped. Some were kinked and broken. As angel feathers went, it was a sorry specimen.

The madam frowned.

"You didn't say what condition you wanted it in."

A brief flicker of annoyance sharpened her pupils, and then she snatched up the feather and brought it to her nose, breathing deeply. "Mm, smells as sweet as you, Anon. Yours?"

He shrugged, letting her think what she wanted.

She tucked the feather behind the cloth strap wrapped around her torso and clicked her fingers, making the two nephilim come up for air. "Give him a show he'll not soon forget."

As she left the room, the two nephilim fixed Severn in their golden-eyed gaze, marking him as their target. Anticipation had Severn salivating all over again. The blond crooked a finger and licked his lips, inviting Severn to play. Heat and pressure had Severn's cock throbbing its want. Maybe if he survived tomorrow, he'd take them up on that offer, feast and fuck them into puddles of their own bodily fluids. Although, if they knew who and what he was, they'd likely rescind their invitation.

He jerked his chin and settled back into the chair, digging his fingers in again, rooting him in place. The nephilim weren't dangerous, not to him. If they knew how dangerous he was to them, they'd likely weep on their knees or run screaming. The madam certainly wouldn't have left him alone with her two precious gems.

"Proceed."

Proceed, they did. Performing in all the right ways, again and again, and Severn drank their ether down, panting out excess power as dawn approached. Nephilim always tasted good, it had to be the angel in them. Severn hadn't had pedigree angel to know for sure, but nephilim rarely tasted *this* good. It was a sign, he decided, his mind far away as his body gorged, a sign that at dawn, he'd fulfill destiny. Nothing could stop him, not even Mikhail.

Fingers grabbed at his arm. Instincts snapped, launching him from the chair, the madam's neck ringed beneath his hands. The nephilim pair let out near-identical screams, scrambled off the bed, and clutched at each other in the periphery of Severn's heightened vision. They weren't the threat, but the madam pinned to the bed beneath him was a heartbeat away from having her heart ripped out of her chest.

"I said... don't fucking touch me..." His voice sounded wrong to his angel-attuned ears, like he'd picked up pieces of something resembling a smoother, rumbling voice and forced those jagged pieces together. From the madam's widening eyes, she heard the slip too.

Fuck. He couldn't come back here again.

But he wouldn't have to.

At dawn, it was over.

At dawn, after a decade, he could discard this wretched shell.

Why the fuck had she touched him?

A cruel smile curved his mouth. He deliberately pressed his thigh and hips against the madam's and brought his mouth close to her neck before taking a deep, soul-plunging breath. Painfully aroused, brimming with power, he could fuck this demon, ruin her mind, strip her down to her basal needs, turning her more animal than demon, and she'd beg him to do it again and again. A good thing then, she happened to be female. Had she been male, he might have already begun.

Her yellow eyes studied his face. She breathed slowly, but her racing heart betrayed her fear. She didn't know what he was, but this close, pressed hip to hip, she'd feel the same buzzing, tingling sensation of wrongness as Severn felt touching Mikhail. "The correctioners are here," she said.

Her words landed like a physical blow, slapping Severn from his heightened state. How? Nobody knew where he was... Nobody... He shoved off her and shuddered, shaking off the primal urges. The nephilim still cowered, eyeing him warily, ready to bolt the first chance they got.

"Go," the madam said, the word hard, but not from anger. Recognition gave her tone gravitas.

A door slammed in the building. Boots thundered outside. Someone barked an alarm.

The madam pointed toward the narrow side-door she often used to come and go.

Severn bowed his head briefly in thanks and reached for his cloak.

The main door burst inward, spewing black-clad

correctioners. The twin prongs of their electric prodbars snapped and hissed, ready to deliver a debilitating shock to any who dared stand in their way.

A pair dashed for the madam. "Run!" she screamed, getting to her feet and dropping her stance, ready to defend herself. They didn't correct full demons, they killed them. Previously illusioned featherless wings sprouted from the madam's back, flicking and twitching outward, increasing her size and threat. She bared her nails and hissed. The first correctioner tried to jab the electric prod at her. She batted it aside.

He could let them kill her and escape in the chaos. It would be the cleaner solution. But while brimming with strength, running was the last thing on Severn's mind.

Three correctioners faced him, their prods spitting their threat. Only their human eyes showed through the slits in their helmets. The rest of them was covered head to toe in matte black demon-resistant armor.

A good thing Severn wasn't a demon today.

"Wait..." one of them spoke up, his voice crackling through the helmet's filters. "You're Mikhail's—"

He didn't get to finish. Severn thrust up a hand, throwing out his unrestrained power like a white-hot whip, tangling it around the correction's neck. Seraphim's Ancient Law dictated no human should die in war. This wasn't war, it was right. The moment Severn's whip connected, Severn yanked, whipping the correctioner's head to the side, snapping his neck. He collapsed, but a second filled his space. The anonymous correctioner lunged, jabbing the prod at Severn like he was some animal to be corralled into a corner. Severn batted the first thrust away, stepped in, and connected his fist against the correctioner's throat, knocking him off his feet.

Spikes jabbed into Severn's shoulder. Electricity snapped down his arm, pulling on muscle and nerves, trying to control a body that was only half real. Another day, it might have been enough to bring him down. But not today. Today, he had destiny's call to answer, and he was fucking alight with power. He barked a cry, whirled, and backhanded the asshole who dared prod a fucking angel, toppling him into his companions.

The madam was on her knees, curled forward, weathering a storm of shock after shock from the three correctioners circled around her. They'd believed her to be the most dangerous thing in the room. They were wrong.

Killing was a lot like fucking. Although for a long time, Severn had been doing a whole lot more of one than the other. There was a moment, a line in which thought became unnecessary and instinct took over. He didn't think about how to kill the three correctioners, just that they weren't living beyond the next few seconds.

He plucked one back from the madam's circle of torment, grabbing him by the back of the neck in that vulnerable part where the helmet met his body armor, and embraced him from behind. Long ago, he'd held lovers the same way, lowered his head to their necks the same way too. But, generally, he didn't tear their throats out with his teeth. Angel teeth were blunt, but after applying enough force, they were capable of tearing through muscle. Gristle popped. Blood gushed into his mouth. He spat to the side and tossed the twitching, screaming correctioner away. Spurting arterial blood declared him dying.

The next correctioner was in his sights, a woman, he

confirmed via her eyes. He saw too in those wide eyes, how she believed angels weren't supposed to attack correctioners. They were meant to be on the same side.

She tried to jab him with her prod. He grabbed the bar, yanked it from her grip with a strength she wouldn't believe possible, twirled the rod in his hand, and thrust the pronged end through the slit in her helmet, lodging it in through her eye socket. Her arms dropped. Her body twitched. And she hung there on the end of the prod like some puppet waiting for commands.

Severn kicked her body off and twisted and swung the prod in an arc, taking out the final correctioner's legs. He or she toppled to their knees. Severn's heel connected with the correctioner's jaw, snapping their head back, dislodging the helmet, sending it flying.

The man quivered on his knees, his gray face exposed.

Severn straddled him in the next breath, one hand around his throat, the other still holding the prod high, readying to smash it down and cave the man's skull in. The correctioner's bladder let go. His terrified eyes spoke of how angels were supposed to protect all humans from the demons, and in return, humans worshipped the angels like gods, while the imperfect cambions and nephilim hid on the fringes of the world, destined to never be embraced by either perfect race. Destined to be *corrected*, a process that killed more than it *saved*.

Ether born of violence thickened the air, and with Severn's act virtually exposing him for what he was, he no longer had to pretend this entire clusterfuck didn't turn all his mental switches to on.

He hovered his mouth over the man's, hearing him

pant, feeling him shake. His short, sharp breaths stroked over Severn's lips.

"I told an angel a secret earlier this night. Would you like to hear it too?"

Sweat-soaked and terrified, and with no real choice, the man nodded.

Severn whispered his name across the man's lips, and then kissed him, sealing the truth inside his mouth. The kiss was hard, a thrusting of his tongue, working his mouth and jaw. The man shuddered a response, his body instantly and painfully aroused. He didn't have a choice in that either. Ether simmered off his skin, its tendrils pouring into Severn as though the man had sported a million arms to embrace him with. He fed, pulling the life out of the human until his ether spluttered and cut off.

The correctioner died smiling.

Normally, Severn wouldn't have bothered with such a display. He hadn't needed the ether, and because it was forced, it was virtually worthless anyway. Still, the stolen kiss—soft lips on his after so long without touch—had felt damn good.

Straightening, Severn turned and found the madam still on her knees, looking up at him, and the two nephilim tucked into the corner, hoping they'd suddenly become invisible. Six correctioners lay dead in various gruesome displays about the room. "Well, that was fucking unfortunate for them." His voice was back to its normal angelic purr. He straightened his clothes and smoothed back his hair. Power tingled at the tips of his fingers. He shook it out and rolled his shoulders, realigning all the different parts of him.

The madam slowly rose to her feet. Scorch marks from

the prods bruised her skin. She folded her wings away, letting them fade completely from the visible spectrum. "You need to leave."

"You think?" He finally scooped up his cloak and threw it on, fingers slowing around the button as he realized the madam hadn't called him anon—*anonymous*. Because she knew him? Or at the very least, suspected. When his gaze tracked back to the nephilim, they whimpered, angel eyes shining.

The madam raised her hand without taking her eyes off Severn, silencing them. She stared unblinking at Severn, like she was staring down some wild, mythical creature. One that might jump her precious boys at any moment.

He supposed she might be within her rights to see it like that. "You should leave too. There will be a lot more correctioners on their way." He made for the door but lingered before leaving, a hand braced on the frame. "There is to be a battle today, after which, everything will change," he said without looking back, but their silence drew his eye anyway.

The trio stared, part in awe, part in love, mostly in fear. He'd seen a similar glassy look on the faces around Mikhail's table. He didn't want anyone's unquestionable devotion, just justice.

He left the madam's building, keeping his head down and his hood up. Not so long ago, Severn would have killed all three and left them for dead with the correctioners as a mystery for someone else to figure out. He'd certainly done worse to protect his identity. But if he succeeded, he wouldn't need to hide, and if he didn't... well, he'd be dead.

"A token for pleasures... Just a token, and I'll make your dreams come true."

Severn threw the old crone a withering look, raising his lip in a snarl. They shrank back, careful to give him a wide berth as he passed.

CHAPTER 3

His fingers were tan and mine black, and as we twined them, I lifted his to my lips, tasting their golden warmth, tasting him.

Severn blinked the memory-dream away. There hadn't been time for sleep when he'd returned to his chambers. Still buzzed and throbbing-hot from his high, he'd donned his armor and joined the ranks of angels making their way toward the frontline. Most flew over London, their wings painted red by dawnlight. Severn had his ranks walk the empty streets to the west, to sweep the grounds for any scouts who may have chanced a look-see at the angels' defenses. They'd found none.

The killing fields opened up ahead. Parts of the city flattened into a vast expanse of churned earth. Buildings had been hammered flat by endless battles. Nothing larger than shrub interrupted the landscape, because nothing took root among the old blood and bones. Angels whisked their dead away from the killing fields. Demons did not.

And so they were left to rot in the mud, left for the rayverns to feast upon.

Rayverns cawed and squabbled in great gatherings in the center of the fields now, anticipating the battle and their breakfast.

The frontline stretched ahead, no-man's-land shimmering in dawnlight, lined by a tide of blackness creeping closer. Demons. Some dotted the sky but most approached on foot. Thousands of them.

Violence scented the air.

Severn checked the lines of angels, the warrior ranks. Their force was generous, at least a thousand. Mikhail was nowhere to be seen.

Anxiety, anticipation, lust. It all tugged at Severn's instincts, buzzing already alert nerves. Without these battles to stimulate him, he might have gone insane long before now. Blood and sex. He couldn't have one, but he made sure to find enough of the other.

Severn withdrew his sword and freed a tendril of power, wrapping it around the blade, making the weapon glow a little brighter. Angels along his ranks did the same, taking his cue to ready up. He knew them all, some as close as brothers and sisters. He wouldn't see their faces at his moment of betrayal, but he could readily imagine their expressions. They'd be confused, lost, like Cassandra had been while she'd tried to gather her wings into her arms. The thought tugged at his smile.

The demons were still some distance away. Their frontline continued to swell, deepening as their numbers increased. So many gathered now that their combined power darkened the sky above, stirring a storm. No angel wanted to fly through a demon storm.

The morning breeze shifted, bringing with it the familiar tingling spice of demon on his tongue. A shudder rippled through him. Gods, he lived for this moment, the moment before the bloodshed, the moment before the killing rush consumed him. Looking left and right, his line of angel-kin stretched into the distance similarly glared into the oncoming storm, each one as close as they were going to get to any kind of ecstasy.

Whatever happened, he'd be free of them before this day was over.

"Will he be among them?" the angel to Severn's left asked. His attention was fixed on the growing demon line, staring into them like he might be staring into his end. The blade in his hand throbbed a pale blue.

It wasn't Mikhail the angel spoke of, but his demon counterpart. Demons didn't have guardians, though, what was a guardian but an angel with a god complex? The demons had lords, and one such lord was probably the only thing the angels feared today. Demons feared him too, though none would admit it. Titles slid off him. The only name that stuck was Argothun. Severn had seen him in battle a dozen times, swinging his great axe, taking angel heads as easily as plucking the heads off flowers, and he'd steered well clear each time.

"He'll be there," Severn replied, like he knew for certain. The angel looked over, and Severn tossed him a genuine smile.

"Mikhail is late."

"No..." At the flash of gold in the sky, Severn looked up. "He's right on time."

The rayverns suddenly took flight, scattering among the angels converging above. Broad angel wings stroked the air, blades and armor shining. But none shone as brightly as Mikhail. Layered in silver and gold, he shone like a star plucked from the sky and brought to Earth. Even his wings glowed, each silvery frond dancing with light. He didn't apply that armor like every other angel here had to, didn't strap it into place. It was a part of him, like his wings, summoned when needed.

His light sliced across the thousands of angels now gathered. Severn felt its tingling touch even at this distance. Like a kiss, another angel had once told him the first time Severn had seen Mikhail up close. Clearly, she'd been kissing wrong, but he had to admit, Mikhail's presence did feel like a steadying hand, like a whispered word of encouragement, like a friend shoring you up for some terrible task ahead, making you think you had all the power of righteousness on your side.

With a private snarl, Severn shook his head, clearing Mikhail's influence. He needed to be clearheaded for what came next.

Lifting his blade, he started forward, and the ranks of angels followed.

As the distance between angel and demon decreased, most angels took flight alongside Mikhail. The mud was always thicker in the center of the killing fields, churned up by countless bloody battles.

Wingless, Severn had no choice but to wrestle in the dirt. A good thing, then, he preferred it. He trudged on, tasting the putrid mud's metallic touch in the air.

The demons burst forward, letting up their battle cry in one long thunderous roar. Severn let loose his own cry, freed the restraints on his immense power, and charged. They were upon him. He took one down with a slash to the legs. He parried the blade of another, adding a duck, and thrust into the demon's middle, unzipping its insides. And on to the next. Sweeping, cutting, stronger, faster, better—his strength and power brimming.

I lifted his fingers to my lips, tasted them beneath a kiss, drew a finger into my mouth, and lifted my gaze.

The memory of Samiel sailed back to him as he cut through the demons' forces, along with regret at having given away the feather. It was meant for Samiel, but Samiel was gone, his bones somewhere beneath Severn's feet. All he had of him now was vengeance—a force as strong as the angel Severn had become.

Deeper into them, he whirled and swung and sliced, using the weight of the blade to hone the lash of his power into each target, either tossing them back or reeling them in. His blade was soaked. He tasted their deaths on his lips and tongue, like he had in the correctioner's final moments.

Forgive me, Samiel. Destiny doesn't give out choices.

Metal rang out and screeched. Demons and angels screamed too. Blood rained from the storm churning above, and Severn found laughter bubbling from his lips. He cut down any who entered his vision, thriving on violence. Never tiring, never missing. This was life. This was fucking everything. He lived for this.

His body jolted to a sudden, impossible halt.

He blinked, hung up on something, and wrapped his left hand around the jagged blade impossibly thrust into his side.

That couldn't be right.

That wasn't how he'd planned this.

"Surprised?" a deep, demon voice grumbled. Argothun

stood at the end of the blade, his thick green fingers wrapped around its handle. He smiled down from his enormous eight-foot height. "Your reign of death has ended."

"No." The word fell from his lips like a gasp. "Wait... This isn't—" This wasn't supposed to happen, not like this.

"Mikhail's precious Severn, the blade at his right side... I've been watching you closely for a long time." The demon lord growled, dropped his shoulder, and heaved. His blade dug upward into Severn's insides, igniting a riot of pain. Argothun levered him clean off his feet into the air, skewered like a prize.

Severn's eyes streamed, and in his blurred vision, he saw the angels looking on. Some fought to get to him, risking their lives to try and stop Argothun. Fools. They were flies to him.

"You don't... understand."

"Oh, I do." Argothun pulled his blade close, bringing Severn eye-to-eye. "Your lies were so good, you believed them too."

"No." Severn's blade slipped from his slick grip and fell into the mud. He clutched at Argothun's blade with both hands, trying to hold himself still, but it didn't matter. The blade had punched right through armor, flesh, bone. The second it was pulled free, he'd bleed out.

He jerked his head up, blinking through the blood-rain. "*I am demon.*" He forced the words around the agony and through chattering teeth.

Argothun shook his horned head and rumbled a belly laugh. "We cannot afford to listen any longer." Briefly, the big demon's eyes echoed some of the sadness leaking from Severn's soul. It had been too long, too late.

All around, angels clashed with demons, desperate to break through, but none would. The demons had closed ranks, as though they'd all known to converge here, to focus on only Severn.

"This battle..." Severn hissed. "It was to be his last!"

"And where is your precious Mikhail? Not where you said he'd be."

No, no, that couldn't be right. Mikhail trusted him. Mikhail was supposed to be here, separated from the others, to take down Argothun. The resulting clash would have been legendary. Both were well matched, but it was Argothun who would win, because Severn had planned to turn on Mikhail, cutting his wings from his back like he had Severn's in a battle just like this one. And vengeance would be paid.

Severn blinked into the rain pouring from thundering skies.

"You are lost."

Argothun slammed the sword and Severn into the ground, driving the blade hilt deep. Cool, hard metal tore through Severn's middle. Blood flooded up his throat.

The demon lord smiled down at him. "Die with dignity, *skree*."

He tore his blade free, taking Severn's breath with it. Taking more than that. Severn wasn't an angel. He wasn't. He reached out a bloody hand to Argothun to beg him to listen, to get more time, but the lord turned away, leaving him to die in the mud. Fallen. Already forgotten.

He couldn't fail.

Not after so long.

Not like this.

What was it all for if this was the end?

His hand fell over the gaping wound, smearing mud and blood. No amount of raw power could save him from this. He tried to slide a hand under himself, to at least get onto his side, but the mud bubbled, sucking him down. An alien sense of tightness clutched at his chest. Icy panic.

He wasn't done.

He wasn't finished.

Destiny had told him it would be this day... this day would change everything. He fell back, gasping. "Damn you..." The hollow coldness tried to swallow him, and it wasn't just the mud. If he closed his eyes, the silence would be complete, the screaming would stop, and wasn't that what he'd wanted anyway? For the screaming in his head to stop? The screams of those he'd killed, those he couldn't save, those he'd vowed to avenge.

A lightning strike shot out of the skies and slammed into Argothun, knocking the demon sideways. And then the golden meteor opened his wings, and Mikhail roared his battle cry, shattering the air, the ground, all of the world, it seemed. His blade snapped and sparked with furious vengeance. He brought his sword down, and when it met with Argothun's, the demon's shattered. The next thrust took Argothun's head.

Severn could watch no more.

His head fell back. His eyes rolled. And in the midst of the battle still raging around, he thought he saw the face of an old friend. His broken mind had found Samiel among the demons, desperately fighting to get through. Samiel's lips formed a name, Severn's real name...

He'd been here all along.

This was wrong... it had all gone wrong...

He didn't...

Understand...

A hand slipped under his head. An arm dug under his waist. Someone held him close, someone who smelled like the clouds Severn missed soaring through, their wetness plastering his body. He felt the kiss of that cold wetness now, felt the air circle around him, and wondered if he was falling. If he was, it seemed Mikhail would catch him, because the guardian angel's face was the last thing he saw before the cold stole Severn away.

CHAPTER 4

He came around slowly, blinking into stabbing rays of sunlight. Then a guardian was beside him, peering close. His eyes lined with fine, dark lashes, irises touched with gold around the widest, darkest pupil Severn had ever seen, like it held entire worlds inside it. Severn blinked again, saw the blade in the guardian's hand, and launched himself away in a sudden, knee-weakening desperation to flee. He made it two, maybe three steps from the bed he hadn't realized he'd woken on, then fell against a dresser, knocking half of the shiny trinkets on the floor, smashing most of them.

He couldn't breathe.

Why couldn't he breathe?

Fuck, was this panic?

"Easy..."

He jumped at the voice. Mikhail's hand landed on his shoulder, scorching where it touched. Severn let loose a pathetic squeak of a noise he'd never in his entire life made before and then followed it with a vicious, "Fuck," before twisting out of Mikhail's reach.

Mikhail's mouth tilted down one side. "Severn, you're safe."

Fucking safe with Mikhail? Wait... he'd been with Argo on the battlefield... the sword, his guts about to be in his hands... He looked down and stroked over his bare abs, searching for the wound that wasn't there. Had he dreamed it? He spread his fingers over his chest, kneading pink skin, making sure all the muscles were still attached and in working order. And he was still an angel.

Gods, where was this? *Who* was this?

And why the fuck was he naked, with all his goods swinging in the wind for all to see? "Shit..."

"Severn..." Mikhail's impossibly calm voice soothed all the frayed nerves, sprinkling warmth through his veins. "Return to the bed," the angel said, taking himself across the room through the gossamer drapes and out onto the balcony. "Give your body time to heal, your thoughts time to catch up." His wings slowly unfolded, and then Mikhail simply dropped off the balcony and was gone.

Severn let out a sharp huff of breath. Frowning, he regarded the bed, then the enormous room. Minimalist, a few pieces of furniture, some white rugs, but little else. The air smelled like sunlight, and it had nothing to do with the light pouring in through all the open windows. He'd woken inside Mikhail's private chambers. That was... unexpected.

He padded back to the bed, poking at the dimple between his abs where Argo's sword had definitely plunged. He could still feel the blade grinding against his lower rib and out his back, still feel the mud trying to devour him.

The wound had been fatal.

But he was alive.

That was... also unexpected.

And he was still a fucking angel.

Because Mikhail was still alive.

Severn dropped onto the edge of the bed and buried his face in his hands. A decade climbing his way through the ranks, a decade playing angel, a decade of lies.

Argothun had called him *skree*.

It wasn't over.

He jerked his head up.

If he could find his blade before Mikhail returned, he could take the angel's wings while he was relaxed. It wasn't the most elegant of solutions, but he was desperate. Opening the dresser draws, he found some lightweight cotton pants and shirt, tossed them on, and dashed for the door. The handle rattled but the door didn't budge. He tugged harder. Nothing.

The bastard had locked him in.

Did he know what Severn was?

He tried to think back to the moment he'd woken. Had Mikhail seemed angry, surprised, happy? No, none of those things. He'd seemed... tired. So very tired.

He couldn't know. There was no reason to suspect Severn wasn't the devoted follower.

He backed away from the door and scanned the chamber again. Mikhail's rooms were said to be vast with an array of interconnecting doors, but there was none of that here. Unless they were hidden? And if there were hidden doors, there might be another way out.

He examined the walls, running his hands over their smooth surface, looking for tiny imperfections. And then he found one. Just a crack. Anywhere else but Aerie, it would be overlooked. But there were no cracks in Aerie. The city was as perfect as the angels it harbored.

Severn ran his fingers down the crack. Pressing his cheek to it, he felt a cool breeze whisper through. There was definitely a void beyond.

There were rumors of another room leading off Mikhail's. A room where he hung all his trophies... a gallery of wings.

Were *his* wings inside?

He shoved away from the wall, heart lodged in his throat.

"Did you rest?"

Severn jumped and whirled.

The guardian padded softly across the room, his wings low, their edges trailing behind him. He'd lost his armor and wore similar lightweight clothing to those Severn had stolen from his drawers, making him decidedly less threatening. "No... I... I wasn't sure if you'd be back and this... this is your room. I didn't want to..."

"You're welcome here, Severn."

Welcome? He tilted his head, regarding the locked door while approaching Mikhail and the bed again. "You locked the door."

"Yes." Mikhail turned to face him. One of his dark eyebrows arched. "Because you're dead."

"I... what?"

"Technically."

"Technically?"

"I removed your body from the battle—we won, by the way."

Fucking great. "Congratulations."

"You kept Argothun occupied, exactly as you'd suggested. Thus, I took his head. I had hoped to heal you, but his blade... You were too far gone."

Severn only half heard the words. It was supposed to be Argo who took Mikhail's damned head while Severn carved his wings off. If Argo hadn't been such an untrusting idiot, the battle, maybe even the war, would have belonged to the demons. One mistake, and Mikhail had won.

"Your death was widely witnessed, leaving me with a problem," Mikhail went on, talking formally, addressing Severn in a professional capacity.

Problems were multiplying, it seemed. "But I'm alive."

"Yes, you are." Mikhail's penetrating gaze roamed Severn's torso, his brows pinching into a frown. "You will stay here until I can think of an explanation."

"What explanation?" He heard himself laugh, heard its flatness too. "You healed me. I'm fine. Let's get back out there. The demons will rally and respond in larger forces than ever now Argo has fallen."

"You're not listening. Your body was too far gone to save."

Wait... had Severn's illusion failed? Did he know? Was that why Severn was locked inside? Severn regarded the angel closer. He hadn't returned with his sword. He'd have his sword if he suspected Severn of being anything other than angel. He didn't appear aggressive, either. If anything, he looked more relaxed now than Severn had ever seen him. So what was all this vague nonsense? "What am I missing?"

"I..." Mikhail hesitated. Mikhail never hesitated. He closed his eyes and breathed out. "I performed the *allyanse*... with you."

Severn's thoughts, his heart, time, it all screeched to a halt. He rolled his lips, planted a hand on his hip, dropped it again, and backed away a few steps. Needing to move. Ideally, he'd have run from the room, but as the door was locked, flinging himself off the balcony was the next option. It almost seemed like a viable alternative. "You... you did... what? Why... why would you..."

An angel had performed an allyanse on Severn—he'd shared his soul. Not only was it rare, but it shouldn't have been possible.

And not just any angel.

The angel destiny demanded Severn kill.

He had to kill him.

He'd sacrificed everything to kill Mikhail.

There was no other way.

And now Severn was... bound to him? Life to life, soul to soul. A bond usually reserved for angels coupling for life.

Oh, the irony.

Severn wasn't an angel. And he most certainly wasn't lifetime partner material for an angel, or anyone.

He laughed and then found he couldn't stop laughing. It bubbled up and freed itself. He laughed so hard, he had to brace himself against the wall, and when he saw Mikhail's hard frown, he laughed harder. The fucking guardian angel Mikhail had bound himself to Severn... Destiny sure had it in for them both. In many ways, it was good news. Mikhail would never have done such a thing if he'd had any suspicions that Severn wasn't an angel. But it didn't feel like good news, it felt like a noose.

"Are you all right?" Mikhail's pinched brow spoke of his ridiculous concern.

"No!" he laughed. He was most definitely not all right. He was crying now, his eyes streaming, and maybe the sobs were real, or maybe it was all some fucked-up piece of his pretend angel act. But Argo was dead, the day destiny had promised would turn the tide of war was yesterday, and things had only gotten worse. Severn was stuck as angel, and now he'd been mated to his nemesis, because why the hells not?

He slid down the wall, bumped his head against it once, twice, and that seemed to rattle the laughter off. A numbness remained. He ran his fingers through his hair. This had to be some fucking nightmare.

"I'm... It was the only solution available to me."

"Liar." Severn rolled his gaze to the angel, arms crossed, hair loose, looking like some vision who only appeared in dreams. "You could have let me die."

Mikhail instantly stiffened. He lifted his chin and a nerve in his cheek twitched. "You're right. I could have."

"You assumed I'd want to be bonded to you, because who wouldn't want the splendid Mikhail half inside them for the rest of their days?" Typical fucking angels. "What's an eternity with a guardian angel sharing my soul, right? Surely anyone would want such an honor?" He liked how his words were slicing pieces of Mikhail's haughty face. "Well, I'm not anyone."

"No, you're not." His deep voice rumbled.

"You stole my choice."

"Yes, I did."

"You *should* have let me die."

Mikhail's cheek twitched again. His fingers curled into fists.

He hadn't let Severn die, because he was a selfish, self-centered prick who thought only of himself and his perfect angels. Why he'd done something as permanent as bond them together, Severn couldn't fathom. Perhaps so he could have his perfect soldier stroking his ego for the rest of his days. Whatever the reason, there had to be a way out of it. There was always an escape route. He just had to find it.

With a sound like the fluttering of drapes, Mikhail was gone again, and Severn was glad to see the back of him. Nothing had changed. He still planned to kill him. In fact, maybe he could use this. He'd never been this close to Mikhail—sharing his chamber, his clothes—nobody had. The guardian had let his guard down, and Severn planned on ripping through it, and him, just as soon as he escaped this room.

CHAPTER 5

*M*ikhail

SAVING SEVERN HAD BEEN A MISTAKE. Mikhail didn't make them often, so it hadn't occurred to him that saving the angel was anything other than right. But the warrior's reaction had been unexpectedly ungracious, and with his vehement words that followed, Mikhail understood why.

An allyanse was a sacred union. Many could only dream of finding their mate to connect with on a soul-deep level. Most angels died alone, especially in these war-torn times. Severn's one chance for such a union had been taken from him.

Mikhail should not have saved Severn.

Yet, he had.

And that was a problem. Not least because Mikhail wasn't entirely sure why he'd gone to such lengths. Severn was an exceedingly talented warrior, as proven by his rise through the ranks. Shortly after his arrival in Aerie, he'd caught Mikhail's eye and had it ever since. Ruthless in battle, and yet not from physical strength—he was lean compared to most warriors. Narrow waist, smaller shoulders that fit neatly beneath Mikhail's hands. But he was quick and deceptively strong. And exquisitely loyal. Mikhail had slowly come to rely on Severn as his connection to the others... Haven knew he needed something to keep him grounded. Severn had been that anchor.

Perhaps that was why Mikhail had saved him, he pondered while leaning against the balcony archway, facing out into the sky as Severn devoured a meal in the room behind.

He couldn't keep him locked behind a door for long. Severn was the type to eventually kick it in. He'd probably have flown the chamber from this very balcony, right after he'd woken, had he been able.

But he couldn't fly... Severn had never spoken of his loss. A horrific butchering most angels did not survive. Severn was not most angels, as he'd earlier made clear. He spoke honestly, with few filters—even more honestly these last few hours, disarming Mikhail. He saw things in others that Mikhail did not. He was a formidable angel. Those were the reasons Mikhail had saved him, surrendering half his soul in the process. There simply were no other angels like Severn. Saving him had been practical. Necessary. He was too important to all angelkind to lose.

And besides, it was done.

"You could lie."

Mikhail's eyebrow darted up at Severn's suggestion. He turned to peer over his shoulder at the warrior and saw the sharp glint of intelligence in his dark blue eyes. Seeing

Severn seated at the table wearing Mikhail's soft linens, his ragged dirty-blond hair a mop of loose curls he seemed to have no control over, it made the angel look vulnerable and tugged on Mikhail's simmering protective instincts.

"I do not lie," he said too harshly, unaccustomed to the strange sensations tying him up in knots. An allyanse brought with it a lot more complications than Mikhail cared to think on now.

Severn shrugged a shoulder and sat back in the chair, his meal evidently finished. Mikhail had brought enough food for four angels. Severn had eaten it all. "I was dying, you healed me. It's really quite simple and technically not a lie."

Technically. Severn always found the loopholes.

"The spirit of it is a lie, and if I lie in this matter, what other matters might I lie in? No, I cannot be seen to lie. I do not lie."

"Then just... don't tell them anything. Surely keeping me here only makes this situation more awkward the moment I walk free. Unlock the door, I'll go about my business, telling everyone whatever they want to hear—without lying, just... a little manipulation of the truth, to save us both the resulting headaches. There is no need to reveal the..."—he waved a hand—"...what you did. You saved me. It's done. Now let's be done with all of it." That last part, he said with a hint of gravitas that would make lesser angels tighten their wings.

Mikhail thwarted a sudden urge to smile. The little breathless patter in his chest wasn't so easily ignored. It had been happening more of late, and always around Severn.

"The alternative is to keep me here forever," Severn

added, "which neither of us wants." He stood and looked about the room as though seeing it for the first time. Stubborn as he was strong, he carried himself with complete confidence. It was in every stride, every gesture. Even dressed in simple garments, with no armor, no weapons, his smaller form still radiated strength. He had *something* that kept pulling on a thread in Mikhail's mind, something that drew the others to him. It had always been there, this pull, this nameless curiosity, this need to observe the way he moved, or the way he tossed gestures about, or how he laughed...

"Unlock the door, Mikhail." And now there was no denying the threat, or how the sound of it from behind, directed at Mikhail, made that breathless patter quicken.

"Who took your wings?" the question startled them both. Mikhail winced, but Severn had already looked way.

Severn's gaze dropped to the floor in shame. "After all these years, you ask me now?"

"Because I am now responsible for you—"

"Oh, please," Severn laughed. "I do not need your protection, Your Grace. As you well know." The flash of violence in his eyes underlined that point.

Few dared speak to Mikhail so frankly, and none in public, not even Severn. His tongue was certainly freer since his revival. Mikhail found its abrasiveness rather... stimulating. So little challenged him, he'd forgotten what it felt like to be uncertain, to doubt... to not already know what would happen next.

Perhaps Severn was right. Keeping him here would delay the inevitable.

Severn approached, slowing the last few steps until he stood motionless before him. Shorter than Mikhail, most everyone was, but what he lacked in stature, he made up for in determination. "I am of no use to you or your armies like this." He spread his arms and then checked Mikhail for a response.

Angels did not feel. They did not rage, or weep, or regret. Emotions were inefficient.

When Mikhail had seen Argothun impale Severn, something in him had broken open and spilled free, momentarily blinding him to the battle and his purpose within it. Power, he'd thought. It had felt like power, like he'd suddenly accessed another level of strength. With it, he'd plowed into Argothun and taken the wretched demon's head. And then he'd seen Severn in the mud, his gaze lost, his trembling hand reaching for some unknown thing, and some all-encompassing sensation had hollowed all that power out. Mikhail had dropped from the sky into the mud beside Severn, so stripped of strength, he'd been unable to keep his wings aloft. Lifting Severn into his arms hadn't been a conscious thought either. It had just happened, like he was watching himself from afar. He didn't know what to make of it and decided, with Severn watching him keenly now, that it meant nothing at all.

"Do you trust me?" Severn asked, blinking sandy lashes over dark blue eyes.

"Yes."

"Then trust this will all resolve itself in a few days. We have greater issues, such as the demons mounting a counterattack."

If the others learned he had shared his soul with Severn, it could bring down the entire army, maybe even Aerie itself. As a guardian angel, he was not destined for coupling. He didn't possess the required emotions for such a thing and had no intention of giving up his title because of this... error in judgment.

He tilted his head. "We will speak no more of this." The door lock loudly clunked. Severn could leave. It was better to forget this entire event.

Severn bowed low, backing away. "There is nothing to discuss, Your Grace." His loping strides ate the space between Mikhail and the door, and he was gone, leaving Mikhail staring after him, wondering if the mistake would be forgotten, or if he'd set into motion his own downfall.

CHAPTER 6

Severn

MATED TO A FUCKING GUARDIAN ANGEL. It was absurd, for many reasons, Severn mentally grumbled as he strode through Mikhail's citadel hallways.

For one, angels were emotional planks and wouldn't know a relationship if it kissed them on the lips. The only time they emerged from their cold shells was for allyanse, resulting in the newly bonded pair being shipped off to Haven to spawn more angels. With mated pairs deemed too emotional for battle, they were never seen again. Which brought his thoughts neatly to point two. Forgetting the race issue and the enemy issue, they were both males, and so far as Severn had seen, angels did not entertain same-gender couplings of any sort because such couplings were inefficient and did not produce offspring. What had Mikhail been thinking?

It didn't matter.

The allyanse probably hadn't even worked, considering their differences. Mikhail had healed him, that much was obvious, but that was all.

A pair of angels stepped aside and stared as he passed. And they weren't alone in their fixation. Severn looked around him, at those he passed and those who looked down from the high balconies above. So many faces, all turned toward him in awe.

He refused to let this be a problem.

He needed his sword, his armor, needed to slip back into his carefully perfected role, and only then would he turn on Mikhail.

An angel broke from the gawking numbers on an intercept course. Solomon fell into step beside him but stayed silent, either thinking of what to say or afraid to say it. A brilliant fighter, if sometimes sloppy, Solo was one of the few angels Severn had grown to tolerate. His wings were blood red, like his hair, and currently illusioned away. He clasped his hands behind his back. "So..." he began.

"I'm fine, as you can see. Rumors of my death were greatly exaggerated. Please tell any and all who care to know it, so I don't have to repeat myself."

"Are those Mikhail's clothes?" Solo enquired, utterly straight-faced, which either meant he was asking a genuine question, or he had his tongue firmly stuck in his cheek.

Severn cleared his throat. "He healed me." A glance, and it seemed Solo's lips were wrestling with a smile. Unlike the others in Severn's ranks, Solo was capable of a small sense of humor. The fact he had an actual personality was one of the reasons Severn had warmed to him. "Was there anything else you wanted to ask?"

"Oh, a great many things, but none that are relevant."

The citadel was connected to Aerie's residential areas by countless glass bridges, each spanning anywhere from fifty meters to several hundred, with nothing but clouds beneath. Severn approached the bridge that would take him to his part of Aerie, and eventually his chambers, but stopped before stepping onto the walkway. He hadn't always hated open spaces or heights. No doubt he'd appreciate them more if he still had his wings.

They'd drawn quite enough attention, and while some angels grew bored and moved on, others openly gazed.

Solo saw them looking and raised an eyebrow at Severn. "They're curious."

"There is no mystery." Severn dismissed the implication and them with a wave of his hand. "Unless you have something else to say, I need to return to my chambers." Hopefully, Solo wouldn't insist on following. If he did, he might find himself surprised by two decaying angel wings on the floor of Severn's chambers.

"I thought you'd appreciate a debrief."

Severn nodded. "I would. Give me some time to get my affairs in order, and I'll find you. How many did we lose?" he added, almost forgetting to ask.

"Fifteen."

Fifteen angels dead. Not enough. "Regrettable."

"Although, easily replaced. At the last count, two hundred and five demons fell, mostly due to Mikhail killing Argo and the chaos that ensued."

Severn turned away before Solo's shrewd gaze could pry too much truth from his face and started crossing the bridge. "A victory, then," he ground out, relieved when the wind quickly stole them and his breath away. He didn't bid

Solo a goodbye, couldn't bring himself to turn and see the smile on his face at so many dead demons.

The war was meant to have ended yesterday.

But nothing had changed.

"A blessing you survived!" Solo called. Severn let the wind have that too, knowing it wasn't over yet, and if Mikhail's allyanse had stuck, he likely wouldn't survive what came next.

MIKHAIL HADN'T ASKED for Cassandra's wings, and as they were now stinking up Severn's chambers, he kicked the useless appendages over the edge of the balcony. Maybe they'd join her in the afterlife. At least she'd be whole again. Mikhail hadn't asked after Cassandra's sentence at all, which showed how little he cared.

Stripping out of Mikhail's clothes, Severn drenched himself in the shower, easing some of the illusionary magic away so the water could trickle and soothe the pair of stumps jutting from his shoulder blades. One of the benefits of pretending to be something he was not, he at least could pretend the ugly remnants of Mikhail's ruthlessness didn't exist.

With his hands pressed against the cold wall, hot water dashed down his back, running in rivulets around what remained of his wings. Old wounds throbbed. He sent his thoughts far away to easier times, when he'd played in the forgotten London streets. Samiel's tawny eyes and quick smile soon found him in the reverie, and he allowed himself a true, honest smile as the water washed him clean of the guardian angel's scent.

Dressing in his own clothes went some way to helping him feel normal again but didn't wipe the unsettling rattle of nerves that seemed to have taken up residence in his gut.

His armor hadn't been returned—thankfully. The nephilim who might have delivered it would have been faced with a pair of the severed wings. Severn ruffled his wet hair and headed out to visit the armory.

He could do without armor for a few days, but he needed that sword.

The deeper into Aerie's lower section he went, the more nephilim hurried about, keeping Aerie running smoothly. It was darker here. Aerie sat atop the cloud-level, which meant its lower levels rested within the clouds, and it didn't take much moisture to block out light. Still, the nephilim didn't care. So desperate to be more their angel halves and less their human halves, they ran themselves ragged in service.

They were all pretty, all built well, all quick to laugh and smile, and were so fucking accommodating. All were slaves.

At least cambions were free to be whomever they wanted to be.

The armory was well protected near the central columns that held Aerie up on its towering foundations and accessed by a wide, spiraling staircase down. Severn breezed through the guards, not caring to linger to see if they were surprised to see him. Instead of summoning a nephilim to fetch his things, he walked among them. He always had. At first, not realizing it was something angels didn't do, and later, coming to enjoy it. Unlike their angel *betters*, nephilim could feel, and it made them infinitely more tolerable to be around.

"My lord." The young, peach-cheeked nephilim male dipped in greeting. Pale skinned, blond, and blue-eyed, he reminded Severn all too easily of the two males that had taken great pleasure in each other as he'd paid to observe. "You'll be wanting your armor?"

The nephilim looked up at Severn like he believed the fucking sun shone out of his ass because he was an angel and closely associated with Mikhail. That was how things were done in Aerie, but seeing how the nephilim were so happy to be enslaved never failed to put Severn in a foul mood. He nodded, not trusting his voice, and followed the male to the back of the noisy, darkened repair shops, where his armor was displayed on a workbench.

A vicious slice split the side-plate almost in two, and the sight made Severn trip against the table.

He should have died. He should not be walking around without a scratch on him. Fuck, if the angels had seen this mangled mess, then it was no wonder they'd stared. He really was a miracle.

"It's going to take us some time to repair—"

"The sword?" he asked, like the wreckage was perfectly normal.

"I..." the nephilim flinched and paled even more. "This was all that was brought in."

"No sword?"

He bit his lip and shook his head.

Severn needed that damn sword.

"I can have the staff search the rack—"

"Do that..." It wouldn't be found. He'd had the sword

in his hand when Argo had impaled him. It had slipped from his fingers right after. The sword was still on the killing fields, probably buried in the mud among two hundred and five dead demons.

He left the nephilim desperately searching the racks of weapons for his, knowing it wasn't among them. Angel-blades weren't easy to come by, and he'd lost the only blade he had access to.

If he didn't know any better, he might think destiny was actively working against him.

"Severn!"

The cry went up as soon as he emerged from the stair-case. The angel running toward him was a female he'd made it his business to know well, if only because she was one of the closer warriors to Mikhail, making her more of a threat than most. Petite, as angels went, Vearn fought dirty on the battlefield. Unlike most angels, she cut her hair short and close to her face, so it didn't hinder her in a fight.

His fingers instinctively twitched, seeking the sword he didn't have, but as she skidded to a halt in front of him, her stricken face made it clear it wasn't him she was targeting.

"There's been an assassination attempt on Mikhail."

An irritating skip of his heart stole a breath before Severn quenched the feeling. "Where?"

"In his chambers."

She whirled, her wings spreading behind her, and launched herself from the nearest balcony. Severn dashed through the halls, still wishing he had the sword, if only to finish Mikhail off. An assassination attempt inside Aerie was unheard of, especially as Severn *should* have heard about it long before now. Mikhail's death didn't belong to anyone else. The guardian was his to kill. And whoever had tried to overrule him would soon witness his wrath.

CHAPTER 7

The angel was on her knees, wings sagging behind her, a cheap dagger broken in two and discarded on the floor in front of her, likely tossed there by Mikhail. Blood dripped from her nose and stained her lip.

Mikhail leaned heavily against the wall, his wings hidden. His white, cotton shirt bore a splash of crimson near his shoulder. The bloodied arrow also on the floor between the two spoke volumes.

Severn read the scene. The assassin had fired the arrow through the window first and entered through his chamber from the balcony, hoping to finish him off with the dagger. Predictably, she hadn't gotten very far. If Mikhail were that easy to kill, Severn would have killed him years ago.

Severn had her by the throat and hauled her off her feet, getting a good look into her brilliant eyes. She glared back without fighting, her chin firm and jaw locked. No *angel* in their right mind would attack Mikhail.

She spat blood into Severn's face and sneered. "You take too long, *skree*—"

Power funneled through his arms, into his fingers. He snapped her neck before she finished her sentence and threw her limp body away.

"Had I wanted her dead, I could have seen to it myself," Mikhail said, sounding only mildly annoyed.

Severn straightened, shaking out the lust for violence tingling through his fingers. "She was demon."

"What?" Vearn alighted on the balcony. She folded her wings and came forward, clearly having heard Severn's words. "Is that possible?"

"It's entirely possible, with enough motivation." He turned his head to Mikhail, waiting for his assessment. The guardian scowled at the carcass but made no comment and didn't move from the wall. Did he see more? Had he heard the demon's last words? Severn found himself needing to fill the silence. "I've known for some time how demons have the means to illusion themselves into angel form." Mikhail jerked his head up, and Severn stammered, "It's only skin deep and temporary, but convincing. It's also brittle. Something as trivial as touch shatters the illusion. At least, that's what I've heard."

"Why did you not tell me of this before now?" Mikhail plastered his hand over the bloody mark on his shirt and started toward the fallen assassin.

Because had you known, you might have realized I've been lying to your face for a decade.

The strange, flickering knot of nerves that had been gnawing on Severn since waking in Mikhail's bed suddenly grew more demanding, beginning to crackle his veins and tighten his breaths. "Because my source tells the vast amounts of power required makes it virtually impossible for most demons to hold the illusion for long." He rubbed at his chest, trying to soothe the horrible sensation away.

"Long enough to reach my balcony."

"That was... unexpected," he said truthfully.

"She came back from the killing fields with our forces." Vearn peered down at the not-angel, poking a wing with her boot. Dust fell away from the feathers. "That's quite some time for an illusion to hold."

"She must have been very motivated," Severn said, hoping his tone was neutral.

Gods, what was this wretched sensation spiraling through him? He backed away from the corpse. "Now she's deceased, the illusion will dissipate within the hour, revealing the demon."

Was he saying too much? Too little and they'd remember the demon's dying words, too much and they'd wonder exactly how much of this illusionary power he truly knew about.

"Then only the most powerful demons can perform this illusion?" Vearn asked.

Severn nodded, not trusting his voice.

"How many demons are this powerful?"

"A handful, I imagine, else we'd see more of this"—he gestured at the body—"infiltration."

Vearn cocked her head, looking sideways at Severn. "Are you...all right?"

The knot had lassoed itself around his insides and squeezed too hard, upsetting his heart and breathing. "No," he choked out. He staggered backward. Poison? Had the demon somehow cursed him with her final words? He deserved it. She'd tried to kill Mikhail. What exactly had

Severn achieved in the last few years, besides become an angel?

Mikhail's steadying hand gripped Severn's upper arm. Severn hadn't even registered he was so close. The touch with Mikhail's power behind it sparked a riot of painful needle-like skitters passing through his skin, up his shoulder and down into his chest, freeing the knot.

"Severn is in recovery..." Mikhail explained, voice drifting around Severn, as insubstantial as clouds.

The fuck he was. This was an attack of some kind... He just... had to...

Mikhail's hand migrated over Severn's shoulder to the back of his neck, where his fingers clasped hard enough to prop Severn up. The breathlessness passed achingly slowly until an involuntary shudder wiped away the last of the unsettling tightness.

Distantly, he heard a part of his mind screeching an alarm to shake Mikhail off, to stop the touch, but damn if it didn't feel good. Its weight, its warmth. There were none of the painful sparks that usually accompanied just the smallest of touch with another.

Severn blinked back to himself on his knees, with Vearn gone but Mikhail very, very close, standing in front of him, his hand scorching through the back of Severn's neck, his eyes two pools of deep blue that Severn found himself utterly incapable of looking away from. The angel's grip softened and came away, but only so he could stroke his knuckles tenderly down Severn's cheek.

Mikhail's touch... shouldn't have been possible, not for this long, not without stripping Severn's illusion from his skin. Still, it was happening. Severn's illusion held, and gods, the male's knuckles stroking his cheek felt divine, like Mikhail's fingers had a direct link to the careless part of Severn's mind—the starved part. Severn's heart thudded for another reason, not least because, as angel, he wasn't supposed to feel desire of any kind, and yet there was one sorely neglected part of his anatomy sitting up and becoming extremely interested in Mikhail.

Mikhail's thumb tugged at the corner of Severn's mouth and then dragged its way across his lower lip, gently parting, pushing in, becoming more than a clinical exploration.

Mikhail's eyes darkened with an intent Severn was a master of.

Lust.

It seemed Severn wasn't the only one experiencing things he shouldn't. Lusting after an angel was wrong, but that had never stopped Severn in the past—he'd eye-fucked and fed from countless nephilim. His circumstances hadn't left him much choice, but he had a choice here. Lusting after Mikhail was a whole new level of fucked-up. But knowing that didn't move him from his knees with the male's hard thumb exploring the softness of his lips.

Severn's tongue probed at the thumb, its warm wetness smoothing over the guardian's rough skin. Mikhail's eyes widened, as though surprised, and skipped down Severn's chest, finding a target. Severn's cock twitched beneath the weight of the angel's attention, and given how Severn was on his knees, he couldn't miss a similarly aroused angel cock impressively filling and reshaping Mikhail's loose pants. With that member at eye level, Severn had the sudden, mouthwatering idea of unlacing the angel's pants and stroking the male's engorged member over his tongue and down his throat, working him over hard and fast, making him cry out and spill his seed.

Mikhail's desires were clearly aligned with Severn's, and would it be so wrong to fuck the angel he was destined to kill?

Mikhail tore himself away so suddenly that his absence made Severn's vision swim.

"Get out."

Severn rocked back on his heels, blinking into the startling brightness surrounding Mikhail's retreating figure. The electric intensity of the angel's touch and its sudden, wrenching loss left Severn adrift. Had those last few seconds been...real? The throbbing evidence of his arousal thought so. Fuck, he hadn't been so hard in years.

"Leave. *Now*."

Mikhail stood in the balcony doorway, his back firmly to Severn, and his tone made it clear if Severn didn't immediately vacate his chambers, there would be violence.

Severn wavered to his feet, stole a moment to look at his hand, confirming his skin was still angel-pale—his illusion had held through all of that, but it shouldn't have been possible—and worse, he didn't even feel its usual tightness across his skin.

"Get out!" the angel boomed.

Severn had no wish to confront Mikhail while disarmed and confused. He fled back to his own side of the city, thoughts in freefall. What if the illusion had held because it was permanent?

He paced inside his chambers.

He'd always known the price for his subterfuge was high. To be angel, he'd had to become angel, but that was the sacrifice he'd gladly made to get close to Mikhail and ultimately kill him, toppling the angel empire with him. But it was an illusion. Not real. An act. A lie. A deceit he'd spent ten years perfecting, knowing that when Mikhail fell, so would his illusion.

But when Mikhail had touched him, there had been none of the usual signs that his illusion was being tested. No pain, no desire to pull away—the opposite, in fact. Like the illusion had become *solid*. His skin had tingled for an entirely different reason.

"Fuck."

Jolting to a halt, he lifted both hands. His skin was pale, his nails short, his forearms and biceps defined but not overly muscular. His body was pleasant enough to admire, as angels went, but as demons went, he was a pretty runt.

He called to mind his true image, before Mikhail had stripped him of his wings. Skin as dark as night, veins of molten lava, and wings... broad, powerful wings that inspired awe. He'd been a creature of strength, of brutal beauty, of unrelenting passion and lust and hunger, the absolute opposite of an angel. Before Mikhail had ruined him.

And just moments ago, he'd been on his knees in front of the monster, tasting angel on his tongue, his cock raging hard for a male responsible for a million demon lives lost.

The assassin was right.

He'd taken too long.

He was *skree*—one of them.

He *was* angel.

Severn crumpled, knees thumping against the floor, and curled into himself. Desperate, he tore free the mental restraints on the illusion that had kept him walking among angels for years, ripping off the lies, layer after layer, but still, his skin was pale, his hands small, his body *angel*. He let everything go, unpicking every carefully placed piece of power that had woven a tapestry of lies, undoing all of the wrappings and gasped in relief as the weight of fighting his true nature fell away.

But nothing changed. There was no dark skin, no powerful muscles. Impossibly, and with horrifying certainty, he remained angel.

He'd become his enemy.

Mikhail

DEMONS COULD ILLUSION themselves into angels. The idea was as terrifying as it was wrong. But not nearly as terrifying and wrong as openly desiring another angel.

After Severn had finally obeyed the order and left, Mikhail had fallen against the door frame, painfully waiting for the visceral sensations of need and want to slowly dissipate from his body while steadfastly denying the temptation to take his wretched member in hand and deliver the kind of pleasures he hadn't sought in several hundred years.

His member had become a useless appendage long ago and hardly worth a single thought in centuries. It was there, the same way a finger was, or a toe, but those digits were more useful.

Angels in his position did not feel. They did not desire,

and they certainly did not imagine their most trusted warrior untying their pant fastenings, taking their treacherous cock in hand, then to Severn's wretched mouth, and doing all those things he'd seen come alive in Severn's eyes.

Mikhail's stunted imagination had delivered more than enough inspiration in a matter of moments, thus arousing his body and completely betraying the dark hole in which his thoughts had plunged into.

And Severn had very obviously desired him in return.

All of this was deplorable.

Unacceptable.

It could not be tolerated.

Oh, but Haven, as Mikhail had touched the male's ever-moving mouth, finding it so deliciously pliable, some long-forgotten primal drive in Mikhail had roared to the surface, so quickly, and so completely undeniable, that Mikhail had instantly become its slave. Had he not wrenched himself back from its grip, he might have debased himself. And that... that was unthinkable.

It could not happen again.

For Severn's sake as well as his own.

He'd dismiss Severn from his service but keep him among the ranks. He was too valuable a warrior to lose altogether. They'd be separated, and that would have to be enough.

The angels would miss his leadership and Mikhail would lose Severn's valuable source of enemy intelligence clearly gleaned from the cambions in the cauldron, but Vearn would step in.

Yes. Severn would be removed, and with him, these absurd temptations.

Sighing hard, his attention drifted down to the demon

carcass now fully revealed on the floor of his chambers. Her bulbous green-tinged body with its smooth, featherless wings was as hideous as it was an affliction on all things good and right. His lip curled in disgust.

The demons' behavior of late had changed, their attacks becoming more sophisticated, and this assassination attempt was proof their tactics were developing.

It was time to order the balconies closed when not in use. Aerie was an open city, with fewer walls than windows, impossible to close in completely. Guards would need to be posted at regular intervals, resources taken away from the frontline.

They'd won a victory in the last battle, but why then did it not feel like one?

Mikhail crouched beside the demon and cocked his head, scrutinizing her face. Demons appeared to be like angels at their roots, but later twisted and warped into a mockery of an angel's beauty. He leaned closer. It was rare any angel came as close as this to one without trying to kill it. Without their enraged snarling and murderous intent, they were decidedly unremarkable.

If this hideous mass of muscle had fooled an entire army of angels, how many more of them were hidden among his forces?

Severn was absent to the gathering, Mikhail noted, as the others settled in around the long table. He waited a few moments longer than necessary, but with no sign of him, he could not delay. He began to speak of how the city would need to be protected from this new threat. The angels stirred and ruffled their feathers at the news of how demons could imitate them, refusing to believe it. An angel's beauty could not be copied so perfectly by such beasts, they proclaimed. At which point, Mikhail's assistants hauled in the demon carcass for those present to witness.

"I witnessed the deceased angel turn from one of us into that." He'd witnessed most of it, when he hadn't been staring out over the balcony, desperately trying not to pound himself to climax.

The thought hooked into him, making him trip over his next words and reawakening the awful and inappropriate stirring in his loins all over again. He pulled over a chair, illusioned his wings away, and sat suddenly, noting how several eyebrows had elevated. He never sat at the table.

"On another matter, it is with regret that I must dismiss Severn from his role among us—"

A surprising cacophony of voices declared their disapproval, and Mikhail let them all say their pieces over one another before one by one, they fell quiet. In Severn's time among them all, he really had proven himself to be irreplaceable.

"The battle took its toll, and—"

"I'm absolutely fine," a smooth, overly confident voice declared. Had he always sounded so careless with his speech, and with the way in which he sauntered in, completely unrepentant in his tardiness?

"You're late."

Severn bowed low, and that too seemed like some statement Mikhail didn't catch. "My sincerest apologies, Your Grace." He rose, and even without wings, his presence commanded the space around him, drawing the eyes of everyone at the table, including Mikhail's. He wore one of the city guard's lightweight breastplates, gold patterns stitched into reinforced white cloth, as though he had every intention of returning to his duties. Had his current attire always been so perfectly formfitting? It nipped at his waist in a way Mikhail would rather like to try with his fingers, spreading them over the small rise of his hips.

Horror doused the unbidden lust, but not before Severn caught his eye. Mikhail made his face blank, tore his stare from the smiling angel, and regarded the others, looking on expectantly. He'd completely forgotten what he'd been about to declare.

Severn pulled out the chair to Mikhail's right and relaxed into it. "You were saying?"

"You would know, had you been on time," he said instead, trying to keep the bite from his tone and failing.

"I apologize again. I was dealing with a...personal matter. I'm sure you can understand."

Dealing with it in the same way Mikhail imagined, with his cock in his hand, back arched, about to unload? Oh Haven, what was wrong with him? Why did his thoughts insist on returning to those carnal images again and again, like some hideously slow torture?

"Are you all right, Your Grace?" Severn asked, and that damn smile of his played upon lips Mikhail so desperately wanted to run his fingers across and then follow with his tongue.

Mikhail cleared the dry knot in his throat and looked up. "Please clear the room." Severn made a move to stand. *"Not you."* The order had been delivered with more growl than was necessary, and Severn hadn't been the only angel to hear it. He slowly lowered himself back into the chair as the others filed out painfully slowly.

"Have I done something to anger you?" Severn asked.

Heated sharpness had Mikhail clenching his teeth. It did taste decidedly like anger. "This cannot continue. You will leave."

Severn blinked. He was a joy to behold, and despite the anger still gripping Mikhail's body, he appreciated Severn's features. He had always been remarkable, but it was only now that Mikhail truly noticed why. Lean, and flighty, and bright, and fast, and strong. All those things and more. He'd been a pillar beneath Mikhail for so long, he'd come to take his loyalty for granted. Keen blue eyes, a smattering of freckles across his nose, lips always pulled into an array of smiles. No, not always. In battle, he was fierce and resolute and absolutely undeniable.

"I will not be leaving," Severn replied.

"I cannot have you..." Mikhail paused at the wrong moment and quickly choked out the next words, "distracting me."

"The demons will retaliate. Despite dwindling forces, they are stronger than ever. They want your head. They want Aerie. You need me." Severn propped an elbow on the table, his smile now a smirk.

"Undeniably." Mikhail forced himself to stand, to create distance, when really, some kind of possession had taken hold of him, making him want to turn, to savagely kiss the male's mouth, to do much more—

He thrust his hands into his hair. "This is madness!"

"No, it's merely the allyanse asserting its control. You fucked up, and now we're both paying for it. If you dismiss me, it'll be your second mistake in a matter of days."

Severn's foul mouth needed discipline, and Mikhail's body knew exactly the kind of discipline to deliver. He groaned and propped a shoulder against the wall, keeping his back to Severn. He had no choice but to try to withstand the torrent of urges. He was a guardian, he stood against countless demon hordes, he could certainly stand against the absurd *feelings*. "Go to the cauldron, get me the information we need. When is the next attack? How many in their frontline?"

"The cauldron? I don't—"

Mikhail shot him a withering look. "I know you visit the cauldron, don't try and deny it." The shock on Severn's face went some way to dousing Mikhail's lust, at least enough for him to wrestle himself back under control. He had always worked well with Severn—together, they'd brought about some of the most stunning victories over the demons. Mikhail had to salvage that, for the safety of Aerie. "And I want to know how many can sustain this illusion for any considerable length of time."

"I've already told you—"

"You've told me what you know. It's not enough. The cambion will know more. If you need more tokens for bribes, I'll see it done. Whatever you need, Severn, you will have it. But I must learn everything they know." Consumed by duty, his lust driven back, he returned to the table and watched Severn rise. Severn turned his face away, his gaze skittish. Then this was difficult for him too. Mikhail had not stopped to consider how difficult it must be for another angel to suddenly experience emotion and a visceral, carnal need, especially one so much younger than Mikhail. Most would be paired up and sent to Haven. Neither he nor Severn had that option.

"In your absence, I shall make some enquiries as to whether an allyanse can be... lessened or potentially... undone."

A haunted look came over Severn. "That would be most appreciated."

Mikhail nodded and watched the angel leave, feeling the entirely unwelcome tug on his heart as he did.

evern

A HEAVY MIST soaked the cauldron, drenching the streets in an oily sheen. Most everyone wore coats and hoods, ducking under awning after awning to keep from the rain. Severn carved through the fray, a shadow among shadows.

He'd already found his usual cambion informants and paid them handsomely for information. Severn had been right, the demons were gearing up for another assault, but so far, none had been able to say when or where. He had one last lead, a wily cambion whose main trade was smuggling. A brute of a beast, more demon than human, Jayke had been Severn's initial contact when he'd first sought to get into Aerie and under Mikhail's nose. Few demons, cambion or full, made Severn sweat. Jayke was one.

The walk through the under took too long. There were few direct routes anywhere and a thousand interconnecting streets, all lined with ramshackle huts leaning against each other so that one collapsing might topple the whole lot.

It had been a long time since Severn had ventured this deep into the cauldron, and much had changed. Streets had moved to suit new uses and the volume of refugees pouring in from all across the lands. While searching for some distinguishing landmark, he spotted a figure behind him. The same figure he'd seen several twists and turns ago. And now he'd seen one stalker, another loomed off to his right, keeping to the periphery, hoping to go unnoticed. If there were two, there were likely more.

He'd been made, possibly by correctioners, although he'd been damned careful to make sure any who'd seen his face at Infinity had died right after.

After casually continuing for a few minutes, pretending to take in the limited sights, he suddenly veered toward a row of ramshackle multistory metal-sheeting-clad structures, and plunged through the door, bolting into a run. The building appeared to be made up of rickety staircases and rotten floors. Severn sprinted down corridors, grabbed a doorframe, and swung himself inside an open room, then dashed across the space, startling the four figures huddled around a fire. He launched himself from the window, landing solidly on a lower roof and set off again. Leaping off the edge, he fell, landed on a balcony, sprang over the rail, and dropped down again before landing on the street, flicking his hood back up and merging with a thin stream of people filing through the narrow street.

The huge, empty warehouses crowding the narrow street were unfamiliar, but at least he'd lost his admirers. Now he just had to find his way out of this rat maze and get back on the path of finding Jayke. Mikhail wanted information, but so did Severn. His kin believed he'd turned angel. Setting aside the fact such a thing was impossible, he planned to prove them wrong.

A huge lump of cambion muscle blocked the flow of people ahead, making them inch around him.

Severn lifted his head and met the cambion's purple eyes. "Fuck."

A bag slammed over Severn's head from behind, and something cold and hard and mind-numbingly painful smacked him across the back of the skull, ripping his consciousness away.

THE BAG WAS SNATCHED off his head and tossed aside. Severn blinked into the gloom, finding the madam smiling down at him. Two other demons lurked at the back of the dully lit, grimy room that appeared held together by spit and prayers.

Well, at least it wasn't correctioners.

"Nice to see you again too." The words rattled his bruised skull, making him wince. Trying to bring his hands around from behind his back had them snagging hard on painful bindings. He sighed. Clearly, he should have killed the madam when he'd had the opportunity, instead of saving her. "Why the rough treatment? I thought we were friends?"

"Me, friends with an angel?" She chuckled darkly and then leaned forward. "I know what you are and what you're not."

"And what is that exactly?"

"Demon."

He snorted and willed his heart to slow, then said, "Do I look at all demon to you?"

"Not in the least, but you have to admit, even for an angel, you have unusual sexual tastes."

"You said other angels visited you."

"There are... but they are more, shall we say, hands-on. None like you. Afraid to touch. And then you went and killed those correctioners..."

He had to admit, killing correctioners was not very angelic. But then he hadn't planned on sticking around to deal with the fallout.

Sighing again, he took a few moments to read her two demon guards currently making fine wall ornaments. They looked particularly fond of eating angel, and not in the good way.

"This is all a misunderstanding."

"Hm," the madam mused, not believing any of it. "News reached me of how a demon had illusioned herself into becoming an angel and attempted to kill Mikhail. She failed, naturally."

"Naturally," he agreed, feeling his heart quicken again.

"And a great deal of the mystery surrounding our regular known as Anon began to reveal itself."

"I'm a horny angel, what can I say?" He shrugged and made an attempt to smile, not entirely sure if it worked.

"No. That's not what you are." She leaned forward again, this time placing both hands on his thighs and digging her fingers in. "You're a demon, and not just any demon. You're concubi. And a powerful one, else your illusion would have fallen long before now. Years ago, in fact. And I asked myself, what kind of demon would go to such great lengths to infiltrate the angels? Becoming so good in his new role, he'd rise to stand beside the great guardian, Mikhail. Who is capable of such an impossible feat? I remembered then, a demon... someone revered and respected, who vanished some ten years ago... about the time you began coming to me."

Severn wet his lips and swallowed. When he next spoke, all the humor, the charm, had vanished from his voice, leaving it cold. "Untie me."

She screwed up her nose. "Not yet."

"You know who I am," he admitted. "We're the same. So, untie me."

"No, not until I know you're not going to slaughter me and mine."

"If I wanted you dead, you already would be, and if you truly believe you know me, you know that to be the truth."

"Finally, he speaks the truth. That must be a novelty for you." She grabbed his jaw, lifting his head, scrutinizing his face. The touch didn't threaten to unravel him like it had before, because the damned illusion wouldn't come off. "The detail in the illusion is remarkable... Blue eyes, pouting mouth, golden locks. A bit dark but good enough. I simply had to study you up close to know for sure."

He bared his teeth. "I already warned you *not to touch*."

"Another clue. It's so obvious now, I can't imagine how Mikhail has fallen for it for so long."

He yanked free of her fingers. "Yes, you're extremely clever. Well done. Now let me free of these bindings so we can talk like two civilized demons."

"How did you do it? How do you continue to do it?" Her fingers stroked under his chin, down his neck, and spread over his chest. "Containing all of yourself inside this weak skin... Remarkable."

Done with being probed, he yanked his wrists apart, snapping the bindings, sending the madam screeching back. Her guards thrust their bulk forward, shortswords drawn in a flurry of posturing complete with bestial growls.

Severn rubbed his wrists, ignoring the theatrics. They wouldn't attack. This was all blustering, because as confident as they appeared, their fear-tinged scent permeated the air, overpowering the stench of the building's underlying dampness. They really did know who he was.

"Let's get a few things straight before this goes any farther." He stood, making sure to keep his movements slow so as not to scatter them. The two guards doubled down on their defensive stances, like they had a chance at surviving a fight. "Shall we assume we all know who I am?"

The madam came forward a step, parting her wall of demon muscle, and nodded.

"Good. Don't speak my name, either in my presence or to another soul. If you do mention my existence, I'll hear no matter where I am and be forced to deal with you, terminally. Fair?"

She nodded again. "Fair." Her top lip curled, displaying sharp teeth.

"Secondly, I need your help."

Mikhail

SAPHIA HAD BLINKED at Mikhail and kept her face wooden when he'd asked if there were a way to reverse an allyanse. Thankfully, she didn't ask why.

He'd have gone to Vearn, but she was too perceptive and would immediately put two and two together, namely Severn and himself. As it seemed Severn had no intention of going anywhere, and Mikhail had no right to ask him to, considering all of this was his fault, he was forced to ask for advice elsewhere.

The angel, Saphia, was well-known for healing remedies, helping to speed along an angel's natural healing process. He could imagine, however, that she hadn't expected Mikhail to arrive at her working chambers that morning.

"Is someone having trouble with the process?" she asked, gesturing for him to enter.

He made an agreeable noise and drifted into her chamber, gravitating toward a long worktop with an array of glass spheres and flames simmering multicolored cocktails inside. He'd had Saphia coat a blade in poison once. One cut, and it had rendered the demon unconscious long enough to return from the frontline with it. Unfortunately, it had managed to kill itself before they'd gleaned any useful information out of it.

She appeared to be cooking up all manner of potions now.

"I'm no expert on the allyanse," she said. "Our cousins at Haven would have more knowledge on such matters."

"Yes, but we are in Aerie, and the matter is an urgent one."

She dipped her head. "Of course. Let me see." Rummaging through colored bottles, she found her target and grinned. "By problems, I assume the attraction is overwhelming? That's usually the first surprise... I hear it can be quite debilitating, although I've never experienced it myself, obviously." She handed out the bottle. "Three drops on the tongue once a day should see those urges dampened somewhat. At least for a little while. But, of course, it's better your troubled individual gets themselves declared and sent to Haven as soon as possible."

He took the small blue bottle. "I'm sure they will. Thank you."

"Your Grace, an allyanse is... powerful." Her tone had darkened. "Angels are not accustomed to emotions. The sudden weight of them leaves them vulnerable and volatile. I assume your pair are warriors?"

"They are," Mikhail answered carefully.

"It would be best for your pair to cease all active duty immediately. Anger can be especially destructive."

"I'll take your advice into consideration. Thank you."

THE CONTENTS of the bottle had warmed in his hand by the time he'd returned to his chambers to take the first drop. It tingled on his tongue. He swallowed, rolled his shoulders, aligned his wings, and considered if he felt any different. He didn't, but perhaps it only worked in Severn's presence.

He'd go find him rather than waiting for the elusive angel to visit with his information from the under. Mikhail's sources had been clear that Severn had been on his wanderings again. He always returned at dawn, to his chambers to sleep. He'd be there now.

Mikhail made his way through Aerie's glass halls, Saphia's words coming back to him. She had seemed concerned, and with good reason. The fact angels lacked an emotional spectrum made them strong and efficient. Emotions were distractions—evident in Mikhail's wandering thoughts. But anger was the emotion that concerned him the most. He'd heard old tales of avenging angels laying waste to the world in rage. Those tales had not ended well for anyone.

He didn't knock on Severn's chamber door, never needed to, but considering the sight before him the moment he opened Severn's chamber door, he immediately wished he had. The angel stood shirtless in the arched doorway, safely away from the balcony's edge.

Morning sunlight kissed his skin, making him glow golden, but it was the two gruesome stumps protruding from his back that gave Mikhail pause.

Severn hissed, and with a flick of his fingers, the stumps were gone, illusioned away. "Knock, damn you." He stalked to the bed, snatched up an overshirt, and stabbed his arms through the sleeves, glowering. "What did you expect? Smooth scar tissue? Or maybe you'd prefer not to see such ugliness at all?"

The viciousness of the words, driven by shame and hate, made Mikhail's reaction sluggish. He knew Severn had lost his wings, but Severn was so capable without them, the horror of it had slipped his mind. An angel without his wings was wrong in the way a bird without its wings was wrong. One should not exist without the other.

A curious knot of emotion tried to choke him. Mikhail's own wings ached in sympathy. He illusioned them away with a thought.

Severn saw. His snarl twitched. "You think hiding yours makes me feel better? Think again, guardian. Nothing of yours—"

Mikhail had crossed the floor and was kissing him, cutting off the male's tumultuous rant. It happened so fast, yet also painfully slow. Mikhail only wanted Severn's pain to end. His fingers found his hard jaw, tilted his head up, and then they were mouth to mouth, Severn's soft, despite the snarl.

Severn's words had fallen silent, his body hard and still beneath Mikhail's other hand pressed against his chest, either to hold him back or hold him steady. The angel's mouth parted, like it had beneath Mikhail's thumb, and Mikhail quickened the kiss, spurred on by Severn's acceptance. His tongue was warm and soft and a hungry tease, pulling Mikhail into the tangle of emotion and sensation, all parts neglected for centuries.

Severn's hands slammed into Mikhail's chest, knocking him back with force.

Severn retreated, wiping his mouth on his sleeve. "Fuck, angel... What the fuck?"

Haven, Mikhail didn't know why he'd kissed him. He always knew his thoughts, always knew the next course of action, but this... this was... insanity. He couldn't think around Severn standing there, overshirt open, inviting Mikhail's hands on him all over again. Severn was shocked and enraged, and another, new sensation assaulted Mikhail's senses: shame. The kiss hadn't been welcome. He'd forced it on Severn, and now he couldn't take it back. He'd hurt him when all he'd wanted was to help him.

Mikhail backed up a step, but he had never retreated from battle. Why should this be any different? Severn had enjoyed the kiss, hadn't he? Thoughts spiraled through Mikhail's mind like water down a drain, and they all circled around one point. Severn. The angel took up every thought in this moment and the next.

Mikhail was going insane. He popped the cork on the potion bottle and poured half its content over his tongue, swallowing hard.

Severn's eyes narrowed with suspicion. "What is that?"

"From Saphia," he gasped. "She said it would help with our..."—he gestured between them—"...situation. I didn't name us."

"The witch?" Severn didn't wait for the answer. He snatched the bottle from Mikhail and upended it, swallowing the last of the bottle's contents in two gulps.

Breathless, he scrutinized Mikhail, his gaze running over Mikhail's face and then lower, with entirely inappropriate but highly provocative intensity. The tip of Severn's tongue ran along his bottom lip, and Mikhail found he couldn't have looked away had he cared to try.

He'd always watched Severn, sometimes without the angel knowing, inexplicably fascinated by his easy mannerism and liquid charisma. But his body's reaction was new, the same reaction stirring now, a hardening in eagerness. There was no hiding it inside Mikhail's thin cotton trousers. Severn's gaze flicked down and then back up, his face unreadable.

"It's not working, damn it." He threw the bottle at a nearby wall. Glass exploded, fragments tinkling against the floor.

And now Severn was coming closer again, not moving away like he should, his blue eyes drinking Mikhail in, his breathing slowing. He approached as though he might be stalking down an enemy, and Mikhail's absurdly aroused member twitched at the thought. Gone were Severn's smiling eyes, replaced by sharp ruthlessness. Some distant part of Mikhail's mind screamed a threat. He tensed to defend.

Severn's hand swept around the back of Mikhail's neck and drew him down to his hot, hungry mouth. His tongue thrust in, and Mikhail opened, surrendering to the warmth and pressure of *Severn*. He tasted of the sweet potion they'd both consumed in an effort to prevent exactly this. But this kiss was more than taste and touch. It wasn't just the one thing, but a cacophony of an assault. Severn was suddenly and completely everywhere. In Mikhail's mind, all over his body.

Severn's free hand looped around and clutched at Mikhail's ass, hauling him close.

Mikhail captured the smaller angel's hips, needing him to be still so he could hold on, lest he fall and not know how to find his way back from this madness. He didn't understand any of it, just that he needed Severn closer in a way he'd needed nothing else in his entire life. He needed to consume this angel in all ways, to kiss him until he groaned or pushed Mikhail off, to touch him all over, making him writhe. He wanted to pleasure him even though he had no idea how to, to see him laugh and gasp and cry out for more. And all those thoughts were at once terrifying and thrilling and utterly insane.

Mikhail pulled from the kiss, catching his breath to find the words to end whatever this was, but then Severn's scandalous mouth was on his neck, his tongue a swirl and his teeth nipping, and Mikhail let his head fall back, openly inviting more of Severn's sinful mouth on every part of him. Haven, if he was falling, let him fall, because nothing had ever felt so right.

CHAPTER 11

evern

THE TASTE of angel buzzed over Severn's tongue and sparked its way through his veins, setting ablaze long-neglected parts of his body. He'd been starved of touch and sex and *all of this* for so long, that once Mikhail had kissed him, there really was no alternative but to chase him down, rip off his clothes, and fuck him senseless.

Luckily, Mikhail hadn't fled, though he'd clearly thought about it. Now, Mikhail's greedy hands on Severn's hips made sure neither of them was escaping this terrible, fucking dazzling moment of pure, unadulterated onslaught of pleasure.

Mikhail's obscenely gentle kiss had surprised him. The fact his kiss hadn't hurt like it should have with his illusion still in place surprised him even more. Now, with his illusion stuck, he was angel, and he didn't want this at all. He fucking *needed* it, like he needed to breathe, like he needed to *feed*, like he needed Mikhail beneath his hands, his powerful body opening and submitting just for Severn.

Repressed sexual power lit Mikhail up. The fool was a dam, holding back several lifetimes worth of raw need, and now Severn had the key to the gates. The fact angels self-repressed their desires was a crime. Mikhail was fucking gasping to be set free, and Severn was more than willing to open those gates, so he could drink that power down and fill himself right up. In this battle, Severn would win, because of what he was. And Mikhail had no idea he was feeding and fucking his enemy. Revenge really did taste sweet, made all the sweeter by Severn's unexpected freedom to thoroughly enjoy it.

Mikhail's breathing stuttered, or perhaps he was shivering? His heart raced, making the pulse in his neck beat hotly against Severn's tongue. He could mouth that fluttering spot forever, but there was so much more of the guardian to explore.

Strong, warm fingers encircled Severn's right wrist and forced his arm down, the target clear. Severn hummed against Mikhail's throat and cupped much of the angel's cock and balls, kneading and rolling his thumb against his sizeable erection. Mikhail's gasp was his reward. But then the guardian's fingers were back on his wrist, holding his hand back. The angel was warring with himself, wanting and not wanting. His body wanted, but Severn could imagine his mind was struggling with what this meant. If it were revealed that Mikhail was emotional, he'd be whisked off to Haven quicker than he could wrap his tongue around a lie to deny it.

Fuck, this was perfect.

Severn didn't have to kill him, not yet. He could destroy him first.

"We can't..." the angel whispered, his voice wrecked.

Severn nudged Mikhail's chin with his nose. His hand was still captured, hovering an inch from Mikhail's cock, but his mouth was free. He'd made many a demon weep with less.

"There is no one here to stop us..." the words fell softly against Mikhail's firm mouth, "and no reason why we should stop."

"I mean..." Mikhail turned his head, his mouth now close. His grip on Severn's wrist tightened, turning painful, and fury burned in his golden eyes with such savage intensity, the sight of it had lust clutching at Severn's lungs, stealing his breath and all thoughts. "I don't know how. I've never... this is—"

Holy fuck, to see Mikhail so vulnerable! Severn planted a finger over the angel's pink lips. "Tell me where you want me."

Mikhail tore his grip from Severn's wrist, his decision apparently made, and slammed his hand down on Severn's shoulder, shoving him to his knees.

All right then. This was more like it. He tore the angel's pant fasteners open, freed the silken rod, and closed his mouth firmly around the flushed crown, taking him in, tasting salty sweetness—so very angel.

He meant to tease, to begin with, to draw the pleasure out and wring the angel dry, but all thoughts of going slow, of teasing, had been ripped free and discarded the moment he'd seen fury in Mikhail's eyes. The guardian knew this was a mistake, that it would cost him, and he hated it, maybe even hated Severn in this moment, and fuck, that was the hottest part of all of this.

Steely fingers sank into Severn's hair, locking him between Mikhail's palms. Angel cock slid deep, riding against the roof of Severn's mouth before plunging lower. If he'd had a gag reflex, the thrust would have been less pleasant. Severn took all of the penetration, ringing the thick, veined member with his lips. Mikhail's grip pinned and trapped him. The guardian's hips thrust, his cock relentlessly beating against the back of Severn's throat. Mikhail's mindless fucking could suffocate anything less than concubi, but the angel was too lost in ecstasy to care, and Severn had always preferred his sex walking the fine edge of pain.

When the guardian's ether hit Severn, a strike of lust and power and heat and madness plunged through him, searing muscle and bone, scorching his soul. His body bucked, back arching, his own cock suddenly spilling its load without a single touch. Mikhail let loose a ragged cry. Hot seed spurted down Severn's throat. He greedily took it all.

Mikhail shuddered, his rhythm jittery as Severn milked the last dregs, then the angel's grip in Severn's hair softened. He pulled his fingers free, allowing Severn to lift his gaze while still holding Mikhail's oversensitive cock in his mouth, and gods, Mikhail looked every part the wild being of terror Severn knew him to be. His wings had sprung into sight and spread wide, arched backward slightly. His beauty was breathtaking, made all the more stunning by his ragged, thoroughly fucked glow.

Their gazes met, Severn's tongue still performing, and Mikhail's heated stare almost enough to instantly harden

Severn again. He pulled his mouth off Mikhail's cock and rose off his knees, opening Mikhail's shirt and licking the golden skin up from his waist, venturing higher, until he was pressed chest to chest with Mikhail, looking up into the male's guarded face. He'd enjoyed fucking Severn's mouth, and was doing a spectacular job of hiding it from his expression. Thick waves of ether throbbing off the angel did not lie.

The bedroom would be Severn's preferred next stop, but if he pushed Mikhail in this moment, there was no telling which way the angel would fall. Fight or flee? Severn kissed him on the mouth, making it slow and messy, acutely aware of Mikhail's semi-hard erection against his hip. His own cock had recovered, though the wetness from his unexpected release was proving a distraction he could do without.

He found Mikhail's hand at his side and threaded his fingers in his. "Come to bed," Severn whispered against his lips. It was bold, but he always had been with Mikhail. He looked up, seeking Mikhail's gaze and the answer. He'd tensed, indecision and doubts holding him still.

Would the guardian let Severn fuck him? Probably not, at least not yet, but gods, the thought of having Mikhail beneath him, his glorious wings open and exposed, Severn's hands gripping their ridges as Severn pumped his cock into Mikhail's tight, angelic ass.

Fuck.

A shudder spilled through him, making him achingly hard. Severn bit his own lip to keep from moaning, and Mikhail's demanding mouth was on his again, tongue thrusting. His strength bowed Severn backward. The angel's arms looped around his waist, pulling him so close the buttons on their half-undressed layers of clothing jabbed uncomfortably. Severn needed them both naked and would strip down in seconds to have the angel's furious tongue on all the heated, swollen and sizzling parts of him.

A fist locked in Severn's hair and yanked his head to the side. Mikhail's mouth burned against Severn's throat. "I need you," the guardian whispered. "In ways I can't make sense of."

The words revealed the melting heart of this stone-cold guardian, a male Severn had always despised, often feared, and could never feel anything but lust for.

"I need to touch you." Mikhail spread his hands across Severn's chest, his warrior hands deliciously rough. "You feel... remarkable."

Severn leaned into the touch and fell into Mikhail's soft eyes. He'd tasted angel, was still high from the unique ether, and he wanted more. Anything beyond that or outside of it meant nothing. Just Mikhail. His hands on Severn. His cock in Severn's mouth or his ass, didn't matter. Lust and need rode Severn hard. He'd say and do almost anything to see them quenched.

"Fuck me..." Severn breathed. He clutched at Mikhail's shoulder and back, holding him close, not wanting to let this source of sexual energy go. Severn would fuck him dry, destiny's plan be damned. He'd been too long alone, too long trapped in isolation, too long hiding in a shell, needing to be touched. He deserved this.

This *was* destiny, he realized.

He hadn't failed.

Destiny had given him this gift, this *allyanse*, to better destroy his enemy.

Mikhail marched Severn backward, mouth and hands still exploring, and when a step almost thwarted Severn, Mikhail's arms wrapped around him like they had on the killing field when he'd pulled Severn from the mud.

Severn hoisted himself up and hooked his legs around Mikhail's waist, trapping his hard cock against Mikhail. The angel's broad hands cupped his ass, fingers digging in, asserting Mikhail's will.

They had never been closer, and with Mikhail's ether sinking into Severn, he might never want to part. To fuck and to feed, it was what he was made for, and to drink down *angel*... all those years, all the lies, it was all for *this*.

The sound of drapes fluttering drew Severn from the mindless lust. He lifted his head and saw the huge rayvern on the edge of the balcony. The drapes rippled again, and the bird was gone, but there was no mistaking it, or the way it had cocked its head, giving them all of its inquisitive attention.

Severn angled his hips, grinding his cock against Mikhail's waist. The angel smiled into his neck, and his pace quickened toward the bedroom. When Severn looked to the balcony again for the rayvern, just the breeze and blue skies remained.

Mikhail

MIKHAIL CARELESSLY DROPPED the smaller angel onto his bed and was about to unleash upon him in all the ways his body seemed to know but his mind had yet to catch up with, when the startling sight before him froze him rigid.

Severn lay on his back, his hair a mop of golden locks, his overshirt askew, riding up around his waist, revealing a tantalizing slip of pale skin that Mikhail's fingers eagerly twitched to skim across. The lopsided smile was the same he'd worn when he'd first challenged Mikhail, so long ago, it seemed like another lifetime. The cocky, confident angel had broken from the lower ranks and demanded Mikhail's blade meet his in combat. The ranks had been performing for the humans in a display of grace and poise, and there was this unranked angel making demands of *Mikhail*. He'd almost gotten himself arrested, but Mikhail had seen something in him then, a spark none of the others had. And so they'd fought. Mikhail had won, naturally. But when he'd grasped Severn's hand and hauled him to his feet, the fool was grinning, like he'd enjoyed almost having his head severed from his neck.

Severn wore the same grin now. He'd worn it often and won more than a few of the ranks over with that charming smile and quick-witted backchat. Mikhail had watched him rise through the ranks, and he'd grown to admire how different Severn was in everything he did. The angels had sorely needed his freshness.

Those years were recent in the long span of Mikhail's lifetime, but they'd felt brighter than the rest.

He wondered now if maybe he'd fallen for this angel long before these last few days. If perhaps it had all begun on that first day, when the runt of a wingless angel had dared challenge a guardian.

Severn was no runt now. Ripped with muscle but lithe too. A surprising delight in Mikhail's hands.

"Are you going to stare all day, or shall we fuck, because I know which I'd prefer, *angel*."

He said angel like he meant it as an insult, and Mikhail's simmering anger shifted, heating his veins. Yes, he hated this, himself, even Severn for making this so easy, and he hated that Severn seemed to love seeing that fury and feeling it beneath Mikhail's touch, feeding these choking emotions, making them spin and swirl, and making Mikhail dizzy to it all.

Bracing an arm beside Severn on the bed, he propped a knee beside Severn's thigh, holding himself poised over his devilish angel.

Severn had thrown an arm back, his body languid, like

an invitation, not in the least concerned or afraid. Mikhail had already fucked his unruly mouth, and there was little more he wanted in this world than to fuck the rest of him. He couldn't explain it, didn't know where it had come from, and had no hope of understanding what any of this meant, and somehow that made this moment more thrilling.

Severn's quick fingers flicked opened the rest of Mikhail's overshirt buttons, and then his hand was a warm pressure running down Mikhail's chest, until turning and capturing Mikhail's revived member. Pleasure whipped down his back. Severn had some kind of tingling touch that tore open any and all of Mikhail's restraints, destroying any attempt to stop this or hold himself back. He groaned aloud, surprised by the sound on his lips.

Severn's free hand looped around the back of Mikhail's neck and pulled, drawing him down, so they were eye-to-eye, Severn's other hand stroking Mikhail's cock. "Fast," his pumps quickened, "or slow?" and slowed, drawing long, stuttering breaths from Mikhail.

Severn's tongue swept across his bottom lip, inviting Mikhail's mouth to his, but not to kiss. Mikhail tilted his head, lips brushing Severn's, gazes mixed, and said, "Will you cry my name?"

Severn's dark pupils expanded, the idea acceptable, and as Mikhail rubbed Severn's member inside his pants, it pulsed against his palm like a hungry thing. Feeling Severn want him in return was like some unwrapped gift. He wanted to keep it safe and hidden and all his. Nobody else could have him.

Mikhail pushed up, using the weight of his wings to help balance him, and straddled Severn's thighs.

Severn tore off his own shirt, revealing a glorious spread of honed abdominal muscles and sun-kissed skin. He was a feast. With his wings, he must have been glorious. The feathers would have been golden, just like his hair. One day, he'd ask Severn to tell him who had hurt him, and if they weren't already dead, Mikhail would hunt them down and destroy them, if Severn wished it.

Severn's hand went to work on his pants, but Mikhail fell forward again, trapping it beneath them. Just the thought of someone hurting him made Mikhail want to rage and scream at the world. The allyanse rode him hard. He needed this angel, needed him close, to protect him. "Will you serve me forever?" he whispered.

Severn's wicked mouth twitched. "Yes, Your Grace."

This time, Mikhail did groan his want. "Say my name."

"*Yes, Mikhail*," Severn purred, his pink mouth sensuously shaping the letters.

Thought became secondary to need. Mikhail flipped Severn over, tore his pants down over the tight rise of his ass, hoisted his hips up, and grasped himself. He knelt, poised behind Severn, wings spread, cock pinched against the smaller angel's puckered hole.

Fear tripped him.

He wanted this, needed it so badly, he was afraid of his own strength. He'd almost lost his mind fucking Severn's mouth, and now this... He was not sure he wouldn't hurt him. Was this even how it was done? It seemed so *primal*.

Severn threw a vicious look over his shoulder. "Fuck me now, *Mikhail*, or are you afraid?" He had his own cock in his hand, Mikhail saw his arm moving with the rhythmic motion of pumping himself, and the last thread of self-restraint fell away. He pushed inside. Severn jerked back, impaling himself. Blinding ecstasy stole a gasp from Mikhail's mouth. He clutched Severn's hips and fell forward, sinking his teeth briefly into Severn's shoulder and biting down.

"*Fuck*!"

Shivers cascaded down Mikhail's spine. "Your filthy mouth is a sin," he growled against Severn's shoulder, rocking his hips, pumping his member into the tight and inviting warmth of Severn's hole. There seemed to be no need for oil, the fit was smooth and exquisitely perfect.

Severn laughed, and the sound of it had Mikhail growling lower with every quickening thrust.

"You fucked... my filthy... mouth," he said, breathless between thrusts, "so what... does that... make you?"

Mikhail's mind unspooled. He gripped the smaller angel's thighs, threw his head and wings back, and pounded thighs-to-ass, as deep as Severn would take him, to a barrage of Severn's rhythmic grunts. Pleasure like he'd never had pooled low in his back, tightening, threatening to release.

He pounded faster—instinct a relentless whip—until it all blurred into one long, exquisitely tight moment.

Severn's beautiful back shone, and two hideously twisted stumps emerged. The bone had long-ago healed over, its edges rounded. But the angles of the single cuts to each wing were clear. He hated that such a thing had been done to Severn, that he could not fix him, that Severn had suffered then and suffered every day since. It was not right, was not fair. But even without his wings, Severn outshone them all, and Mikhail knew in that moment, allyanse or not, he'd protect his broken angel from the horrors of a world that would take his wings. Love him, if Severn would have him. But even if he didn't, Mikhail would see to it that Severn was never hurt again.

The tight pull of pleasure snapped. Mikhail came hard with a roar, his member pulsing, spurting its seed deep into Severn's quivering sweat-glistening body.

Mikhail rode seconds of numbing bliss until his eyes fell to the stumps again. His heart stuttered. He couldn't look away. He reached out a hand to touch the mangled flesh and discolored scar tissue, as though he could smooth away Severn's agony, but pulled back at the last moment.

He'd brought this marvel of an angel back to life, but he could not fix the butchering done to him.

The twin stumps faded from view and were soon gone, hidden behind Severn's illusion. He may not even have known he'd revealed them. Maintaining an illusion in the midst of coupling could not be easy. Mikhail would say nothing of seeing them, but he'd carry the image with him and never forget its truth and his promise.

He had the sudden urge to wrap Severn in his arms and pull him close. He was Mikhail's now. And nobody and nothing dared cross a guardian. But Severn had made it quite clear that all this was the allyanse at work and he wanted no part of it. Mikhail had made the same clear too —there was no use in embracing him, or telling him he was protected. Severn was too free for that.

Mikhail dragged a hand down his face, waking from the rampant possession that seemed to have overcome him. They'd done quite enough. Mikhail could not, in fact, protect Severn from the very real threat of being deemed too emotional to continue as a warrior.

Severn eased forward, parting them, and fell onto his side, eyebrow arched at Mikhail still knelt over him, member semi-hard and slick. The rogue angel's gaze was still too hungry and bright a thing, like he could never be satisfied.

Mikhail gazed down at him, experiencing a bewildering array of emotions, all tangled together so he had no hope of understanding a single one. But he was not afraid of them, not anymore, not with Severn. Here, together, in this moment, this seemed perfect.

"You are quite skilled... in this." Mikhail lowered himself beside Severn, careful to let his wings drape off the edge. He should probably have illusion them away, but his thoughts were fuzzy and soft, and he had no wish to do anything other than rest with Severn tucked close.

"It's instinct, don't you think?" Severn had rolled onto his back now and gazed at the ceiling, golden lashes fluttering. His cheeks had a dash of color, the same blushed hue as his lips. "You know, demons don't care what gender fucks what, or who fucks whom." He flicked a careless gesture at the dresser. "Even furniture, if the mood strikes."

Mikhail regarded the dresser and couldn't imagine ever wanting to insert a part of himself anywhere inside such an inanimate object. He found Severn's gaze again, the corner of his mouth tilted in a strange way, as though fighting with a laugh. "Is that true?"

"Would I lie to you, Your Grace?" He let his head fall to the side so he faced Mikhail, and his blue eyes sparkled with mischief, or perhaps it was the after-coupling glow that he'd heard angels speak of. Mikhail would never be able to hear *Your Grace* again without remembering the sinful sound of it on Severn's lips. "Do you think all demons bad?" he suddenly asked, eyes still sparkling.

"They are the enemy," Mikhail replied. Good and bad didn't come into it.

"Why, because some ancient angel made them to fight us? Don't you think it's all... redundant? We fight them, they fight us. What if both sides just stopped fighting?"

"They do not know how to stop. They are beasts, driven by emotions and desires. They cannot stop."

Shrewdness turned his sparkle sharp. "Have you ever tried talking to them?"

Only Severn would think to even consider such a thing. "Should an angel commune with the rats in London's sewers?"

Severn's cheek flickered. "I suppose you are right. Animals do not know how to stop being animals."

"You know a great deal about demons. More than any other angel."

His fingers started dancing down Mikhail's chest, flicking the stray locks of dark hair aside. "I make a point of knowing my enemy so I can better destroy them when the time comes."

"For which I do not thank you enough." Mikhail blinked at the ceiling, relishing Severn's tickling touch roaming his chest. "When we become *guardian*, we leave so much of the world behind. I left *everything* behind. I had friends... once."

"You did?"

"It was long ago. I remember caring, I think. I forgot what it means to feel."

"I know what it's like to lose a part of yourself," Severn said, his tone soft.

Mikhail was struck again by the urge to pull the male in and wrap his wings closed, tucking them both safely inside. If this was some part of the allyanse at work, he fully understood why the angels caught in its throes were eager to leave, to keep each other safe, away from the threat of war.

But he could not take Severn away. Their lives did not permit such freedoms, and the allyanse for them wouldn't result in a happy ending in Haven anyway. Two males could not produce offspring. The allyanse was forced. In fact, all of this was inefficient fantasy, and it had to end. Now.

Mikhail pushed up and swung his legs over the edge of the bed, bringing his right wing around, careful not to brush Severn with his trailing feathers. He lifted their expanse forward, stretching their feather tips. When Severn's hands pressed against his back, Mikhail stilled, recalling the tattered remains of Severn's stumps.

The male's hands swept down his spine, kneading over tight muscles, relieving the weight of the wings, and then roamed back up again, between his shoulder blades, massaging higher. The touch left the same kind of tingling sensation behind as it had on more intimate parts of Mikhail.

"Do you remember"—his lips skimmed Mikhail's ear —"when you returned from battle so broken you could not retract your wing?"

"I do."

Severn had been there, like he'd known Mikhail *needed* him. Wings were sensitive, and his instincts then had him refusing any help. Any but Severn's. Severn had stroked along the wing's arch and snapped the bone with devastating ruthlessness, allowing it to reset and heal correctly. And during all that, Severn had never left his side.

Severn's tingling touch stroked over the powerful joints

now, climbing higher, massaging out knots and kinks along the wings' arches.

Mikhail had taken him for granted for so long. Unable to see Severn for who he truly was. Thoughtful, *powerful*, caring.

Warm, strong fingers looped Mikhail's hair around a fist, and then Severn was pressed against Mikhail's back, his tongue a hot tease against his ear. "Leaving so soon?"

By Haven, he could not let this strange emotional magic consume them. "What information did you discover in the cauldron?"

The harsh, cold words worked. Severn's grip on Mikhail's wings tensed. "I was right. An attack is imminent. But none know when or where. I was about to try another lead when I was..." he trailed off.

Mikhail turned his head and caught Severn's frown. "When you were what?"

He withdrew, shifting to the other side of the bed, where he turned his back on Mikhail and scooped up his shirt. "An angel asking questions in the cauldron attracts the wrong kind of attention. I'd worn out my welcome."

"Did the cambion cause you trouble? You must alert the correctioners—"

"I dealt with it." He jerked the shirt on and buttoned it up. Clearly, whatever had happened had been difficult, because now he did not seem to be able to meet Mikhail's gaze.

Mikhail had brought the war into the room with them to push Severn away, and it had worked, but now he wished Severn would climb back into bed and beckon Mikhail to ravish him all over again. Just the simple act of watching him shrug the shirt over his shoulders had

Mikhail's mind wandering to exactly how he'd ease that shirt off those shoulders and kiss the revealed skin all over again.

He would have to navigate these emotions better if the secret of their allyanse was going to stand up to any scrutiny.

"What of the illusion skill. Did you find out any more on that?" He stood, forcing himself from the bed. If he lingered, he might demand Severn stay all night, and their absence would be noticed.

"No. As I said, it's rare... limited to a few subspecies."

"Such as?"

Severn's scowl cut deeper at the question. "Concubi, mostly."

"Then it's a good thing the majority of those are dead." Mikhail had seen it as his divine duty to eradicate the ruthless and debase concubi demons—incubi and succubae. They were well-known for their grotesque power harvested from the emotion of others, like leeches. But with the assassination attempt, Mikhail hadn't been as thorough as he'd thought. If they were breeding and bolstering their numbers again, he'd need to act.

Mikhail hastily dressed, and now with the war and their work between them, he could look at Severn again as the warrior he relied upon. With any luck, his lust would end at this, now they were both *satisfied*.

Finally, his thoughts were clearer. Perhaps they'd both just needed this release to move on. He illusioned his wings away and headed for the door.

"I want current concubi numbers. Can you get me that information?"

"Why?" Severn asked.

"To kill them. Why else?"

"Of course, Your Grace."

The bite in Severn's voice gave Mikhail pause, but when he turned to ask, the angel had turned away and was straightening his own clothes. Mikhail hesitated at the door, feeling the necessary distance opening between them. "What happened here, between us—"

"Shall not be spoken of."

"Will never happen again."

Severn bowed his head. "As you wish."

His memory provided him with the image of Severn on his knees, Mikhail's hands in his hair and his cock down his throat, and it was all Mikhail could do to leave before the lustful fuel in his blood reignited and he succumbed all over again.

evern

WITH THE WAY his body throbbed and ached and pined after the touch of angel, Severn might have forgotten how coldhearted the guardian bastard was. Thankfully, Mikhail'd reminded him with that last statement regarding killing all concubi. Now his back throbbed with the memory of having Mikhail's blade slice through his wings.

Severn embraced the hurt. The pain of their loss had kept him living the lie this long. It would shore him up for the last hurdles ahead.

Topped off and buzzing with power, he headed straight for the training quarter. The day was still new. Vearn would be training the younger angels, those plucked from Haven before forming memories of their parents and thrown into battle training.

Severn observed the huge open platforms, each one

suspended on a single pillar at different heights to its neighbors. Angels performed aerial acrobatics from one platform to another, mock-clashing with spear and sword. From a distance, they looked like butterflies above a meadow, if the meadow were made of steel flowers. The last time he'd seen a real meadow, he'd been sprawled on his back, buried among the wildflowers, Samiel's hand in his. It turned out Samiel was allergic to pollen, resulting in a sneezing fit and Severn crying with laughter.

Seeing Vearn, he whistled, drawing her attention from her class. She stepped from the edge of a platform, threw out her wings, and soared in, circling above him before landing gracefully. He'd stopped being envious long ago. Mostly.

"Severn," she bowed her head respectfully, "is something wrong?"

"There is..." He looked around him. There were no angels nearby, and though the wind could carry their voices, Vearn's class was far enough away not to hear. Though it wouldn't hurt if a few happened to catch some of what he had to say, helping the rumors spread.

"I'm not sure how to approach this." He played at looking away, squinting into the light, as though ashamed to meet her gaze.

Vearn's brow pinched, making her eyes seem sharp. "Go on."

"It's Mikhail... and well, myself. You see... there's something you should know."

He told her everything. At least, everything he cared to: the allyanse used to resurrect him after his death in the killing fields, Mikhail's attempt to conceal their attraction with Saphia's potions, his desire to keep their affair hidden. And of course, Severn's lack of choice in any of this. Severn was the victim, really, and he had no one else to turn to but the stalwart and reliable Vearn.

"You are bonded?"

"I..." he spread his hands, looking sheepish. "Yes? My emotions are unruly. I can only imagine what Mikhail is going through."

She sniffed, lifted her chin, and folded her wings shut. She'd seen their behavior around each other in the past few days, and now those strange changes began to make sense. "Meet me in the council room in an hour." With that, she took off and was a tiny blot in the sky moments later.

When he arrived at the council room, the table was empty, and Severn was alone. He wished he had his wings back just so he didn't feel so small among Aerie's cavernous spaces. Would he ever stop wishing them back? He'd stopped wishing Samiel back years ago. Death was final. But his wings still ached like they haunted him, like he could feel their towering weight, could throw them open again and take to the skies. Several times after Mikhail had mutilated him, he'd forgotten he was wingless and tried to take flight from the edge of the clifftops along the coast, stopping only at the last second by a voice that whispered him back from the edge. Destiny's voice. He'd followed her ever since, leading him here, he supposed, to this room, and this moment.

Solo entered first, his gaze hard and fixed somewhere in the middle distance. Although they hadn't been especially close, Solo's refusal to acknowledge him unexpectedly jabbed at his chest. Vearn had told him. He wore his armor with his two-handed angelblade strapped to his back, so he was here for battle.

Severn's heart picked up its pace. He'd wanted this. This had to happen eventually.

"Severn..." Solo said, stopping a few feet from him. The warrior's hardness softened, and the angel's lips turned down. "I should have seen it..." Bizarrely, the warrior came in close and threw his arms around Severn, embracing him hard enough to knock the air from Severn's lungs. "Love is precious, brother." He looked as though he might say more, but other angels were entering, and Solo retreated to the side of the room.

The jab of guilt grew sharper.

Severn watched the others file in, waiting for any more to fling themselves at him, but all steered well away, keeping to the fringes until they had the room encircled. Vearn was the last to enter, done up in her battle attire but with no helmet. She nodded at Severn once and then took the head of the table—Mikhail's place.

Where was Mikhail?

Severn glanced around at the thirty faces, all of whom he knew to be demon killers. Had they gathered here, surrounding him, because they knew he wasn't one of them? No, Solo wouldn't have embraced him. This was the allyanse.

Silence descended—the thick, ominous kind.

They didn't appear to be waiting for him to speak. Vearn's eyes were on the open balcony and the fluttering drapes, expecting an arrival.

And then a figure filled that space, his wings so broad they blocked out the sun.

Mikhail strode in, frowned at them all, and stopped at the foot of the table. "What is this, Vearn?"

"We know, Mikhail."

Mikhail's gaze flicked to Severn, and Severn's throat prickled, his mouth instantly dry. "Know?" the guardian asked.

"Your allyanse with Severn. It has been confirmed with multiple sources and cannot be denied."

"What of it?"

Only Mikhail could shrug off the full force of the battle council.

"You are both to be immediately transported to Haven."

"No." Mikhail pressed his hands against the tabletop, leaning down a little to do it. His wings slowly opened, just enough to remind everyone here who and what he was. "I am not going anywhere."

Vearn faced him down. "The allyanse is a sacred bond and must be obeyed."

"In case you haven't noticed, Severn and I are both males. There is little use in us being sent to Haven. The demons are due to attack any day, and we still do not know their plans. Aerie needs Severn and I. We will not be leaving."

Mikhail's words sounded a great deal like Severn's when Mikhail had tried to dismiss him. It seemed the angel had been listening.

Vearn nodded a silent command, and the angels positioned around the room closed in. "Be that as it may, the allyanse means you are too emotional to lead us. I will take command."

Mikhail straightened. A muscle fluttered in Mikhail's

jaw, and Severn felt the guardian's anger prickle his skin, or maybe it was the allyanse responding to Mikhail's emotional state, because although he appeared calm, the prickle running sharp fingers across Severn's skin felt a lot like fury. His heart was a rapid *thump-thump* in his throat. This was the moment Mikhail would fall. This was the moment destiny had promised him. His angels would turn on him.

Vearn held the guardian's stare.

An angel reached for Mikhail's arm. Mikhail shot them a sharp, warning look, and the warrior's reaching hand stalled midair. "Don't make me fight you."

"Mikhail," Vearn interjected with cool authority, "you know this to be right. Your emotions are blinding you. Stand down."

Another guard had closed in and reached for Mikhail's wrist, and the guardian inhaled, spreading his wings. The prickling sensation turned to acid beneath Severn's skin. Severn stepped back, straight into the iron-like grip of two guards, but had no wish to fight them. Events were playing out exactly as he'd expected. Mikhail, however, was done playing nice. He threw the first angel onto the table with a crash and burst of loose feathers, spurring the rest to plunge forward in a flurry of wings.

Severn shrank back, forgetting the guards holding him, and watched Mikhail unleash on his own people. They swarmed him. He knocked each back as though they were mild annoyances, moving with the kind of liquid grace that came from several lifetimes worth of killing instinct. An angel made the mistake of catching Mikhail's left wing and was plucked clean off his feet and thrown against the wall for his effort. The more they attacked, the faster Mikhail retaliated, pushing them back as though his will alone was enough to fend them off. But he did not hurt them. All were climbing back to their feet, shaken but unharmed, until one produced a blade.

Mikhail saw, reached for his own blade, and in the fray, his dark-eyed gaze flicked to Severn, seeking something unknown. Severn stared back, feeling that same rage skitter down his back and tasting it on his tongue. None other in the room could sense the rising heat and the crackle of power. Then Mikhail pulled his blade free and tossed it onto the table. The massive weapon skidded toward Vearn, who hadn't lifted a finger throughout the entire mêlée.

"Stop!" she barked.

The angels instantly ceased and withdrew, almost all breathless, wings sagging, and all knew they hadn't bested Mikhail. He'd surrendered, saving their lives.

"You know this to be the right thing," Vearn said.

A pair of guards locked iron shackles around Mikhail's wrists, pulling his arms behind him. He bowed his head, defeated, and illusioned his wings away, instantly making himself appear less threatening.

"Transport them immediately." Vearn came around the table and waited as Mikhail's guards led him toward the door.

Mikhail pulled back on his own guards, stopping them from dragging him through the door, implying there was a strong chance he could simply break free and be done with all of them.

Vearn lifted her face under Mikhail's scrutiny. "You should have let Severn die," she said.

He should have. Everyone in the room knew it,

including Severn. If he had, Mikhail would not have been compromised.

Mikhail lifted his chin and told Vearn, "You'll make a fine guardian."

~

BECAUSE MIKHAIL COULDN'T BE TRUSTED to go quietly, both he and Severn were transported down to Aerie's foundations, into the underground station terminal, and ushered into two cages, both made of thick iron bars. The cages were at least positioned together inside a timber carriage, the only light spilling in through cracks in the wooden cladding.

Solo had the privilege of chaining Severn inside his, only once meeting his eyes as he locked the shackles home. He almost behaved as though he cared Severn was being shipped off to some faraway land with no hope of ever returning.

Severn wet his lips to say some parting words to him, but in the end, the words wouldn't come.

The doors slammed shut, a whistle blew, and the carriages shunted into motion.

Severn pulled at the chains. He had enough length to circle the small space and set about examining the hinges and welds. Both cages were made for demons. Having Mikhail locked inside one was a surprising indignity from Vearn. "Not the first-class trip to Haven you imagined?"

Mikhail sat propped against his bars, one leg drawn up, his head resting back, eyes closed. The cage was small enough to hold him while he had his wings illusioned away, but if he were to summon them, their feathered expanse would be forced into the tiny space and likely shatter into a thousand bones. Severn had heard of demons trying to escape the cages by summoning their wings, hoping the bars would break. All were crushed.

And angels believed themselves the civilized race.

Severn snorted, dropped to the floor, mirroring Mikhail's seated position, and watched the guardian through the bars. His untucked shirt was smudged with iron dirt. The same smudges marred his cheek and forehead. His long hair was still miraculously knot-free, though it likely wouldn't stay that way for long. He appeared calm, but Severn's skin still prickled with what he could only assume was a volatile emotional mix the allyanse was transferring to him from Mikhail. Considering Mikhail had to be an emotional wreck inside, he was holding up well.

"Why did you tell them?" Mikhail asked, eyes still closed and head still tilted back.

"Because it was the right thing to do."

Slowly lowering his head, he opened his eyes. "Aerie is now vulnerable."

"Vearn is capable. Our ranks are intact. The city will survive without its guardian."

"Did you want this?" A hint of anger grated the edges off his words.

Brittle anger was in his eyes too, and Severn was grateful there were two sets of iron bars between them.

He folded his arms and dropped his gaze to the bars between them. "Vearn was right. You should have let me die. I've witnessed you sacrifice dozens in your pursuit of victory. Why did you save me, Mikhail?"

Mikhail turned his face away to stare at the carriage door. "Is it not obvious?"

"If the allyanse were active before the battle, yes. But it was not. Your saving my life made no practical sense."

The carriage clattered and rumbled, its iron wheels galloping down the tracks, taking them far outside the city to a fate neither wanted, where Mikhail's wings would be clipped, and they were due to spend the rest of their long lives fucking and producing angel spawn. There was a huge flaw with that plan that nobody seemed to want to acknowledge.

"Because saving you had nothing to do with being practical," Mikhail finally said, speaking so quietly Severn almost missed the words beneath the clattering.

He cared. He had cared before the allyanse, and Severn had missed it, or they'd both missed it until Severn had died in the mud. Mikhail, the greatest guardian angel of their time, ruthless, powerful, and entirely incapable of emotion, cared for Severn. The irony was so acute, it was almost painful.

"I could not let you die," the angel admitted with a sigh. "Nothing else mattered in that moment. The battle, whether we won or lost, I didn't even care if the demons breached Aerie in my absence." He choked, like the admission was so foul, it made him wretch. "It was... instinct. I barely recalled killing Argothun, just that it had to happen because he... because I saw what he did to you, and I could not let that stand." His last words trembled with the same rage he'd been clinging to. "I'd have killed every last demon on the killing field to save you." He looked down. "It is surely a madness and no doubt the reason why I'm in this cage, but it did not feel wrong..."

He met Severn's gaze through the bars. "It does not feel wrong."

Severn found any response had fled his mind. The things he spoke of, the passion with which he'd fought to save Severn, angels were not capable of those emotions, and certainly not an angel like Mikhail. They were little more than machines with wings, driven by the desire to kill all demons. At least, that was how Severn had always known them.

Mikhail's confession didn't change anything.

So, Mikhail had cared. It just meant his downfall would be all the more devastating, and that downfall was almost finished.

Destiny had put Severn here, in this moment, and destiny had one last hand left to play.

"How far outside the city do you think we are?" he asked, steering the conversation far away from Mikhail's confession and its meaning. He could do little about his racing heart or the strange tightness in his chest. That was the allyanse fucking with his head. Soon, this would all be over. The allyanse would be dealt with, and he'd be free from this wretched angel-skin. Everything would be right again.

"A few miles. We have some ways to go..."

Severn settled in his spot, resting his arm over a bent knee. "Have you seen Haven?"

"Never. And those who go do not return."

They fell into a strangely comfortable silence, one that even the rattling carriages couldn't break. Severn rocked with the motion of the train and occasionally glanced at Mikhail. The angel had his head tipped back again, his eyes closed. He wasn't sleeping, but he was elsewhere. He had a few hundred years of memories to call upon to keep him company, whereas Severn only had half a century. His half a century was easily worth an angel's several lifetimes. What did Mikhail dream of? He'd wondered a great deal about the guardian when first arriving at the bottom of his ranks, and wondered a lot more after Mikhail had finally noticed him. He'd seemed infallible back then. Like the god so many thought him to be. He'd led the angels for centuries, and in that time, more and more demons had died. Cities destroyed. Families ripped apart. Demons now were numbered one to every thirty angels. As a race, they were desperate.

The war might end when Mikhail did.

That had made Severn's actions right, didn't it? Why then, did the wretched guilt still squirm inside?

Brakes screamed, and the carriages shunted, clattering together as movement suddenly slowed.

Mikhail's eyes opened. "Too soon to be Haven."

Severn slowly got to his feet and stared at the closed door. He listened but heard only the ticking of hot metal and his own racing heart.

All those years, all those sacrifices... it all came down to this.

The door rattled and then rolled open on wheels, spilling ambient streetlight inside. "Stand back," a demon grunted, applying a sweet-smelling paste to the cage lock. Severn stepped back, acutely aware of Mikhail rising to his feet and approaching the internal bars.

The lock blew with a short, sharp blast and smattering of metal, and the door swung open.

Severn took a step forward.

"Don't, Severn," Mikhail urged, his usual firm voice quivering. "They'll kill you..."

The door in Mikhail's side of the carriage rumbled open next, revealing his closed bars. He raised an arm, shielding his face from the light, but he couldn't miss the further two demons outside, one carrying an angel-style recurve bow.

Severn jumped from the carriage and held out his hand for the bow. The madam handed the weapon over with a short dip of her chin.

Necessary, Severn silently reassured himself.

"What is this, Severn?" Mikhail asked, blinking into the light.

"This..." Severn nocked an arrow into the bow, pulled back the string, and aimed up through the bars at Mikhail. "Is vengeance." He let go. The arrow smacked straight into Mikhail's chest, slamming him back against the bars, rattling the iron, and dropped him to his hands and knees. At such short range, the arrow had penetrated straight through Mikhail's unprotected chest and lodged itself in muscle.

Severn took a second arrow from the madam. "This..." he backed up, lifting the bow again. "Is ten years of preparation in the making." The arrow flew, snatching Mikhail's right shoulder and jerking him back. He was up on his knees now, clutching at the arrows, breathing hard through bared teeth, and oh, how his fury burned beneath Severn's skin. The angel's ether, this time spawned from rage, was the icing on the cake.

Revenge really did taste sweet.

A high-pitched whistle sounded somewhere near the front of the long, snaking train. Severn checked the abandoned streets branching off around them, into deeper London. They wouldn't be alone for much longer. If the train guards didn't reach them, correctioners soon would.

"Finish him," the madam hissed.

Severn nocked the third arrow, lifted the bow, and aimed between Mikhail's eyes. Mikhail's mouth had found its warrior snarl, and rage filled his too-dark eyes—Severn could taste the seething ether boiling around the guardian and had to repress a pleasurable shudder. Fury was too small a word for what Mikhail was experiencing. Blood pulsed from around the stuck arrows, already soaking Mikhail's chest. Trapped, with no weapons and no allies, he was just an angel on his knees, just like Cassandra, the angel Severn had pushed from his balcony. Only Mikhail's death would be far more satisfying.

"Why?" Mikhail whispered.

"They're coming!" the madam screeched. "Kill him now!"

More alarm whistles had joined the first, and they were getting closer. If they were seen, the chances of escaping would drastically reduce.

"Why?" Severn smiled a cold, hard smile and approached the bars, the arrow still poised to fire. "You took my love from me." The guardian's face softened with confusion. "And you took my fucking wings!"

"*No,*" Mikhail gasped and slumped forward on a hand, hurting like the arrow had already struck him. "No, I could ne—"

"*Now!*" the madam screeched again.

The heavily armored guards were incoming, at least half a dozen from either end of the train, bearing down fast.

The madam grabbed Severn's shoulder and pulled. His finger slipped from the bow's string, the arrow flew, jerking Mikhail's head back with a spray of blood. The madam pulled Severn away, but not before he saw Mikhail fall and felt the wretched, sickening allyanse finally snap, tearing out what felt like half his heart. Maybe its absence would kill them both.

Whistles screamed. Shouts went up.

Mikhail moved...

He fucking *moved*. Severn turned on his heel, and alongside the madam, he sped into the abandoned buildings with the screech of whistles sounding behind.

CHAPTER 14

Mikhail

THE ENTIRE LEFT side of Mikhail's face beat hot and loud, thumping through his skull. He tried to press a cool hand to it but found the skin slippery and numbed. His vision blurred, his body a riot of pain, and the relentless screaming whistles wouldn't stop, but more than all of that, he'd felt the allyanse snap, tearing out half his heart.

He didn't understand any of this... Nothing made any sense. Why would Severn hurt him?

Gripping the arrow in his shoulder, he yanked it free, but the one running through his middle and out his back made his vision spin and his body convulse.

He knew only one thing with any certainty.

This cage would not be his coffin.

With a thought, he summoned his wings. Fire ripped down his back. Iron crushed his bones. The sounds of horrible snapping flooded his ears, like tree branches surrendering to a storm.

His wings...

As the iron pushed in, he pushed back, flexing powerful muscles, forcing his body to *obey*. One bar twanged free. Then another. Another. And with a roar, the bars exploded outward. He fell from the cage, vision swimming and wings ablaze in a wholly wrong way.

Then the first shot was fired. The pain came first, striking him in the leg, and then the sound, echoing off the high buildings, their black windows looking down on him. Another shot, another dart of pain, but there was so much of it now, he barely felt it.

Crawling, then staggering into a loping run, he illusioned the wings away, still bearing their pain, and fell into the nearest vacant doorway. He couldn't fight, not with his body wracked by pain, the arrows still sticking from his chest...

Severn had done this...

He doubled over and dropped. So great was the pain, his mind concocted the image of an old woman hobbling toward him with what appeared to be an iron bar in her hand. Then the bar came down and he imagined no more.

PAIN PUSHED DOWN on Mikhail's back and wrapped him in glass thorns. He groaned awake to shifting candlelight and the smell of warm food. His eyes told him that an old woman was stirring a pot over a small, round stove, but his instincts told a whole other story. Trying to sit up, he pulled on his wrists, snagged at his back. He'd been bound.

Out of one prison and into another. He could at least sit upright against the wall, teeth gritting against the pain.

He'd broken the cage with his wings, but the weight of agony suggested the cage had broken much of him too.

"Ah, there you are... About time too. Thought you was never gonna wake."

She left her simmering pot on the stove and planted a hand on her hip, frowning down at him. Her face, wrinkled with age, bore kind, forgiving eyes, and when she hobbled closer, her body advertised a lifetime of hard labor.

It was all very convincing, and all lies.

Mikhail lifted his chin. "Release me."

"No, can't do that." She waggled a finger, her thick, cracked lips stretched into a grin, and she set about gathering some herbs from an array of pots, using her gnarled hands to mash some kind of paste together. "You ain't my prisoner."

He pulled on the wrist-bindings. "Then why tie me?"

"Well, I ain't stupid, am I." She chuckled to herself and peeled the potatoes, her old hands working remarkably fast with the little knife.

"You struck me."

"Yup."

"Why?"

"Because dragging an unwilling angel back 'ere ain't exactly subtle, now is it?"

A crow landed at the one broken window and squawked an alarm at seeing Mikhail. Not a crow, he realized, noting its size. A rayvern. It hopped inside, onto a shelf, strutted along until reaching the woman, and pecked at her herbs. She patted the bird on the head.

Whatever this act was for, he was content to let her focus on her concoction while he twisted and tugged on the wrist-bindings.

"I took the arrows outtah yah handsome torso. Nasty things. You're welcome."

He looked down at himself and saw two wounds, both packed with some kind of herb paste. Whatever it was, it thoroughly dulled the pain. Or it could be the fire raging down his back overshadowed all the other wounds. "What are you?"

"Demon, obviously."

He'd known that much the moment he'd woken, but she wasn't just any demon. Her old woman appearance was almost flawless and would fool a great many people, but not Mikhail. Because he'd seen her ilk before. Killed most of them, he'd thought.

"Are you even female?"

"No. And I ain't male either. Best bits of both."

The rayvern squawked, and she tossed it a piece of something pale and limp that looked suspiciously like a dead chic. The bird caught it out the air in its thick black beak and eyed Mikhail as though concerned he might steal it for himself.

"Your illusion does not fool me."

"Reckoned it wouldn't." She tossed all her ingredients in the bubbling pot and stirred the steaming concoction with a wooden spoon. "I have some skill. Was a concubi trait. Did you know that, angel? The twin races incubi and succubae was the strongest of us all. Could change their shape into anything your cold angel heart desired."

"Angels do not desire demons."

Her rheumy eyes held some sparkle. "Maybes you

wouldn't even know what it was you desired? Besides, they're all dead, ain't they? I'm a half, by the way, a cambion. Only have a jot of their gift. Now get yer wings out." She used a ladle to spoon some of her slop into a bowl and approached him with intention.

The thought of revealing his ruined wings to this creature made his stomach knot. "Why?"

"You smell of bitterness and defeat, and as an angel only cares for one thing—or two, to be more accurate—reckon your wings are broken. This salve will help them heal."

"You can smell emotions?" He hadn't known that about concubi.

"Did I not just tell you I'm part concubi? How else would I root out my next meal?"

Mikhail pulled harder on the bindings. He should have been able to break them by now, but his body was weak, his mind weaker, parts of it fragmenting off and chasing the hurt, stuck in the loop of wanting to know the how and why Severn had done this.

"Don't be shy. I seen angel wings before."

He peered at her. If she truly was concubi, she wouldn't be helping him. She'd kill him, slowly and painfully, like he had done to hundreds of her kin.

"C'mon now, get 'em out." She crouched in front of him. Her rayvern jeered, mocking him. "The longer you leave 'em broke, the worse it'll get."

He desperately pulled on the bindings. "Release me, demon!"

"Now that didn't work the first time you asked, did it. So let's be reasonable."

"Do you know who I am?"

"I have a good idea. Only one idiot angel struts around London shirtless."

He gave up tugging on the bindings and slumped, panting. "I do not *strut*."

"Uh-huh. And I suppose neither do cockerels." She beckoned with her free hand. "If I'd wanted you hurt, I'd have done it while you were spread-eagled on my floor. I did consider it." Her shoulder lifted. "Can't blame a demon for looking, even if all you angels are self-righteous pricks. Especially you."

He bared his teeth in a snarl. "I'd be a fool to let you touch me."

She sighed. "Maybe, but look at it this way. You ain't goin' nowhere 'til it's done. The longer you wait, the more it'll hurt putting those wings right again."

"I don't want your help, or need it." What he wanted to do was get out of this dark, foul-smelling little hut and away from this demon so he could try and wrap his mangled thoughts around why Severn had so viciously attacked him.

The old hag moved away, muttering to herself or her pet rayvern, and Mikhail pushed himself tighter against the wall. She was right. She could have already hurt him, even killed him, but that didn't prove her intentions were good.

Why would a demon help him? It made no sense. A great many things in the past few days made little sense. His angels had turned on him. He'd known they might once the allyanse was known. The rules were strict. Mikhail had enforced them himself over the years. But none were willing to even consider how removing him would leave them vulnerable. And Severn... Severn had accused Mikhail of terrible things. He believed his words and had almost killed Mikhail because of them.

He touched his face where the arrow had skimmed his cheek, finding crusted blood and some of the crone's paste. His nail snagged on a stubborn lump, making him wince.

"Don't pick!" the crone snapped. "It'll scar."

Someone must have told Severn that Mikhail took his wings and made him believe it. The demon who had broken Severn free of the cage, perhaps. There was no other explanation. But why would Severn ever believe a demon over Mikhail? Years, they'd worked together. And more recently, with what happened between them... How could Severn believe Mikhail capable of hurting him in such a savage and barbaric way? He had to have been bespelled. The breakout, the attack, none of it had seemed like the Severn Mikhail knew. The demons had gotten to him. Probably during his last time in the cauldron, when he'd mentioned something had gone wrong.

He fell into a fitful sleep, dreaming of Severn's twisted face and that last arrow zipping open his cheek. The sting of its barbed cut woke him with a start.

The crone's rayvern squawked. The beady-eyed creature had hopped down onto the floor and pecked at Mikhail's boot.

"Leave him be. He ain't dead yet, Jasper."

The bird cawed and ruffled its wings, put out that Mikhail was not yet edible. He kicked at it, making the thing squawk and fly back onto its shelf, where it chittered some more.

"Shush now, both of you! Like bickering children, you are."

Pain snapped up Mikhail's back, and for a few blinding seconds, he forgot the room, the bird, and the crone, concentrating instead on breathing and surviving and making his heart beat once, twice, and the next, until the horrible agony finally passed. Wrecked and gasping, his vision slowly cleared.

The crone tutted.

He couldn't stay here. He couldn't go back to Aerie, but there would be other places an angel could rest. Angels were revered all over London. He would find sanctuary among the nephilim, even the humans.

"I'm going to tell ya a love story."

"Don't waste your breath." He eyed the only door. Made from corrugated tin, it gapped at the top and bottom but had three latches holding it in place. The only way he would be getting through it was by overpowering the crone, and she was not as weak as she appeared.

"It's that, or you show me yer wings." She lowered herself into an old creaking stool by her little stove. Opening the stove's iron door, she tossed a log into the low flames. Embers spat until she slammed the door closed again. "Do you know what a seraphim is?"

He leveled his glare on her withered face.

"All righty, then. As you're acting like an idiot, I'm gonna assume you are one—"

"You cannot disrespect me like th—"

"Yes, yes, I can. I'm sure the correctioners will come arrest me for insulting your almighty honor, but until that happens, you're all mine, and I'm gonna tell you a love story."

"If it has anything to do with rutting demons, I'll not hear it."

"You'll hear it, and after, you're gonna let me fix those wings. A seraphim is not a race of angels, as so many now assume. He was just one. A mighty warrior with six wings and so much power the stars themselves bowed to him."

"I know," he grumbled, more than familiar with the story of Seraphim. An angel myth, like that of Aerius the Rayvern King, the demons' kingly counterpart, who was so fond of corvids, he bestowed them with power, creating the much larger and more demonly boisterous rayverns, one of which was staring at him from its shelf now.

"Good for you."

The rayvern squawked.

This demon and her bird were impossible. She had to sleep, and when she did, he'd take the poker, strike her down, and be gone from this place. Until then, he shuffled back and closed his eyes.

"Seraphim took those stars, and with each one, crafted a warrior to protect the human race. Angels."

She sounded like a child reciting things they did not understand. "That's not what happened," opening his eyes again, he caught her grin, "but you're demon. Everything of yours is warped, including your knowledge, so I can hardly expect you to know the truth."

She huffed. "Who is telling this story?"

"What you're telling me is fiction."

"And you'd know because you were there?"

He huffed a humorless laugh. "No. I'm old, but not that old."

"Then you don't know."

"I know—"

"You don't know," she said again, firmly. "History is

written by the survivors. You don't know the truth, and that's your problem."

"My problem is I'm stuck in a hut with an insane demon and her wretched crow when for all I know your race could be attacking Aerie at this very moment and I can't do a damned thing about it. History is not my problem. The war is my problem. The demons are my problem. Severn is—" He cut himself off, and the cambion watched, her eyes as keen as her rayvern's.

"If you'd let me help you, you'd be halfway to healed by now."

"You're not touching my wings, hag."

Smoothing out her apron, she planted her feet and went on, "And so Seraphim sent his angels to live peacefully among humans. At first, they did so in hiding, but as the humans made more and more mistakes, the angels were forced to reveal themselves, guiding humans to what the angels believed to be a better future. But angels did not understand humans. They could not. Because the stars they were crafted from do not understand emotion. And so the foolish humans made more mistakes, driven by the messy things, like love and hate, and Seraphim's angels became more and more controlling—like overbearing anxious parents, the kind who suffocate their spawn out of kindness."

He shifted position against the hard wall. "This is not a love story."

"Know much about love, do you, angel?"

"I know what it is not."

"There he goes again..." she told Jasper, who'd tucked his beak into his feathers and settled down to sleep. "Thinking he knows it all."

"Get on with it."

"The angels began to control humans—"

"We did not."

"Seraphim saw his mistake and tried to correct it, but the angels were too many and too powerful and would not listen... Sound familiar?"

Rolling his eyes, he refused to reply.

"Fearing his angels might destroy the only thing Seraphim loved, he created their counterpart by collecting molten rock and shaping it into—"

"Demons."

"There, he does know something!" She clapped her hands so loudly, Jasper took off, flapping about the room until finally disappearing out the broken window.

Mikhail sighed. "Demons, full of all the emotions angels were not, were set upon the land to stop angels... How's that working out for you?"

Her beady eyes narrowed. "Meanwhile, Seraphim realizes he's made two mistakes and fucks off instead of fixing it—typical angel—leaving his children, made from the skies and earth, to squabble for eternity."

"Bravo. And you're reciting this fantasy because?"

"Because it's not every day Mikhail lands in my lap and I have the opportunity to speak to a guardian angel without him trying to kill me."

"So speak..." He'd get to the killing part later.

"I..." She pursed her lips and shook her head. "You ain't ready. Look at you. Still so far up yer own arse."

"Not ready to hear your lies? No. I am not. Kindly release me so I can go on my way."

"Release you?" she snorted. "You'll kill me."

He wasn't going to deny it. She had brought this on

herself. And she'd admitted she was part concubi, thus revealing she was too dangerous to be left alive.

"Why were you limping through my neck o' the woods, huh, angel?"

"Lost my way." It was true enough. He was lost. In more ways than one.

"Remember how I said I can smell emotion?" She heaved her bulk from the chair and hobbled toward him, making a show of her old bones groaning. "Angels smell cold and hard, like ice. You do not smell like an angel, yet I know you to be one. You smell hot and fiery, like demon."

Perhaps it was her words or just bad timing, but pain flared up his back again, ripping a cry from his lips. When he blinked his vision back into focus, the room was cold, the stove out, the crone nowhere to be seen. He'd blacked out for some time.

Tremors rattled through his bones. He'd clenched his teeth for so long his jaw ached. His shoulders had numbed, along with his wrists, both still bound behind him. If he could make it to the door... But what good would it do him? In this state, the correctioners would soon find him before he could seek sanctuary, and they'd likely send him to Haven, even without Severn.

Breathing out, he let the illusion fall away. Pain beat against him in hot nauseating waves, stealing his thoughts and the air in his lungs. His wings—what he could see of them—were bent and twisted, feathers ripped free. More feathers fell now as the enormous arches trembled, filling the crone's tiny hut with their mangled sinew and shattered bone.

Mikhail let out a sob and fell into darkness, where at least the hurt didn't chase him.

evern

"I MISSED." Severn paced. "I fucking missed."

"It doesn't matter. He's ruined. Wasn't that the idea?"

"No." He stopped and faced the madam, hands clenched into fists. "Ruined is not enough."

And to make matters worse, the allyanse had felt as though it had broken, and here Severn was, still wholly and thoroughly a fucking angel.

He dropped into a chair, one of many mismatched pieces of furniture tossed about the large warehouse. Moonlight poured in through the windows high in the walls and onto a suspended gallery, but below, where he and the madam were, only a string of lightbulbs dangling from steel trusses above lit the space. They'd entered through a back door and avoided the rooms where muffled voices seeped under closed doors, probably because those inside were cambion and Severn so-obviously angel.

He couldn't return to his kin as an angel. And he couldn't return with Mikhail still alive. And he couldn't go back to Aerie. The madam and this warehouse, somewhere near the east end dockyards, were his only sanctuary.

"Fuck." He slammed his head back into the chair and stared at the string of lights.

The madam had stayed quiet since breaking him out of the cage, but she'd also stayed close. She had played her part to perfection just as they'd discussed when she'd caught him in the cauldron. Tracking the train, breaking him out. Until that last second. If she hadn't pulled on him, dislodging his aim, Mikhail would be dead. Another stupid mistake, another backhanded slap in the face from destiny.

He needed to think, to clear his head, to feed. To remind himself of who he was. "Where are your nephilim?"

The madam's smile maneuvered her lips into a sly grin. "You have acquired a taste for angel?"

"More of a taste for *male*. No offense."

Chuckling lightly, she dipped her chin. "I'll see they're brought in, my lord."

"Don't call me that," he grumbled as she passed him for the door. He wasn't anything right now, certainly not a lord, and definitely a failure. Argothun had called him *skree*, as had the other demon—the word was the highest insult. Something pretty but worthless. *Angel.* He'd been disassociated, his name and title deliberately forgotten. If he returned to the demons as he was, they'd kill him.

He closed his eyes. Thick emotion tried to choke him

—emotion he shouldn't even be feeling if he truly were angel. He had to get out of this wretched body. He had to find Mikhail and kill him. Mikhail was probably in Haven by now... Protected among his own kind, squirreled away for safekeeping.

How could he have missed? He had only been a few feet away. The arrow was poised...

The madam returned and told him the nephilim pair was preparing and would join him in the gallery above. He grunted an acknowledgment. At least stuck as angel, he could feed with all his senses, including touch. That was the only benefit of the illusion becoming permanent. If the nephilim were anything like Mikhail, he'd soon be brimming with power and lost to its thrall.

"What did you sacrifice for your illusion?" the madam asked. She knelt by stacks of boxes and rummaged through their contents. With her back to him, he saw mostly wings and a leather-clad ass. As his only ally in this entire clusterfuck, he had little choice but to trust her. She feared him because of who he was, but that fear may not last once she realized how restrained he was in angel form. His name could only get him so far. She'd appreciate some honesty, and fuck knew he could do with someone to listen.

"A memory."

She blew a layer of dust off an old dark bottle and grabbed two cups from another box. "Must have been an impressive one?" Handing him a cup, she used her sharp teeth to twist off the bottle's wire brace and pulled the cork.

Power like the kind he'd used to build himself a withstanding angel form did not come easily and did not come to many at all. He'd built the act on rage, on injustice, and on vengeance, but he'd needed one last spark to lock it all together. One last sacrifice: a memory.

"I don't recall."

The madam filled his cup with the cool, red wine, and he lifted it to his lips, thinking of the memory he might have lost. It was likely one of Samiel, and it would have been a prominent one. Something painful to give up. The transformation took it, and now he didn't remember it at all, and as Samiel was dead, it hardly mattered.

After tasting her own drink, the madam cocked her horned head and ran her clinical gaze over him from head to toe. "I am not concubi, but as a pup, I admired those who were. To be able to draw on ether, it seemed like a magical gift. I watched those who could, and later, when old enough, I became the madam so I could be among the concubi, live *through* them. Their strength, their honor, and their beauty. I saw you many times from afar. You reminded me of the myths of old." She blinked. "To hold such an illusion for ten years. It's unheard of and beautiful work."

He pinched his lips together. "Yeah, fucking wonderful. Only problem is, it won't come off."

"Perhaps give it time?"

Rolling his eyes, he stood, making her back off, and headed for the exposed steel stairs. "Send them up."

"My lord?"

He stopped partway up the steps and arched an eyebrow down at her.

She bowed her head low, adopting a submissive position. "May I... watch?"

Seeing as he'd watched her fuck the nephilim more

times than he cared to remember, it seemed only fair she did the same. He dipped his chin and continued up the steps, reaching the gallery. A large four-poster bed filled much of the space, but his gaze lingered on the view from the windows of the River Thames snaking toward Greenwich. Aerie's towering foundation loomed like a wall, slicing the world in two, making London seem small in its shadow, but the old city's splash of colored lights twinkled defiantly.

Was Mikhail out there somewhere? If he ever got free of his own rules regarding Haven and that cage Severn had left him in, he'd probably come straight for Severn and vengeance, especially now the fool was a walking emotional bomb. He'd always been ruthless, but now the guardian was something of an unknown threat. Angels were predictable in their efficiency. Mikhail's current state of mind would be fragile, tumultuous, and volatile.

"You fucking missed..." he whispered to his reflection in the grimy glass, taking a few more drinks of the bitter wine. Blaming the madam was easy. The truth was more complicated. He'd had plenty of seconds to let that arrow fly. There would be no coming back from an arrow through the skull, not even for Mikhail. He could have taken the shot before the madam grabbed him. He'd hesitated and hesitated and hesitated some more. If the madam hadn't grabbed him, would Severn have fired at all?

Of course he would have.

He saw Mikhail's face again now, the fierceness of his defiance but also the confusion. *Why?* It was in his eyes and on his lips. *Why?* That damned stupid angel had convinced himself he *cared* for Severn. Despite its obvious nuisance, the allyanse had been a stroke of luck, leaving

Mikhail completely vulnerable to an emotional attack—and emotions were weapons in Severn's hands.

He raised his cup and toasted his reflection. "It ain't over yet."

The madam led the two male specimens of perfect nephilim genetics up the steps. She ignored him by the window, but the pair smiled coyly. The red-haired male blushed and bit his lower lip, and it was all Severn could do not to grab him and shove his tongue down his throat. He didn't particularly need to feed, he wasn't low on power—he still buzzed from the high of being with Mikhail—but sex had always had a way of settling his thoughts and focusing his mind on the task at hand. Plus, after being without physical contact for years and failing so miserably at his mission, a little self-indulgence would go a long way.

Not so little, apparently, as he saw Red's loosely clad cotton trousers already revealed an impressive eagerness. The blond guided Red to the bed, where they both began to undo each other's shirt buttons. Severn had watched them perform numerous times, but this was the first time he'd be able to join them. The anticipation had him salivating like a pup, already erect and wanting like one too. Gods, having Mikhail touch him had awoken all his suppressed desires. He'd managed it for years, kept control, stood back and absorbed the ether, but refraining was no longer an option.

He handed the madam his cup and forgot her presence a second later. The two males parted, shirts open, chests bare, waiting for instructions. They were equally matched in height, and although they played at submission, both were physically impressive, baring sinewy muscle dictated by angel DNA.

"How much can you take?" Severn approached, working open his shirt buttons.

"Whatever you've got," Red purred, his eyes widening as he watched Severn slowly reveal himself, button by button.

"Careful," came the madam's warning. She didn't want them broken. "He is not one to behave carelessly around." The well-behaved pair stiffened at her tone.

"I won't hurt them." He dismissed her concerns with a wave. "Unless they want me to." With the same hand, he caught Red's jaw, brought him close, and planted an arrogant kiss on his mouth. Red melted into him, pliable and easy, his ether tickling Severn's senses. To touch another male was a gift Severn planned to relish during the next few hours. He kissed his way down Red's neck, cradling the man's back as he arched into Severn, surrendering himself to Severn's touch.

The blond's hands found Severn's waist, and briefly, Severn remembered Mikhail's strong grip at the hips, his cock a firm, stroking pressure filling Severn from behind. Mikhail's ecstasy-ridden face hung in his mind, and Severn purred while mouthing over Red's collarbone. The male shuddered, his body answering Severn's innate summons, and behind him, the blond pressed in close, the rod of his arousal snug against Severn's ass.

The redhead and the blond came undone beneath his skilled hands, tongue, and cock. Their ether misted the air, sinking into Severn's skin and over his tongue, filling him up. If he'd had wings, he'd have spread them, drenching himself in sex, and their absence made his heart ache. Samiel had stroked Severn's wings as they'd coupled, and when their sex grew rough, he'd grip Severn's wings, arching his back and thrusting into him.

He had Red on his knees on the bed, his ass spread, Severn embedded inside, his thighs slapping Red's ass, while the not-so-gentle blond deep-throated Red's sweet mouth, his blue angel eyes eye-fucking Severn. The pair were cresting, losing themselves to sex, building to simultaneous climax, guided by Severn's hidden power. And this should have been the peak, the moment Severn gorged on nephilim. He'd stroked them, licked them, kneaded and probed, tasted and bit, sinking his teeth into tight flesh, bringing them to the glorious crescendo... only the peak wouldn't break. His power stuttered, making his heart jump. Confusion broke his rhythm, making his thoughts trip. Red came violently, his cry muffled by the blond's pumping cock. Then the blond threw his head back and let loose his seed.

Severn tried to mentally snatch at their climax and swallow the swell of power it should have granted him, but the moment darted through his mental fingers, lost to him, and his own cresting climax waned, unspent. He thrust harder, desperately trying to chase the pleasure again, but the nephilim were softening, their ether waning.

Severn pulled free, still inexplicably hard and desperate with need. But the climaxing peak was long gone. He'd failed in the final moment, in the most basic of concubi skills. Pups were born hard and sexually mature, clawing at their own member for release, spilling their seed in those first few moments of life like human babes needed to bawl. And Severn had failed.

He reeled, thoughts tumbling, the power still a heady whisper against his skin, still luring him on and teasing him with the promise of more. A mistake. That was all. Just one small mistake. It didn't mean anything. It couldn't. He did not fail at sex. He could not. The thought was ludicrous.

"My lord?" Red reached for him.

He snarled and batted his hand away. Was it because he was turning *angel*? Was he losing more of himself to the horrible curse?

The nephilim's gorgeous eyes dropped to where Severn's cock still strained. For one terrifying second, Severn feared he knew he'd failed. He'd lift his head and laugh. They'd all laugh at the incubus who wasn't, not anymore. But Red sealed his warm, wet lips over Severn's cock and tongued low, taking him in deep. Pleasure sparked down his spine. He plunged his hands into Red's sunset hair and thrust deep, making the half angel gag. He didn't care. He needed to know he could perform and grasp that precious release, that sweet spot all incubi drank from. He had found that exquisite moment with Mikhail. Nothing had changed since then. He had to fucking do this.

He pounded into the angel's mouth, teeth gritted, fingers locked in his hair, while Red gripped his thighs and held tight, and he chased that crescendo, feeling it build again, racing toward release, but still, it proved elusive, like trying to catch water in a sieve.

Thunder rumbled through the walls. Severn didn't care to notice it at first. His ability to feed was far more important. But the thunder rumbled louder, shaking the walls. Rust rained from the crossbeams holding up the warehouse ceiling.

Severn pumped his hips, feeding himself over and over to Red's forgiving mouth, chasing the sweet ecstasy.

The windows exploded inward, sending a thousand jagged projectiles into the room. Pain zipped through Severn's shoulder and neck. He twisted, turning his back to the vicious onslaught. The nephilim's mouth vanished off his cock. Then the thunder poured into the warehouse in a wave of heat and noise. The brick walls bowed inward, blasted open, and suddenly Severn was weightless, falling through a hail of noise and heat and grit.

CHAPTER 16

$\mathcal{M}$ ikhail

THE SHIVERING WOULDN'T CEASE. There wasn't an inch on Mikhail that didn't ache, and the crone's wretched paste burned his nose and throat. He woke with his wings caked in the stuff and proceeded to retch up what little he had in his guts to begin with.

She pottered about behind her stove, muttering to herself while the rayvern eyed Mikhail from its shelf, waiting for him to die so it could peck out his eyes. And he'd rarely felt closer to death. It was said when angels died, their souls returned to the night sky as silent sentinels still tasked with watching over the human race but no longer able to protect them. It sounded terrible, and Mikhail had never had any desire to let death claim him, and certainly not in this demon's den. But his body wasn't listening. The damage to his wings was worse than

155

he'd let himself realize. Had he been thinking without emotion, he would have known to stay in the cage and await arrival at Haven. Once there, he could have pleaded his case, and if necessary, escaped them. He could have escaped them in the council chambers if he'd chosen to fight. A few untrained angels in Haven wouldn't have stopped him.

But he'd been emotional and foolish, and now he was suffering because of it, and Severn was out there somewhere being led astray by demons.

He'd drawn his knees up to hug them while his wings were spread and throbbing against the shack walls, almost reaching the entire circumference, feather-tip-to-tip. The sight of their mangled fronds was enough to make his gut roil again, but the pain was easing some. Having them so exposed made him feel as though he were naked. The cambion had had her hands all over him while he was out, and he felt her invasion beneath his skin, like she'd violated him.

He eyed the door.

He wasn't strong enough to make a break for it. She looked weak but was far from it, and he couldn't take another hit.

Jasper the rayvern cawed an alarm. The hag glanced behind her and tutted. "Settle down now." She patted the bird on the head, making it preen. "He ain't goin' nowhere, Jasper."

That damn bird was a problem. When she wasn't watching Mikhail, it was. "He likes you," he told the crone. His voice sounded as rough as dirt and nothing like his usual smooth drawl. All of him was breaking apart. He'd have been embarrassed if everything didn't hurt so much.

"He's a good boy, aren't you, Jasp?" She made kissing noises, and the bird cawed again, then turned a single beady eye on Mikhail in warning to back off his woman.

Mikhail snorted.

"They're intelligent, you know. More than crows. More than some angels, I reckon. They mate for life too. Rayverns know what love is."

He snorted at that too.

"The Rayvern King made them with a stolen angel feather. Black, it was. Bit like yours."

Mikhail's wings weren't supposed to be black. The glorious feathers were a frosty gray with silver edges. But admittedly, in this place with the paste all over them, they looked black. Lost and aching, he propped his chin on his knees and resigned himself to listen to the cambion's stories, as wrong as they were.

"Aerius was Seraphim's first demon creation and his most loyal servant. Seraphim ordered him to lead his new demon army against the angels. Aerius loved Seraphim in all ways, and as Aerius was demon, his love was a powerful and undeniable force—he'd have done anything for Seraphim. He made the first rayvern as a gift for him, but when Seraphim saw how his demons began to fall against the angels, and he lost all hope that his fuck ups could be fixed, he fled. The myth is Aerius has been searching for him ever since."

Jasper squawked and ruffled his wings.

Mikhail could stay silent no longer. "Utter fantasy."

She huffed and wiped her hands on her gown. "And I supposed you know better, bein' angel an' all."

"I do. Aerius was a monster—"

She pffted. "Absurd!"

"On the eve of the Battle of a Thousand Stars, he tried to murder Seraphim in his sleep. Seraphim's guards caught him, and it was Aerius who fled, so fearful of Seraphim's wrath was he. The next day, Seraphim's angels almost destroyed the demons. Seraphim vanished among the fray. His bones likely lay at the bottom of the tens of thousands in the killing fields, if he even existed to begin with."

The crone arched an eyebrow. "And how do you think Aerius was able to get so close to Seraphim the night before the battle?"

Mikhail hadn't given it much thought. Demons were always full of tricks and lies. Like the concubi he was, Aerius had probably illusioned his way into Seraphim's chambers as an angel. These stories were so old, Aerius and Seraphim were practically myths, fairytales. And discussing all of this now was pointless.

"They were fucking," the crone said.

Mikhail laughed humorlessly and then wished he hadn't when his wings spasmed. "Angels do not couple with demons. Seraphim would have never debased himself in such a way. He was the greatest of all angels. The first. His beauty and strength brought humans and angels to their knees."

She waggled her eyebrows and planted her hands on her ample hips, thrusting out her breasts. "You ain't never wondered what it might be like to stick your piece of meat in some demon's ass? All that rough muscle." She made grabbing motions with her hands. "Those leathery wings, perfect for tugging on."

She thrust out her hips, and Mikhail turned his face away, swallowing a sudden bout of nausea. "The suggestion is disgusting and an affront to the natural order of things. I'm done talking with you, hag."

"Hm... offended your fragile sensibilities, have I?" She chuckled to herself. "All the power, but you can't ever have fun with it, and that's a damn shame. Seraphim was a prick. He made you all pricks in his image, impotent and emotionally stunted."

She ranted on, but Mikhail sent his thoughts far away, eventually circling back around to Severn. The demons had him, he was sure of it. There was no knowing what they'd do to him. Demons rarely captured angels. They killed them. Was Severn dead already? Mikhail would feel it if he were, wouldn't he? The allyanse was broken, but that didn't mean it had vanished. Everything he knew said an allyanse couldn't ever be destroyed, but something *had* happened to the bond when Severn had attacked.

Mikhail's gaze drifted over his ruined feathers. Was the broken bond a part of why his wings weren't healing like they should have been, or was it the hag's paste keeping him weak? His thoughts circled around and around until they tugged him into sleep.

The approaching rumble of a train woke him. A strange reddish hue poured in through the hut's broken windows, over the old crone trying to grab for each of her rattling pots and pans. Some clattered and bounced off the shelves. Jasper made a shrill squawking, flapping about his perch. And then the blast slammed into the hut. The entire structure screamed and jolted sideways. The crone's metal panels bowed and rattled and shook so hard it was a wonder they didn't break apart. Dirt and dust and heat blasted in through the window, like brittle smoke. Mikhail threw himself sideways, curling away from the worst of the shrapnel. When it was over, he lifted his right wing, revealing the crone muttering and swearing, protected beneath his feathers. Her bird had vanished. She realized the same and started lifting up bits of fallen metal sheeting, calling for her pet.

Mikhail got his hands under him and heaved himself onto his feet. The restraints had broken, he realized. He pulled his wings in, hissing at their reluctance to fold away, but managed to retract them enough to mentally illusion them away, making his stagger toward the crooked doorway all the easier.

"Wait! You can't leave now! We are not finished!"

He shoved on the door, heaving it open, pushing a mound of debris behind it, and clambered out onto the rubble. Sunlight poured down and sparkled off broken glass, and beyond that, the winding River Thames reflected its powerful rays. Buildings smoked. Some had been torn in two, left in shards. And where Aerie's foundations should have towered high into the sky, there stood just half a mangled structure, dripping with sparking wires and falling debris.

The debris... the dust, the rubble, the chunks of glass thrust into the ground...

Mikhail shielded his eyes from the light and looked higher, into a sweeping blue sky. Half of Aerie's enormous disks had vanished, like some huge beast had torn half the structure away.

"No..."

It wasn't possible.

He staggered into the sun, joining dozens of people staring skyward, watching broken bodies silently fall from Aerie's distant platforms.

The residential half of Aerie's great disks had fallen to Earth, flattening most of the cauldron shantytown and neighboring high rises. The dead would number in the thousands. Angels, human, nephilim, cambion. But not demon. Because there were no demons in the cauldron.

Demons had done this.

They'd retaliated. But this... this was impossible. It was too much, too terrible.

He had to get up there.

He tore free of the new illusion and thrust out his wings to a chorus of gasps, then bore the monumental pain as he beat them, taking to the air in a cloud of dust. His body convulsed from pain, and a burning sweat nearly blinded him, but the wings held, and with each beat of their great weight, he climbed higher, witnessing the destruction with every painful stroke. Higher and higher, he flew into the cloudless sky until Aerie's exposed spine was within reach. He landed among panicked nephilim somewhere in Aerie's exposed middle, the broken walls and roof unrecognizable.

His agony faded to numbness as he witnessed hundreds lying dead or dying on the cracked glass floors. So many...

He fell to his knees beside the first nephilim, but she died before he could say a word. The next wept and clung to Mikhail's arm, begging for help. She, too, died in his arms. Everywhere he looked, angels lay unmoving in pools of feathers and blood. Some descended from above, landing with stretchers, organizing a rescue attempt. They were his charges. He was supposed to protect them all.

The floor groaned and tipped beneath Mikhail's feet. Bodies slid sideways, the living went too, screaming their terror. He reached for a young nephilim scrabbling for purchase on the shining floor, just a boy. Mikhail snatched his hand, reeling him in. The floor fell away, and for a breathless moment, they both tumbled through the air among chunks of glass and stone until Mikhail flung open his wings and caught enough wind to carry them both from the debris. Others were not so lucky. They tumbled and fell, screaming. Angels flew in, catching some but not all. He watched them plummet, his grief a cold, hard fist around his heart.

"Who did this?" the boy whimpered, clutched so close to Mikhail's chest that he could not see the worst.

"Demons."

He carried the boy to safer ground and left him in the care of a wide-eyed angel, then returned to find the entire disk gone, and the people with it. All of them had fallen to London below.

Rage set Mikhail's soul ablaze.

He'd kill them all for this. Every last damned demon.

CHAPTER 17

Severn

SEVERN—NAKED but for the shirt he'd dragged with him —climbed from the debris, coughing up dust, and squinted into the sunlight. London lay beneath a quilt of glittering gray dust, lit by sudden, glaring sunlight, where before, there had been only shadow, because half of Aerie was gone.

Its absence defied belief.

The city had been there for so long, to see half of it gone was to see the impossible.

The madam clambered from the rubble, and behind her, other demons emerged too, crawling out of the dirt like their ancestors must have. Severn wasn't safe among them, but few even cared to see him. They all looked up, squinting in the suddenly bright day.

The madam handed over a pair of dusty trousers. "You look like you could use them."

He grunted his thanks and quickly pulled the trousers on, his thoughts racing. "The nephilim?"

"Carl is dead." She added, "The red-haired one."

"Damn." And he'd had such a sweet mouth.

She nodded behind him at the blond, sitting slumped on a rock, face in his hands, sobbing. He wasn't the only one distraught. All around, cambion and demons wept. Aerie had clearly been the target, but those in the cauldron crushed beneath the fallen sections of city would be too many to number.

Severn looked up, numbed as he watched debris tumble down from what remained of Aerie. Some of those specs of black were bodies. Some probably still alive. If he had his wings...

"You can't stay here," he said, his voice thick. "They'll come for you." The angels would kill everything they saw as having anything to do with this. They'd tolerated a few demons in London before, content to sweep them into the correctionals, but now, they'd wipe any demons left out of London. The cambion too.

Turning, he saw the numbers increasing as cambion emerged from their makeshift homes, stunned. "You have to leave! They'll come for you!" He raised his voice, letting the wind carry it far. "Leave—now. Go anywhere but here."

They saw him now, wondering why an angel stood among them, telling them to run. And they started back, too shocked to do anything.

"Run! Go!" the madam ordered, blood oozing from her

many scrapes and cuts. "THEY WILL KILL US ALL FOR THIS!"

Finally, they began to move away.

Severn looked up again. "I have to get up there." There was no way Mikhail would stand for this. Wherever he was, he'd heard of this, and nothing would stop him from returning to Aerie.

"Who did this?" the madam asked, her voice trembling with something like awe and fear.

"Someone who doesn't care." He had an idea who among the demons was capable but didn't want to think it. Because if he was right, the war had just gotten a whole lot worse for both sides. He started forward, barefooted over broken glass. If he'd had his wings, returning to Aerie would have been easier, but he didn't, and so walking through the smoking, twisted wreckage was the only way.

"Where are you going?" the madam called.

"To kill an angel."

She was beside him suddenly, having used her wings to hop the distance. "Don't." Her eyes appeared sad, and the madam became less of a rigid caricature selling sex in Infinity and more of a demon who had seen enough death. "You don't need to. Let him go."

"I *have* to."

"My lord—" Her hand landed on his arm.

He shook her off. *"I am stuck as this until he's dead,"* he hissed. "He's up there, out of his mind on emotion. While they're in chaos, I can walk right in. I won't get another chance. He'll eventually tell them what I am, if he hasn't already. I have to do this now. For me, for... what he's done—"

"Konstantin—"

He grabbed her jaw and pulled her close. "Never EVER say that name. If I didn't need you, I'd tear your tongue out and your throat with it." Throwing her back made her stumble and fall in the rubble.

"Just..." Her bottom lip quivered. "What was done here is wrong. You know it. Go back to your home. Lead them. They need you. *We* need you."

"I can't!" When would she get it into her horned head that he was a fucking angel now? "Go," he dismissed. "And get every demon you find out of London. Because if I'm right, there will be nothing of the city left standing by the end of the week."

THE WALK back to Aerie's foundations, across rubble and over broken glass, took a day and a half. He'd managed to find some boots but not before cutting his feet to ribbons.

One elevator was still in use, ferrying the wounded down from Aerie. The nephilim told him that all of Aerie was being evacuated, the city no longer structurally safe. Severn rode the elevator up, listening to two nephilim talk of how Mikhail had returned, and of how this never would have happened if Mikhail had been with them instead of being sent away. They blamed Vearn, blamed it all on some conspiracy to remove Mikhail. He was hurt, they said, his wings shredded from some unknown attack. Severn couldn't find it in him to feel anything. All of this should have made him smile, at least. But he hadn't wanted the death of so many innocents. The nephilim were not the demons' enemy.

He couldn't even bring himself to smile at the news of

Mikhail's damaged wings. He felt hollow, and as the elevator climbed into the clouds around Aerie's remains, he wondered if all angels felt the same.

AERIE'S vast open spaces usually echoed with voices. Now, a brittle silence hung in the still air. With the residential disk gone, Severn could only imagine the number of angels killed with it. Some would have escaped, but many would have been trapped inside as it fell into the cauldron. Had he not alerted Vearn to the allyanse and gotten both himself and Mikhail shipped out of Aerie, he might have been among the dead.

On his way to the library, where the nephilim had told him Mikhail was currently helping organize the evacuation, his ill-fitting boots clomped over the cracked glass floor, and his new sword bumped against his back. He'd found it among several abandoned in the armory, their owners likely perished.

Voices reached him as he jogged down the library steps, and there was Mikhail, talking with a couple of angel guards about doing a last sweep to remove anyone left behind. They all looked up as Severn entered. The guards appeared more surprised than Mikhail, whose level gaze showed no emotion. Severn's heart stuttered. He looked... wrecked. Torn clothes hung off his bruised frame, his hair—always so perfect—lay knotted and unruly about his shoulders. Mikhail had his wings illusioned out of sight, but given the rest of his appearance, talk of his wings being ruined was likely true.

How far the guardian had fallen...

Severn should have been happy to see him so beaten, but the emotions roiling through him were far from happiness. They left him breathless and stunned and inexplicably grief-stricken. But he knew emotions and knew how to push them aside.

He put a wooden half smile on his lips and dipped his head. "Your Grace."

"How did you—" Mikhail cut himself off. The guards looked to him for instructions, and Mikhail's veil of dark lashes fluttered, his mouth forming words he couldn't speak. The infallible guardian angel, who always knew the right thing to say, was speechless.

Severn gestured for the guards to leave, testing whether they'd actually follow his orders and how much they knew about his escape. Surprisingly, they bowed their heads and obediently passed him by. Mikhail hadn't told them. Interesting.

He watched them go and then brought his gaze back around to find Mikhail watching him with the oddest blank expression. An angry scar marked his right cheek, where Severn's arrow had punched through. He'd healed well enough. Of course he had, angels always healed. Severn cleared his throat of the annoying knot trying to choke him.

"I..." He struggled to find the words to encompass all of *this*. "The city... I'm sorry, Mikhail. I'm sorry I wasn't here." Mikhail started forward, his dark blue eyes suddenly intense. "I'm sorry for what I did... in the carriage," Severn hastily added, but the guardian's glare grew harder with murderous intent. Severn reached for his blade. "I'm sorry—"

Mikhail's fingers slid around the back of Severn's neck,

the touch igniting some unknown crackling power across Severn's skin, and the angel's mouth slammed into Severn's, so rough and demanding that Severn's heart lurched, his blood hot, his body sure it was under attack. He almost wrenched free before realizing Mikhail was *kissing* him, not killing him.

His sword fell from his fingers. He spread his hand against Mikhail's hot, scarred cheek and sealed the kiss, falling into the feel of Mikhail so soft against his lips, so warm beneath his tongue. He answered the male's demands with no hope of thinking beyond the glorious taste of angel. But it was more than angel, it was bright and hot and everything. It was *Mikhail*. He tasted of sunlight, of heat and power, and Severn's power unfurled, stretching wide, trying to wrap itself around Mikhail and swallow him down.

Mikhail slowed the kiss first, lips gently parting. Severn followed Mikhail's withdrawal, nipping at his mouth, trying to pull him back down. He didn't care they were in public, didn't care about anything, just that he needed more of Mikhail on his tongue, down his throat, filling him up. It almost worked too, but Mikhail's mouth brushed the corner of Severn's, then his cheek brushed Severn's forehead, and the angel sighed.

To Severn's horror, Mikhail slowly revealed his wings.

They were black.

That was his first thought.

Followed by: *they're broken.*

Once so glorious, Mikhail's wings were mangled wrecks rising from his back. They were still shaped like wings but hideously deformed, like old, crippled talons curled inward. Severn's back ached in sympathy. He knew that pain, knew it so well he barely went a day without feeling it. But seeing such horror on Mikhail felt wrong on a level Severn should have wanted.

He grabbed Mikhail's face, forcing his stare away from the wings and into the guardian's tired eyes. They'd been tired before, but now his beautiful eyes were dull and flat and distant.

"Eight thousand dead," Mikhail whispered. "More… lost." His arms folded around Severn, wrapping him in warmth and strength, but the strength trembled and the warmth waned, and the broken angel shivered in Severn's embrace. Mikhail's grief touched Severn's soul. He could taste it, feel its empty, devastating chill, and knew his pain went far beyond the physical.

"Mikhail…" Severn pulled from the embrace and grasped the angel's face again in both hands, searching his eyes for the bright spark that had always fascinated him, but it was gone. Lost to grief. Mikhail really was ruined, and Severn had done this, just like he'd wanted. Mikhail deserved it. He did, but gods, Severn hurt inside too, because somewhere in the past ten years, he'd come to admire this brilliantly bright angel, and now the city was broken, Mikhail was broken, and the truth left Severn breathless.

"I'm sorry…" Severn whispered, pulling Mikhail's head down to brush the words against his forehead. Yes, Mikhail deserved to be hurt. Yes, he was Severn's enemy, but in this moment, all Severn wanted was to make that hurt go away.

Mikhail's fingers brushed Severn's cheek. "Those things you said? About love, about your wings…" His fingers skipped lower, brushing Severn's neck. "Angels do not know love. How could I take it from you...?"

"I... It was... The demons..." Severn grasped for the story he'd concocted while walking through the fallen city. "I meant... my chance at love, I didn't... I wasn't thinking clearly." The lies spilled free, broken and bitter.

"They hurt you?"

Severn swallowed, tasting the acid of his deceit. Mikhail's strong fingers tipped his chin up. "A drug, I think." He lied again, looking into Mikhail's eyes. "I didn't know what I was saying..." The lies burned his throat and churned in his gut, sickening him. "The wings... I was wrong. About it all, about everything."

All of this was... wrong. The emotions he felt toward an enemy he'd long despised, they couldn't be real. Because if they were real, then Severn was lost to his own illusion and it was all over.

No, he needed to kill Mikhail. If he did that, the illusion would finally break, these emotions would scatter, and he could return home, and maybe even stop this never-ending battle between angels and demons. But none of that could happen with Mikhail alive. He had to die. Here. Now.

Severn slowly crouched, dragging his hands down Mikhail's firm chest and thighs until he knelt at Mikhail's feet. He looked up at the grief-ridden angel with the broken wings and knew this moment was exactly where destiny had led him. Mikhail would never be weaker or more exposed and vulnerable. No demon had gotten this close to ending him and the war with him.

Severn carefully reached for his fallen sword.

Mikhail's warm hand touched his cheek. "I feel… everything," he whispered. "And it burns."

Severn's fingers brushed the sword's hilt. He pulled the handle into his grip.

Now. He must.

Through the heart.

Mikhail would die, and Severn would be free. Vengeance and justice served.

He tried to lift the sword, but its weight had inexplicably doubled.

One strike through the chest. Simple justice.

But it wasn't simple.

Because on his knees, in front of this guardian angel, he couldn't lift the sword and plunge it into his enemy. His mind screamed at him to stop. Mikhail's grief, his pain, it made him something else, and damn if Severn didn't feel it too. It was the allyanse, or maybe it had always been there. But he couldn't kill Mikhail. He just… couldn't. He should. Everything relied on him delivering the final blow. Ten years he'd waited for this. Every day and night, every hour, every silver-tongued lie, had brought him here, to his knees, a blade in his hand, ready to strike down the angel scourge.

But his heart, that hidden core of him that had been so broken when losing Samiel, was hurting, and it had nothing to do with vengeance. Gods, *he cared for Mikhail.* It couldn't be, it was impossible, but there was no other explanation for why he could not fulfill destiny's wish, for why his arrow had missed, for why he could not lift his sword, for the times he'd fought beside him, protected him—telling himself it was all for destiny's grand plan.

But he hadn't been lying to Mikhail. He'd been lying to himself.

The sword fell from his fingers a second time, the final time.

Somewhere in all of this, he'd become lost in his own lies. He *was* angel. That was his fate.

A great swell of horror and grief and regret poured over him. He clutched at Mikhail's thighs, buried his face against Mikhail's warmth and strength, and tried to hold the savage flood of emotion back, but what was the point? He was skree just like Argothun had said. He really had died on that battlefield. Maybe he'd died long before that, when Samiel's hand had fallen from his, when he'd known the demons weren't ever going to win the war and he'd chosen to end his life and build another.

"Forgive me?" he whispered, not sure if he was speaking to destiny, to himself, or to Mikhail. Nothing made any sense anymore. For the longest time, he'd chased vengeance, and without it, he no longer knew his purpose.

Mikhail knelt too, trying to catch Severn's gaze, but he couldn't look at him. Everything hurt. His body, his mind, and most of all, his heart. He turned his face away, ashamed, lost.

"*Severn*," Mikhail said, tearing Severn from the miasma in his head. His fingers on Severn's urged him to face him again. "We must leave. The foundations are weak... Our city is broken. But this is not the end of us. We will rise up stronger than before."

A broken city, a broken guardian. This was all Severn's fault.

He couldn't be here, he couldn't stand Mikhail looking at him, his eyes soft with sympathy, thinking he knew exactly who Severn was and why the useless tears swam unshed in his eyes. He wanted to yell the truth at him, but if he did that, Mikhail would pick up Severn's sword and run it through Severn.

He pulled from Mikhail's terrible grip and was up and moving, needing to get out, to get away, to escape these feelings tearing down all his barriers. He *cared* for Mikhail. He couldn't kill him because the allyanse had crept into his life and strangled his heart.

"Severn, wait... We're regrouping in Whitechapel. Please... meet me—meet us there..."

Severn stumbled from the library, unsure if he'd go there, or where he'd go next. He wasn't demon, not anymore. He was a ghost, a nameless phantom. He'd failed. Failed at everything. He was skree, and he loved his enemy.

"I'm... angel," he mumbled, falling into the elevator and slumping against its walls. "Angel..." Over and over, he said it, in time with the beat of his treacherous demon heart. "Angel... angel..."

He'd lived the lies so long they'd become true.

CHAPTER 18

*M*ikhail

IT HAD BEEN two days since the library and Severn had not joined the angel's temporary camp in Whitechapel.

Those moments in the library played over and over in Mikhail's mind as he set his angels to work on shoring up the neighborhood as a temporary stronghold. Vearn was missing. Angels were still being pulled alive from the rubble, so not all was lost.

Mikhail's ranks were broken and battered, rocked by Aerie's destruction, but rarely had he seen them stronger. He walked the Royal London Hospital hallways—a huge glass-fronted structure built to resemble Aerie's architecture—visiting those recovering from the attack. Angels and nephilim bustled around him, each one a beacon of light in the dark. Emotions assaulted him, leaving him exhausted in mind and body, but he could not stop, could not rest when there was so much to do.

Saphia spotted him speaking with the young nephilim and approached, smiling her polite smile. "Mikhail, may I have a word?"

She was clearly exhausted, run ragged by dealing with a never-ending stream of injuries, some worse than others. He'd been aware of her efforts since Aerie's fall and had sent every nephilim he could spare to help her treat the wounded.

"How are you?" she asked, keeping her voice low.

"Fine." His gaze wandered back to the boy on the bed while his mind conjured the moment they'd both fallen. He should have saved more. He should have been there.

Her smile turned sharp. "Follow me, please."

Knowing better than to argue, he followed her down the hospital's hallways and into a treatment room. She flicked on the bright lights and gestured toward a bed. "Sit."

Saphia had been a constant in his long life. She'd patched him up enough times over the centuries that she knew every inch of him, and some parts of him even he wasn't accustomed with. When he was a fledgling, in the absence of a mother, he'd often turned to her for answers.

The little room she'd commandeered was in the half of the Royal London Hospital Mikhail had claimed for angel use. Humans were still treated in the other wing, but most were evacuated to outside the city limits—as Mikhail had instructed. He'd only ever wanted to protect them, but now his angels were on the London streets, among humans, putting human lives in danger. He'd failed like no angel ever had before him.

It wasn't supposed to be this way.

"Mikhail?"

"Yes, I... apologize. My thoughts were elsewhere."

She smiled, and he smiled with her. "Are you all right?" she asked.

He opened his mouth to answer, but the denial that anything was wrong stalled on his lips. He'd caught sight of his reflection in the hospital glass. He was not all right, and Saphia knew it.

Slowly, he exposed his wings, watching her face fall.

Over the past few days, he'd become accustomed to the pain, bearing it like he bore the guilt of abandoning his people when they'd needed him the most.

"Sit, my dear," she reminded grimly.

He lowered himself onto the edge of the creaking bed, keeping his wings aloft.

She backed up and ran her clinical gaze over their crippled expanse. "Can you open them?"

"Not fully."

"Try."

He pulled in a deep breath, bore the weight of the pain, and cracked his wings open, inch by inch. When their trips reached the walls, he gasped and slumped forward, hating how his body trembled. If his enemies saw him this way, they'd kill him and go on to kill every other angel, knowing they were all similarly hurting and wounded.

Saphia touched the arch of his wing, and the pain almost made him weep. He kept his head bowed and focused on breathing. "A demon... she put some kind of paste on them," his voice trembled, and he hated that too. He had never been this weak. He was a shining light of strength, a guardian angel. He could not be seen to be broken. "I think it made it worse."

"You were with a demon?"

"She captured me," he looked up. "I was in a confined space when I opened my wings and... shattered them."

"The cage... I heard." Her mouth twisted. "A terrible thing. You should never have been locked inside."

He might have agreed with her if he hadn't considered killing all the angels in the council room just to protect himself and Severn from banishment. "I... It was necessary. After I... broke out, the demon found me. She claimed to be helping..." He caught sight of the tar-like substance coating his feathers.

He couldn't bear the thought of trying to wash the wings clean. A single touch was enough to drop him to his knees.

"I'll take some samples and run tests. The damage is... extensive." She took a swab from the wings and busied herself packaging the sample away, then pulled off her gloves and frowned down at Mikhail. "You haven't told your ranks?"

"They need to see me strong."

Her eyes softened. "You cannot fly like this, Mikhail."

"I know."

"You should be resting."

"I know that too." Panting, he pulled the wings back in, folding them closed as much as their brittle bones allowed, and then illusioned them away. The entire effort took too long and almost ripped his consciousness from his body. Sweating and trembling, he found strength from somewhere and got to his feet. "Is there anything you can do for me now?"

"Mikhail, my dear... I have known you so long... When you were a tiny ball of feathers and determination telling me you'd change the world for good, I knew you'd be one in a million. But we need you... Please, give yourself time. More hinges on you than you realize."

He sighed. "I could say the same of you."

She gave him the look of someone who had seen and heard it all before. "Until I know what that coating is, I'd rather not touch them. Give me time to run some tests. I'll try and be quick, but resources are strained."

He nodded and eased his bruised body back against the chair. "There's something else..."

"The allyanse." She frowned, like he was a fledgling again, coming to her with a bent wing because he'd tried to fly too fast. "I've heard all the rumors. You're meant to be in Haven. Admittedly, we're all grateful you're not. Tell me about it."

Metallic-tasting anxiety spiked his tongue. "What I tell you must not leave this room."

"Do not insult my professionalism."

He told her all of it, finding some relief in sharing the entire truth, including how he cared for Severn in ways he couldn't explain. "I am as ruined on the inside as my wings are. Emotions smother me. They cling to my every thought. It's distracting, and in some cases... debilitating. I thought the bond broken, but its effects remain. I am angry all the time, and there's a pain inside that I'd gladly cut from me if I could find its source. I... do not trust my own judgment."

"The mixture I gave you didn't work?"

He cleared his throat and averted his gaze, trying to

fight the potent image of exactly what had happened after both he and Severn drank her potion. "No."

"I would normally advise you get yourself to Haven, but as that is not an option until reinforcements arrive, the only thing I can suggest is keeping Severn close to lessen the impact of your... emotional urges."

Mikhail turned toward the window and the view of Aerie's fractured spine. "He left."

"He'll be back. No angel can resist the allyanse."

Mikhail winced. "Severn is different."

"Oh, I know it. The times I've had that angel brought to me all cut up, refusing treatment. But the allyanse is undeniable. No angel can fight its pull for long."

Mikhail wasn't so sure. The things Severn had said beneath the will of the demons and his abrupt exit from the library were all indications that he despised the allyanse, and Mikhail couldn't blame him. "I forced it on him. I stole his choice. He is right to hate me."

Saphia's soft sigh spoke of her own exhaustion, but her smile stayed. "You might have initiated an allyanse, but Mikhail, it wouldn't have worked without the will of both parties. He doesn't hate you. He's confused. Whatever happened between you, he cares for you and probably had long before you instigated the allyanse. You forget I've observed the pair of you for years. You were always insepa-rable. Severn will come around. You have enough to worry over, the allyanse need not be a worry. Take strength from it. You are lucky to find your mate."

The allyanse with Severn didn't feel lucky, it felt like a noose.

Saphia answered a knock at the door to find Solo

outside. The angel bowed his head. "Your Grace, Severn has returned."

Mikhail kept his face blank, nodded his thanks at Saphia, and left alongside Solo. "Is he... well?"

"He's Severn," Solo said, smiling, implying Severn was always well. And he was. Until recently. "He's asking after you."

"Take me to him."

Keeping his pace slow was more difficult than it should have been. He'd feared Severn would never return, or the demons might pick him up off the street again. They knew how important Severn was to Mikhail. The allyanse would be common knowledge now, making Severn a high-value target. He had been before the allyanse, but now everyone knew Mikhail had a weakness—an emotional weakness he'd preferred not to have, but there was no undoing it. The best he could hope for was that the bond stayed weak, allowing them to live separate lives, as Severn clearly wished for.

The Whitechapel streets were quiet but for the occasional angel landing on the rooftops. No human traffic passed through, vehicular or on foot.

Clouds hung low above street level, obscuring what remained of Aerie, making it seem as though the floating city had vanished. Perhaps it could be rebuilt one day, once the demons were driven back or defeated for good. But only if the angels survived whatever the demons planned next.

This war had to end. The demons had struck at the very heart of London, and Mikhail planned to strike back equally as hard. Now Severn had returned, he already felt stronger. Saphia was right.

"Your Grace." Solo gestured ahead at the angel leaning against a lamppost.

Severn had his arms crossed and his hip cocked. Traffic lights silently blinked red above him. He still wore the too-big boots, laces undone. His shirt gaped, a buttonhole missed in his haste to dress, and that too looked like he'd tossed it on without a thought for an angel's usual attention to detail.

Relief hit Mikhail, then fury and shame and fear and everything all at once, but the important thing was Severn really was all right.

Solo peeled off, leaving Mikhail to walk the last few meters alone. They'd drawn a few glances from nearby angels. All would know about the allyanse. Mikhail found he didn't care that they thought him emotional or compromised. He didn't care for what they thought at all.

"Your Grace." Severn's half smile did curious things to Mikhail's insides, like spill a pleasurable shiver down his back. Mikhail wanted to tell him he was glad he'd returned, that he'd worried he might never see him again, that he was sorry for everything and he wished it could all have been different, but none of that made it to his lips. Because if he started saying such things, he might never stop. This damned rogue of an angel had Mikhail's heart in his hands, and he had no idea.

"Your absence was noted," Mikhail said, wincing at its coldness.

"By you?" Severn pushed off the lamppost and sauntered close, barely stopping a hairsbreadth away.

"By everyone."

Severn tilted his head. His blue eyes dropped to Mikhail's mouth and back up again, his gaze suddenly suggestive. "But the question is, did *you* miss me, Your Grace?"

Mikhail sighed through his nose while struggling to keep his body from revealing exactly how much he'd missed him. He'd thought he could ignore it, but every time he saw Severn, he wanted him in all the ways. That warm peppery taste on his tongue, how his tight body moved and answered to Mikhail's, the way he smelled, of heat and spice and deliciously devious things. Whether this deeply visceral reaction was normal or not, he didn't care to analyze. He just knew he needed Severn close, so close the lines between them blurred. The first time Mikhail had taken him from behind hadn't been enough, and the angel's sly smile said he knew it.

Mikhail had lain his eyes on Severn for no more than a few minutes, and already, he could see himself shoving Severn against that lamppost and taking him hard from behind, and he didn't care that such a display would shock and horrify the nearby angels.

He stood so close now, they shared the same breaths. His eyes were bright aquamarine pools.

A needy crackle began beneath Mikhail's skin, demanding he reach out and grab the angel, then savagely devour him, right here on the street.

Severn pulled away, stepping around Mikhail, and walked back the way Mikhail had arrived, like he hadn't just made Mikhail painfully aroused with a few words and a suggestive glance. "This war isn't going to win itself," the impossible angel said, lifting his voice so all heard his much-needed confidence.

Severn was back, and Mikhail had never needed him more.

~

MIKHAIL HAD BEEN ALLOCATED a brick-faced terraced townhouse, wedged between its neighbors. He'd been inside once in the past few days, found it dark and oppressive and typically cluttered with human trinkets, and hadn't returned since. But now, with Severn in tow, he needed a private space to discuss everything they hadn't and all the things they should. He needed Severn's help to regroup the angels and reorganize a united front. Once that was secure, he needed a way to hit back at the demons, and Severn would know one, because when everyone failed, he always had an unexpected solution.

Severn entered the house first, drifting down the dark hallway, between walls of patterned wallpaper. He seemed bigger in these small human spaces, his scruffy presence already brightening the dark. He turned, frowning, apparently disliking the house as much as Mikhail did, and that was as far as he got before the full force of Mikhail's shove drove him back. He hit the wall, his breath puffed out of him, and Mikhail caught his face, his mouth, his body beneath his. Just tasting the angel had all the frayed parts of Mikhail's mind coming together again, proving more than ever that Severn was his.

Inside the kiss, the agony of his wings and loss vanished. Feeling Severn gasp, feeling his hands grab at Mikhail's arms and pull him in, feeling the male come alive beneath his touch—it chased all the hurt away. Mikhail didn't know what love was, but if this savage relief was love, he wanted more of it *immediately*.

Severn clutched Mikhail's shirt in his fists and shoved with a startling amount of strength. Mikhail's back struck the opposite wall, but Severn's tongue stole any surprise by stroking a path down Mikhail's neck. Mikhail clutched at his shoulder, torn between pushing him off and pulling him closer.

Severn's mouth on him felt too good to be wrong. A part of Mikhail wanted this to end here and now before the allyanse made life intolerable for Severn, but he couldn't stop it, not when Severn's blunt teeth nipped and his thigh forced its way between Mikhail's legs, claiming. It seemed as though Severn should be the one pinned. He'd wanted to be beneath Mikhail when they'd coupled in Aerie, but something had changed. Severn's grip was stronger than ever, his body inexplicably harder, as though he were furious. Perhaps he was.

Pinned beneath the very hard and real feel of male, Mikhail dropped his head back and closed his eyes, relishing Severn's scandalous mouth and the way his tongue flicked a nipple. He tore the rest of Mikhail's shirt open and mouthed lower, his hands fixed on Mikhail's hips.

He was caught, inexplicably owned, and Mikhail struggled to level his breath and control his heart. Part of him fought to break free and push Severn back, but another part liked the sensation of being held down, being controlled. There was a freedom in it, a relief almost. He didn't have to be strong now, he could let this happen.

"Come here." Severn's rough hands grabbed Mikhail by the throat. His mouth smashed into Mikhail's and ravaged his so viciously, Mikhail tasted blood. He tore free, groaning like an animal, and arched his hips, his arousal a devastating need demanding to be answered.

Severn had hold of him again and pulled him through a

doorway into a room. The drapes were half-open, daylight pouring into the dark in one thick shaft. Severn backed him against a desk, his hands tearing at Mikhail's trouser fastenings, and Mikhail forgot the unfamiliar room and the fact anyone might see inside if they cared to look. Severn's snarl scorched Mikhail's mind, then the snarl broke apart, revealing his half smile, and he purred, jaw to jaw with Mikhail, his hand pressed against Mikhail's chest, holding him right where he wanted.

"You like it hard," Severn growled, nudging Mikhail's mouth and then teasing away as Mikhail tried to seal the kiss. *Haven*, he was going to throw Severn down and take him on the floor if he kept this up.

"You wanna fuck me, angel?" Severn shoved him down, forcing Mikhail to brace himself against the desktop. "Or shall I fuck you this time?" Severn's mouth was halfway between a snarl and a smile again, and Mikhail got the distinct impression if he tried to stop this now, Severn would refuse. There was no going back, and there would only be one winner here.

Something fragile fell off the desk and shattered on the floor.

Mikhail lurched forward, drove Severn hard into a bookcase, spilling books from their shelves, and captured the male's cock through his trouser fabric, freezing him. Severn's emotive eyes blew wide. He grappled with Mikhail's arm, clutching him like Mikhail had clutched at his shoulder, trapped between shoving him off and wanting more. And now he did snarl while panting hard through his nose.

Severn needed this. Mikhail could only guess at why—he needed the control, and Mikhail needed to let go of it.

He relaxed his hold. Severn's reaction was instant, his warrior instincts fast. He twisted Mikhail's arms behind Mikhail's back, and in two strides, slammed Mikhail face-down against the desk. Sunlight bleached Mikhail's vision. Haven, if anyone saw them through the window... His heart thudded harder at the thoughts, and his cock pulsed, seeking closure.

Severn yanked Mikhail's trousers down his hips, exposing his ass. Fingers kneaded, spreading Mikhail's cheeks, and then one of those fingers drove inside, widening Mikhail's hole as it probed deeper to the exquisite bundle of nerves that tore all thought and reason from Mikhail's mind.

"Say it..." Severn hissed against Mikhail's ear, his weight pinning Mikhail still. "Say you want me to fuck you, angel."

Mikhail hissed each breath through his teeth. His body strummed, hot and alive and wrung tight with need. Nobody dared speak to him the way Severn did. The angel's mouth was a foul trap, full of snarls and harsh words, and Mikhail hadn't known such things could tip him toward the edge of ecstasy.

Severn still had hold of one arm, still holding him down. He could fight him off—perhaps. Or maybe not. That uncertainty made Mikhail's balls ache. "*Yes*," he breathed.

"*Say it.*"

"*Fuck me.*"

Severn's finger left, and within seconds, the warm, hard press of his cock took its place, easing inside the tightness, spreading Mikhail wide with slick ease. Severn's gasping groan combined with the full pressure filling him up almost undid Mikhail. Then Severn's free hand was on Mikhail's raging cock, and it was Mikhail's turn to splutter some foul word.

Severn chuckled and leaned in close, his fingers ringed around Mikhail's cock while his cock pressed hilt deep into Mikhail's ass. "You have a filthy mouth too, angel." Severn's teeth nipped at Mikhail's shoulder, and then they were moving, rocking, Severn rolling in and out, pushing pleasure higher with every stroke.

Mikhail wasn't going to last, not spread and vulnerable with Severn pumping him like he was. Every instinct had his nerves on edge and his cock raging, Severn's hand perfectly bringing him up against the sweet crescendo but holding him back from tipping over. Mikhail begged him for release, the words barely coherent. Severn's thrusts grew savage. The desk rocked. Severn's hand pumped, and Mikhail lost his mind. He came so hard his legs gave out. The desk held him up, or was it Severn's grip keeping him safe?

The animalistic grunts accompanying each of Severn's thrusts built to a growling shout, and Severn's relentless pace stuttered, his cock pulsing, spilling *inside* Mikhail, and it was all Mikhail could do to ride out the last dregs of his own orgasm.

"Fuck..." Severn gasped, falling against Mikhail's clammy back. "You taste too fucking good..." He clutched Mikhail's ass, squeezing so hard it hurt, but the pain was the good kind, not the kind Mikhail had been carrying with him for days now. He waited for that pain to return now. A dull ache beat where his wings should be, a reminder they were broken but little more.

Severn hooked an arm around Mikhail's waist and

evern

MIKHAIL WAS an endless supply of ether that Severn could easily find himself addicted to. Any concerns that he couldn't sexually perform had been banished with Mikhail spread beneath him. Severn had come so bone-achingly hard that he'd almost blacked out from the ether overdose their fucking had churned up.

Content, well-fed, and fucked dry, he pulled Mikhail upstairs and into one of the beds Mikhail seemed surprised existed. The room was dark, like the others in the tiny house, but it didn't matter, because Mikhail's skin glowed, and Severn was sure his did too. And there they lay, legs tangled, hands stroking and exploring, discovering the mysteries of each other, like the way Mikhail shuddered every time Severn's fingers rode over his hip, or the way Severn couldn't resist teasing Mikhail's mouth with his tongue whenever it was within reach.

Severn climaxed again, courtesy of Mikhail's hand, while the angel looked him in the eyes, and Severn had taken him into his mouth right after, building him to the breaking point slowly.

Their fucking was raw and wild, and when Mikhail looked deep into Severn, he was sure the angel could see through him. The thought made Severn spill his seed harder and faster than he'd ever known and wrecked all his defenses.

Severn later drew the sleepy-eyed Mikhail slowly from the bed and threw a shirt at him.

"Where are we going?" the angel groused, his black silken hair a mess, fallen about his face and shoulders. He tugged on the trousers and shirt, missing a few buttons, so the shirt sat askew on his broad shoulders. He caught Severn watching him and waited for the explanation that wasn't coming.

Severn offered a smile, and taking Mikhail's hand, led him through the house, up a narrow, winding staircase, through an attic room, and onto the terraced house's flat roof. He'd found the rooftop exit earlier in the evening, when Mikhail had dosed from exhaustion.

Rods of rain patted the low wall and hissed into puddles, making the city sparkle and shine. Severn pulled Mikhail to the edge, leaned against the wall, and nodded at the view.

Mikhail frowned. "What am I looking for?"

"Just look."

London's jagged buildings poked against a darkly orange sky. Mist rolled through empty streets, blurring the streetlights, smudging color in the rain. Mikhail's keen eyes observed it all, as though searching for a threat. It took a few moments for the view to sink in, and when it did, the tension in his face eased.

Rain weighed down Severn's clothes and dripped from his hair, plastering it to his face and neck. The cold tried to seep into his skin, but he was too wired on power to care. "You've never seen London from below."

"No."

The city's ambient light warmed Mikhail's stern face, softening his jaw and dark eyes. Rain glued his shirt to his skin, painting it on, and all Severn could think as the angel tipped his head was how he wanted to peel that shirt off again. Right here on the rooftop. No angels flew in the rain.

"It's... beautiful." Water dripped from his lashes. He turned to face Severn and reeled him into his arms, then the angel's mouth sizzled against Severn's all over again, and they kissed slowly in the rain, like they'd only just met and this was the beginning of something neither could control.

Severn surrendered to Mikhail, to the allyanse, to the fate destiny had apparently planned for him. He had come to understand he could not fight this and didn't want to, not when being with Mikhail felt so damn good and right.

Mikhail's illusion washed away. His glorious wings unfurled. Their silver tips flashed, encircling them both until feather sighed against feather, hiding Severn from the world.

The wings looked *whole*. "Your wings—"

Feathers flew open again, and Mikhail staggered from Severn, pulling the wings in again to run his hand along their shimmering surface. Rain dripped from each trailing frond, each one perfect. Severn reached for one, needing to stroke its silky smoothness.

Mikhail dropped to his knees. He let his wings fall too, like a collapsing castle of cards, and lifted his face to the sky. Severn couldn't see his tears among the raindrops but knew they were there. Mikhail was... weeping.

It was so unexpected, so unlike Mikhail, that Severn couldn't move. The rain pounded, his heart thumped, and the most powerful angel alive wept fresh tears into the puddles on a London rooftop in the rain.

Angels didn't cry.

"You did this..."

Fear tore at Severn's chest, trying to get to his heart. "I..." And then the pain cleared from Mikhail's face like the sun following a storm, and he smiled.

"I don't know how, Severn. But you made them whole again. You made *me* whole..." Mikhail pressed a hand into a puddle and hunched over. "Before, there was nothing... now, every breath is loud with feeling... and I can't stand it, but I can't be without it... without you."

Severn knelt with him. "I don't..." What could he say? Words were not enough. He hadn't healed Mikhail's wings. He had power but not the regenerative kind. The ability to heal was an angel's gift. He reached for the proud angel's face, *his* angel, and watched the full force of emotion wreck his beautiful features. "The allyanse, perhaps?"

Rain pounded around them, hissing through the air and drowning out all sound but that of Severn's heart.

Mikhail looked up. Rain wet his face. His lips lifted in that smile, although pieces of it kept breaking off as some other emotion tried to grab hold of him. "You did this."

He croaked, choking on denial.

Wet wings swooped around and scooped Severn into Mikhail's arms. The feathers tickled, cocooning him in Mikhail's warmth.

Mikhail's dark blue eyes turned intense, their depths bottomless, like the ocean.

Severn sighed at the sudden warmth soaking through his bones. He decided, in that moment, there were worse things to be than angel. On this rooftop, wrapped in soft wings, he didn't mind being angel at all.

"I was blind to it, but I see now. I see it all, feel it all. It's not just the need to feel you, to touch you—although that need is undeniable—it's more, and it was always there, between us... I've fallen for you," Mikhail whispered, as though saying it aloud might break them apart again.

Severn playfully shoved at his chest, and the big wings opened, freeing him again. He got to his feet, grinning like a fool at the angel on his knees in the rain. "Say it again, angel." He laughed and spread his arms, wishing he could spread his wings too. But their loss no longer hurt. Maybe this impossible pairing had fixed him too? He hadn't felt as free or as blissfully happy in years. Not since Samiel, but Samiel was gone, the war still raged, and nothing had changed. Except Mikhail. Severn was done with destiny. This was his life now... with an angel, and gods, the relief of letting go of the past almost toppled him over.

Mikhail suddenly pinned him to a chimneystack. The air whooshed out of Severn, and he laughed, unable to hide the bloom of joy.

Mikhail's vast wings stretched high, shielding them from the worst of the downpour, and Mikhail peered at him like he might devour him whole at any moment.

"I fell the first time I saw you. I've been falling ever since. I fear I love you, Severn," Mikhail's voice thickened and quivered. "Since you broke into my ranks and demanded to fight me like you could fight the world."

I fear I love you, Severn. The name was wrong, and the jab of guilt struck at his heart, but he refused to be imprisoned by it. He *was* Severn now, Mikhail's lover. Fate had made it so. "I've only loved you since Tuesday..." Mikhail's eyes widened hilariously, the big angel's heart so fragile. "So, I have some catching up to do." He kissed the guardian's firm mouth, and Mikhail scooped him into his arms. They kissed in the rain on a London rooftop, and Severn knew this memory was one he'd never surrender.

MIKHAIL WAS NOT DYING by his hand. Vengeance had already been served, and Severn would have no more of it. He was strangely all right with that now he'd come to accept it. He'd already been an angel for a decade, what was another few hundred years?

And he knew love.

He'd loved with all his heart before.

And now he loved again.

Destiny was strange, fate was often cruel, but he wondered if both had been trying to guide him here all along.

Maybe it was the allyanse, or maybe it was real. Either way, it felt fucking real, and he wasn't giving it up now he'd found it again. Maybe he'd been looking at this all wrong for years. Maybe it had always been about standing beside Mikhail, not against him. Whatever destiny's plan, Severn was done with it, and would be following his own plan from now on.

As angel, he was going to make some changes. The first of which was stopping the demons from making a bad war worse.

He lay on the bed next to Mikhail, thoughts turning over. Sunlight poured in through the open drapes, up Mikhail's leg, and over his half-uncovered ass. He wasn't sleeping. His gaze had been warming Severn for a while, and Severn soaked it up like he might soak up ether. Angels would soon come looking for them, but until then, this moment of peace was theirs. He pretended, just for a little while, that they could live like this, side by side. But the sunlight soon faded, and the room darkened, and Severn's thoughts turned to war.

"The demon who destroyed half of Aerie is called Djall. She is ruthless and cold." Like an angel, Severn silently added. But not *his* angel. His angel was a winged emotional disaster, and Severn loved him for it.

He twisted onto his side and propped his head on his hand. Mikhail blinked, his mouth alive with a smile. The sheet lay over his waist, half a hip exposed, the dip below his navel so very tempting. "She will not stop." Talking of Djall helped lessen the insatiable need to mount Mikhail and fuck him into a puddle all over again. Mostly. Gods, the attraction was like some strangling curse, one Severn gladly let swallow him.

Mikhail considered the words like he always did. "How do you know this?"

With his sleepy eyes and mussed up hair and thoroughly fucked fluidity to his limbs, Mikhail looked the very picture of sin. Severn delicately ran his fingers down

Mikhail's hip, delighting in his sharp hiss. "It's better you don't know."

Mikhail nodded, too lenient, but that was his way. He trusted. It was who he was. A trust that made a whole lot more sense now. Severn still wasn't sure how Mikhail could have loved him before the allyanse took hold, but if any angel could, it would be Mikhail. As to how Severn could, he'd always been capable. In that, he was thoroughly demon.

"How do we stop her?"

"Lure her out from behind demon lines and kill her." Severn pushed the edge of the sheet back from Mikhail's hip and skipped his fingertips toward the erect cock lying flat against Mikhail's lower belly. He skimmed around the wanting member, making it twitch for attention.

"That sounds... easier than it is."

Mikhail turned onto his side, and Severn roamed his hand behind, kneading his ass with a roughness he'd learned Mikhail liked. Mikhail's penchant for submission had been a pleasant surprise. One Severn planned to explore a whole lot more at any given opportunity.

"Demons always flock together," Mikhail added.

"Ah, but you have me."

Mikhail's finger trailed down Severn's cheek. "I've had you for years, I just wasn't capable of understanding it."

Maybe not always, but Severn wasn't going to argue with Mikhail or himself over this. Things were what they were now, and he was content enough with that.

"What else do you know of this demon?" Mikhail's hand stroked down Severn's arm all the way to his hand. Their fingers entwined, catching Mikhail's attention. He lifted Severn's hand to his lips and planted a small kiss on the backs of his fingers, then parted his lips and gently stroked his tongue across the back of Severn's hand. With his dark eyes and suggestive mouth, Severn was reminded of how he hadn't yet had Mikhail's mouth on an exceedingly harder part of his anatomy.

"She is concubi—a succubae, preferring to stay as female," he said

Mikhail fingers tightened around Severn's. He looked up, and the heat had snuffed out of his eyes.

"And powerful," Severn went on, eager to be done with the facts and all of this talk of demons and war. "Now she's succeeded in bringing down Aerie, the others will rally behind her."

"This succubus was hidden from our forces all this time?"

Severn nodded. Djall wouldn't call it hiding, more like preservation of the species. She'd always preferred to observe from the sidelines before making her killing move, and she'd been watching a long time. "She believes humans to be the angels' greatest weakness. It is a belief few demons entertained. Whatever our differences, they have always followed Seraphim's Law: humans must never be threatened."

"And they have broken that sacred law."

Severn rolled onto his back and stared at the ceiling, his fingers still linked with Mikhail's. And he needed that touch, more than he cared to admit. *Kill the humans*, Djall had once whispered to him, because such a thought was blasphemy, *and the angels will fall.*

For generations, it was angel against demon. That was the way of things since Seraphim had created both races. Nephilim were sometimes fair game for demons, and the angels tolerated cambion, preferring to try and *correct* them by extracting their demon halves instead of killing them. But humans had always been off-limits. Taking out Aerie and not caring for the mix of races huddled below was exactly the kind of idea she'd have championed.

Mikhail looped a leg over Severn's and pulled himself close. "How do we lure her out?" He spoke softly, his mouth tantalizingly close to Severn's ear. When he sucked the lobe between his teeth, an unexpected shudder rattled through Severn, ending in his leaking cock.

"Fuck..."

Nothing satisfied Mikhail, and Severn couldn't get enough of him either. They were both so sexually starved, a week alone wouldn't have been enough.

"She will come for one thing." Mikhail's mouth trailed a warm, wet path down Severn's neck. Severn moistened his lips. "Did you ever hear of a demon known as Konstantin?" He was glad for the distraction of having Mikhail's mouth on him, else his voice might have cracked speaking the name.

"Hm." Mikhail bridged over Severn, arms braced either side. Tension strummed between them. The silken tip of Mikhail's cock brushed the length of Severn's, and it was all he could do not to grab him and demand he sink himself over Severn's need. Mikhail brushed his mouth to Severn's. His long hair tickled everywhere it touched, striking and licking like his tongue had. "An incubus," Mikhail whispered against Severn's lips. "One of their fiercest warriors. He's dead. I have his wings on my wall."

Severn's intake of breath sounded too much like a hiss. He turned his head away and clenched his teeth against a sudden rush of nausea. "She's one of a rumored thirty siblings. Most are dead, Konstantin apparently among them. She's his sister." He almost spat the words and suddenly needed distance from the angel beside him before he said something too close to the truth. He'd known Mikhail had his wings, or he'd suspected. But to hear him say it ripped open old wounds.

His wings were gone.

They were a part of the old him. The dead him.

He pushed Mikhail back, steering away from his puzzled look, and snatched his clothing off the floor. "We've wasted enough time."

Mikhail winced at the tone and swung his leg over the opposite side of the bed. Severn glanced, watching his naked back flex, the fully healed wings hidden. "How does Konstantin help us?"

How did he, indeed? "I've heard from the cambion that she thinks he's alive." Severn ran his fingers through his hair and sighed hard. The old part of him wanted to flee the room, but his new self wanted to climb back onto the bed and lick his way up Mikhail's back. Never mind the war raging outside; he had one raging inside of him too.

Where his wings were didn't matter. They were dead to him and had been for a long time. War was war, and Mikhail had been protecting his people like Severn had been protecting his. It was different now, not least because he cared for Mikhail. "Make it known you have her brother, and she'll come crawling out of the woodwork to see."

"With an army behind her?" Mikhail stood in the sunlight and threw on a shirt. Severn mourned the loss of that body beneath him.

"Not if we agree to a trade," Severn suggested.

"For what?"

"Konstantin for a temporary truce while we regroup."

Mikhail's fingers paused while buttoning his shirt. "He was important enough to pause the war?"

"He was... important, yes. Demons have a complicated hierarchy. Konstantin was respected, feared by most, admired by all."

Mikhail considered it and nodded. "Where do we find a demon that looks like the dead incubi?" He gathered his hair together in a loose knot

"Let me deal with that." Dressed and with the room between them, Severn's gaze was hung up on the heat radiating from Mikhail's.

"I don't believe I can refrain from touching you for an entire day," Mikhail admitted.

"Well, then." Severn fastened his fly and headed for the door, casting Mikhail a long look over his shoulder. "That should make today an interesting one." He turned in the doorway, hand on the handle. Mikhail waited for him to speak, tension humming off him. It took a monumental amount of self-control not to cross the room, throw the angel against the wall, and rip those clothes off him all over again. "Would you like to fuck me over the council's meeting table, Your Grace?"

He laughed at Mikhail's wide-eyed expression and left, noticing how Mikhail hadn't declined the offer.

CHAPTER 20

The council meeting took place in a church. Appropriate, as humans often integrated angels into their own religions. Stained glass windows had multi-colored angels trapped midflight over human scenes of suffering, their rays of light shining down. Naturally, all demons were displayed as tucked in dark corners, grasping at that light.

All the pews had been pushed aside to make way for the council's table. Fuck knew how they got the table down from Aerie. It wouldn't have fit inside their elevators. Flew it down probably. Severn shot Mikhail a raised eyebrow, and heat touched the male's cheeks, his eyes too, and Severn's forever-unsatisfied cock began to pay attention. He took his usual seat to Mikhail's right and scanned the angels present. Most were as old as dirt. Some were missing. He hadn't seen Vearn since she'd banished them and assumed she was among the thousands dead from Aerie's collapse. All were loyal, proud, and deadly efficient warriors.

"We will not stand for this atrocity," Mikhail began. He went on to confirm the number dead and the efforts being made to make Aerie's residents as comfortable as they could be with their feet firmly on London's dark, gritty earth. It wouldn't hurt the angels to slum it with humans for once, Severn mused. It might even remind them what they were fighting for.

Many glances kept tripping over Mikhail to Severn and back again. They all knew they were fucking, and Severn relished the feel of their fascination and horror. What would they think if they knew how Severn had pinned their guardian to a desk and made him come so violently their reserved angel spat all the curses under the sun?

"Correctioners are rounding up cambion and any stray demons—"

"What?" Severn interrupted. He'd been enjoying the thought of spreading Mikhail over this table and hadn't been listening until the mention of demons. "Why?"

Mikhail glanced at Severn and then studied those around the table. "It's likely explosives were used at intervals through Aerie's foundations. The only people capable of such a thing are the cambion. We've traditionally ignored their presence, but they can no longer be tolerated."

"Why would the cambion set into motion an event that would destroy their own homes? They had families, lives, just like the rest of us. None of you cared to visit the cauldron, but I did. As chaotic as it was, they loved it. They did not do this." The act of terrorism might have easily come from a disgruntled nephilim, but the angels would never consider that any creature with angel DNA could be capable of mass murder.

"They're demon. Perhaps they weren't aware who it was they helped or what the outcome would be," Mikhail argued. Although it wasn't so much an argument as a statement of fact. "I'll have no more demon influence within London's limits. Will thousands of dead angels not convince you of their deceit, Severn?"

Angels nodded and mumbled their agreement, and Severn pressed his lips together. He'd walked among the debris of what had been the cauldron and swallowed the thick miasmic grief in the air. The cambion did not do this, but he was hardly surprised Mikhail was clearing them out. He'd warned them he would. Another benefit of fucking the guardian meant Severn could work on him later, while he was sleepy and sated and might be more inclined to let the cambion retreat to demon territory instead of having the correctioners try and "cure" them.

"We are battered and bruised, but we will stand united against this new threat of terrorism. We may be outnumbered, but we have the forces of good and righteousness on our side. Demons crossed the line. They killed innocents. But we will rise above it. It is time we ended this war. We will prevail." Of course, the angels all agreed. Dismissed by Mikhail, they left the church with their spirits lifted.

Severn watched how they avoided getting too close to him or Mikhail, afraid they'd catch *emotion*, which would have been hilarious if it weren't so sad. He swallowed the urge to call them back in and tell them they were idiots who couldn't think properly because they were badly made from the beginning. It wasn't their fault. But it would be all right now because they had him, and Mikhail working to make this clusterfuck right again.

As soon as the door swung shut, Mikhail filled Severn's vision, the angel suddenly all up in his face, his lopsided smile a promise Severn couldn't resist. He leaned back, bracing his hands on the table behind him, and parted his knees, allowing Mikhail to slot his thighs firmly between them. "Hm... would you look at this... an entire table we haven't yet defiled."

Mikhail leaned in, his lips so close, Severn tilted his head back, mouth opening in invitation.

Mikhail's heated gaze flicked from Severn's mouth to his eyes and back to his lips. "We should argue more."

Severn purred in return. He could see how much Mikhail liked to be challenged. The male needed to start wearing tighter, more restrictive trousers. His angels might all faint if they saw that undeniable rod making its intention perfectly clear. Severn cupped the member in his hand, instantly feeling its heat, and pressing in, made Mikhail gasp.

He eased the angel back a step and straightened up to him, eye-to-eye. Mikhail held himself back, his hands off the goods, but his quickening breaths made it clear his restraint wouldn't last.

"Put a pin in this." Severn brushed his lips over Mikhail's, testing his restraint and feeling him shudder beneath his hand still on his cock. "I have to go find a cambion before you have them all killed."

Mikhail pulled himself back, impressively cutting off his desire. "They aren't killed."

"Aren't they?"

"You believe something else?"

"Do you honestly think the correctioners actually cure cambions?"

"Yes. They report as much."

Backing toward the door, Severn smiled at his gullible angel. Mikhail didn't lie, so naturally, he believed the humans didn't either. Did he even understand the humans his kind so resolutely protected? Mikhail: so perfect, so terribly flawed. "We will talk more on this." He had to leave now before he fell upon Mikhail and made good on his promise to dirty up the council table, making new memories Mikhail would have a hard time forgetting during every meeting. But leaving was easier said than done, because Mikhail was propped against that table, his aroused body an open invitation to be ravaged and his face a strange combination of stubbornness and confusion.

Mikhail watched Severn's retreat like a wolf considering the hunt. "Where are you going?"

"To find a willing pawn for our game of deceit."

"Don't be gone too long... or I'll have to take matters into my own hand."

Severn almost choked on a laugh. Mikhail with a sense of humor was a damned delight. "I shall do my best, Your Grace." Severn bowed low and left the room, thinking of all the ways he wanted to make Mikhail laugh some more. What they had... It was too good, too perfect, and he should have known it wouldn't last.

"Token... a token... and I'll make you come." He heard their squawks before seeing them and made his way over the piles of collapsed brick and twisted metal. The rainstorm had passed, leaving London overcast, smelling of damp dust and the Thames. And grief. The reek of it was everywhere, plucking on his incubi senses, reminding him he wasn't wholly angel and he couldn't shrug off the devastation like they could.

People wandered about the destruction, picking through the debris like rayverns scavenging the killing fields. Most all were cambion, and he wanted to take each one aside and tell them to leave before the correctioners swept the area.

Luckily, they hadn't yet swept up the crone. The same cambion who had accosted him outside Infinity before Mikhail's allyanse and the fall of Aerie.

He spotted their hunched figure propped on a jagged fallen corner of some building that no longer stood, lifting their bowl to anyone foolish enough to wander within earshot of their screeches.

Considering their chosen hawking spot, he wondered if they might have lost their mind. The middle of a warzone was hardly an appropriate place for sexual endeavors.

He whistled through his teeth, caught their eye, and clambered closer.

Grunting, the cambion held out their bowl, rattling its contents of two tokens. Someone *had* employed their services. Severn was mildly impressed.

"Hm," they said, "the angel who likes cock, is it?" Their voice carried like a gunshot. "I see yours ain't shriveled and fallen off yet, eh?"

He propped a boot on a rock and frowned down. "We talked about this a few days ago. Remember?" After realizing he couldn't kill Mikhail, he'd fled the library and spent the following days wandering the cauldron's remains, seeing the death and destruction firsthand. By the time he'd returned to Mikhail in Whitechapel, he knew who he was and what had to be done, and he had the crone's card up his sleeve.

She waggled the bowl at him. "Talked about payment too."

He dug out a handful of tokens from his back pocket and dropped them in the bowl. "Half now, half when it's done."

They eyed the tokens like he'd tossed in a bunch of worthless pebbles and smacked their lips together, reassessing Severn. "When I get killed, you mean?"

"They won't kill you."

They huffed and straightened, old bones cracking and

creaking. "Reckon you're an expert at demon, are you, *angel?*"

Severn backed up, letting them shuffle down the mound of dirt, but in a few strides, their hunch had vanished, their shoulders came back, and their head lifted. Illusion such as theirs was no small trick. Cambion, they might be, but their demon lineage had to be powerful for them to shift at will without feeding. "What you're askin' ain't easy. Takes power. Who am I gonna fuck?"

They still spoke too loudly, prattling on, making sure everyone scavenging the ruins caught their every word.

"Must you draw so much attention?"

They chuckled, and as they hopped over the rubble, steps becoming lighter, they held out their left arm and whistled. From behind, Severn watched the illusion warp from old crone to a slim red-haired male nephilim, startling similar to Red, who had died when Aerie fell. They'd seen him in Infinity.

"You like this one, no?" Even the voice was the same, although the speech pattern was all wrong. "Maybe I get to fuck you, eh? Angel who likes nephilim cock."

Severn was about to tell them to quit screwing around when a huge rayvern flew in over his head and landed on the cambion's hand. It cawed, ruffled its feathers, then plodded up the cambion's arm to their shoulder and hunkered down against their loose red hair.

"Don't go minding Jasper," Not-Red said. "He likes angels. Don't you, Jasp?"

Liked to pick at their carcasses on the killing fields. "What do I call you?" Severn asked, striding ahead now the rubble had eased and the streets opened. Traffic was minimal, so he walked along the road leading them toward Whitechapel.

"Hmm... a name... a name..." They tilted their handsome head, blue eyes shining. As much as it unnerved Severn to see the dead walk again, this cambion was exactly what he needed. "I have many..." they continued. "I keep 'em like shiny trinkets. Today you may call me Amii. Tomorrow might be summint else. But today, reckon I'm an Amii."

"Amy?"

"You got feathers in your head or what? *Amii. Ah-mee.*" The rayvern's distinct squawk sounded much like *dumbass.* "Angels." They tutted. "Don't ever listen."

AMII and their rayvern provided a running commentary on the walk back to Whitechapel, only falling silent when Severn led them into the church. They made it a few steps and then whistled. "Well, fuck me sideways. Ain't this pretty. Shame all those stories in that colored glass is bullshit, but that's what happens when angels control the narrative."

Severn studied the cambion as they drifted around the council table admiring the church's admittedly impressive architecture. Humans knew how to build temples to their saviors. The cambion was more demon than human, Severn assessed, maybe two-thirds. They were probably older than he'd first guessed at too. He'd been so full of power, he hadn't noticed theirs, but he did now, felt it instantly warming the vast space around them both. They'd be more than capable of carrying out his plan.

They ran their hand down the table. "Shiny... eh, Jasper?" The bird looked like it had fallen asleep, but they still waffled on.

The door rattled and Mikhail entered. He'd changed his clothes into more formfitting attire, dark too. Black trousers hugged his tight ass, an ass Severn admired as the angel strode forward. He wore a black satin waistcoat over a black shirt. All of it spotless. He'd braided his perfect hair too. Fuck knew where he'd gotten the clothes from, but Severn wanted him out of them immediately, and then he wanted to mess up the rest of his angel, undoing all those strict lines.

"This the cambion?" he asked, voice cold.

Severn pushed off the church wall and approached the table, keeping Mikhail to his right and the cambion at the opposite end of the church, near its altar.

Amii turned, ran their suggestive gaze all over Mikhail. "Well, ain't you a peach." They rolled their tongue, poking its tip against their top lip. "You don't need to pay me to fuck this one."

Mikhail sighed. "Does it come with a gag?"

Severn opened his mouth to reply, but Amii got there first, "Only if you want me to, big boy."

A laugh briefly choked Severn. He coughed, clearing it, and rapidly stepped in front of Mikhail before the angel did something like kill their best chance at luring Djall into the open. Severn gently placed a hand on Mikhail's chest, feeling his heart racing beneath that soft satin. Mikhail did not appear amused.

"He's capable of what we need?" Mikhail grumbled.

"*They* are, yes."

"They?"

"Bigender."

Amii propped a hip against the table. "The best bits of both."

Mikhail gently pushed against Severn's hand, his expression suddenly hard. "What did you say?"

They swept a gesture at themselves. "Able to tickle all the balls and bits you—"

"The rayvern... do all cambion have birds as pets?" Mikhail interrupted, frown deepening.

They dramatically flicked their red hair. "Ain't no crime in it."

"All right," Severn raised his voice. Mikhail regrettably wasn't finding any of this entertaining, and Severn had no wish to rile him any more than he already was. "Show him," he told Amii.

They hopped off the table, shooing the bird from their shoulder. The rayvern cawed and circled above before coming to rest on a wooden beam. The cambion sauntered away from the table, checking the space they had to work with, and then rolled their shoulders and sighed out.

"What's it doing?" Mikhail asked.

Severn stepped to his side and slipped his fingers in Mikhail's. The angel squeezed back, and by the gods, Severn needed it. "Watch."

The red-haired blue-eyed nephilim visage blurred at its edges. The colors making up the cambion shifted, churning from pale pastels to an inky black marbled with pulsing red. Two great horns grew from its head and curved backward. Its eyes turned golden, pupils slitted.

Mikhail's grip tightened around Severn's fingers, likely because he heard Severn's heart or felt his trembling.

Severn breathed too fast. His heart thumped at his ribs, trying to escape.

Two great featherless wings peeled open from the cambion's back. So enormous even Mikhail drew in a breath at their reveal.

Severn's sight blurred. He gritted his teeth, making his jaw ache, and pushed back the great swell of grief, grateful Mikhail couldn't sense or smell emotion. Because those were Severn's wings, at least a damn near-perfect copy of them. He looked at himself—at Konstantin, the incubi lord who had sacrificed everything for the chance to kill a guardian angel. The angel who stood beside him, hands entwined.

Mikhail's fingers slipped from Severn's. He drifted forward, leaving Severn rooted where he stood. "Remarkable."

The cambion blinked its fully demon eyes and tilted its horned head downward. "Thank you." The voice was rough, deep, and spoke of unchained power.

Severn couldn't move, couldn't find the words to speak, couldn't breathe. He never thought he'd see his whole self again.

Mikhail's form appeared small in front of the demon. If he had his wings displayed, it wouldn't matter. Konstantin was bigger in every way. Rough to Mikhail's smoothness. Dark to his light. Opposites.

"I remember him well," Mikhail said, his voice distant. "A beast like none other. So fierce, he cut down an entire rank of angels to reach me. We fought... blade against blade. His strength was... boundless." He spoke with awe, but that soon changed. "But emotion blinded him. The fury in his eyes, he could not see through it. He wanted me dead more than the rest. To this day, I don't know why. He struck, blow after blow, each one threatening to shatter my blade or my bones. But his mistake was in caring too much. He had me pinned. I saw death in his eyes. He lifted his blade for the final strike, so desperate for vengeance that he did not see how I had retrieved my sword from the mud. I plunged it through his heart, and he fell..."

"So brave, Your Grace," the cambion purred. Mikhail missed her sarcasm, but Severn caught it. Amii looked over Mikhail's shoulder at Severn, and he looked back into his own eyes.

Konstantin was dead.

He had to be...

"As his heart bled out, I severed his hamstrings—made it so he couldn't flee, and held down his left wing, removing it with a single blow—"

Severn barely made it outside before the sickness in his guts boiled free and he vomited up all the wretched grief. His body rebelled, trying to heave up the past, and all he could do was ride it out and hope Mikhail didn't see. With memories haunting him, he staggered behind the church and into a narrow alley, the type of forgotten space London had so many of, and there he slid down the filthy wall, drew his knees up, and wept.

CHAPTER 22

Mikhail

THE CAMBION KNEW ITS ROLE, and after its impressive performance earlier in the day, Mikhail was certain its Konstantin act would fool Djall. He'd made sure word had been spread of Konstantin's capture, now they just had to wait for a response from the demons. A wait that should have been easy enough if Severn hadn't disappeared again. Mikhail had never known an angel so elusive and slippery. Worse, when he vanished, he did so with typical angel efficiency, making him impossible to locate. For someone who adored attention, he knew how to shrug it off and vanish when the mood struck him.

He filled the strange void of Severn's absence by checking on the status of the repositioned angel and nephilim refugees, and after Severn's strange comment regarding the treatment of cambions, he even asked Solo to report on the methods of the correction facilities. The rest of the day flew by, and still no Severn.

It was no coincidence that Severn's disappearance had come right after the cambion's Konstantin reveal. Severn's trembling hand had spoken volumes, but so had the allyanse. Its twisting pressure had coiled ever tighter in Mikhail's chest and cinched there now, trying to shove him into action. He'd been pacing the last hour, but when that didn't reveal Severn, he wedged himself into a chair, chasing thoughts around his head.

The reason for Severn's reaction had at first seemed baffling. Was he concerned for Mikhail? That seemed unlikely. Perhaps Severn had a history with Konstantin. Mikhail knew so little of Severn's past before he'd joined the ranks. Had he and Konstantin fought on the killing fields?

Had Konstantin been the one to take Severn's wings?

That would explain his reaction.

Mikhail could have shown Severn the beast's wings as proof he was never coming back. He still could show him, if the flighty angel ever returned.

As the light faded over London, Aerie's broken disks poked at the full moon, and Mikhail sat in one of the chairs in the room he'd come to understand was called a study. Severn had fucked him into the desk opposite. A savage coupling, but so desperately needed. Severn was all light and laughter, but in their moments together, when his guard shifted, like that of the illusion hiding his wing stumps, Mikhail saw darkness in him. The darkness of old grief.

The more Mikhail went over the events of the past few

days, the more the cause of Severn's grief solidified in his mind. Konstantin had hurt him.

If Mikhail could raise the demon from the dead just to kill him again for Severn, he would. These wretched and wonderful feelings were impossible to voice, especially to Severn, who seemed to be handling the emotions far better than Mikhail. But he could put them into action. He'd do anything for Severn, he realized, sitting alone in the dark. And that thought had terrified at first, but not so much now. Now he only feared losing Severn.

Time was flowing past them, and he had the unsettling sensation that the fleeting moments they'd enjoyed would soon be their last. Once the crisis was over, the council would want them both transferred to Haven. Severn had wanted the same.

Mikhail could not—*would not* allow it. Laws be damned. He was guardian and above the law.

They'd find another away.

A thump sounded above. Quickly followed by a scraping clunk.

Mikhail made it to the upper landing in time to see Severn fall through the rooftop door and stumble down the staircase. His wet shirt clung to his chest. His hair dripped water. He lifted his head, fixed Mikhail in his sights, and a grin slid off his lips, then he reached for Mikhail, missed the bottom step, and stumbled into Mikhail's arms.

"Are you... all right?" A waft of rain and sweet alcohol assaulted Mikhail's nose.

"Fine... fine, absolutely fine." Severn pulled himself free and swept his wet hair back, then flicked water from his hand. "Thank you, for the, er... catch. I just, erm... I got lost. These fucking streets and your ridiculous house all look the same. A house that's yours now, apparently... Because we're angels, and we take what we like. Never mind that this was... someone's home..." He patted his trouser pockets, mumbling something, then added, "Right, I forgot..." Then he laughed and staggered down the hallway, using the wall to hold himself up. "So easy to forget. Gods, the rain is vicious outside." Throwing his arms up, he declared, "*I love it*."

Mikhail followed behind, unsure whether to be concerned or angry. He didn't entirely recognize Severn in these moments. "Are you drunk?"

"Oh yes, very."

Angels had a high metabolism. Getting drunk required substantial effort and copious amounts of alcohol. "How?"

"Found a human woman hawking gin down near Aldgate East." He shoved open the door to the nearest room—a bedroom Mikhail hadn't yet explored—and fell inside. "Once she saw I was an angel, well, hell, you know what it's like, right. Course you do, you're fucking you." Severn turned and gestured at Mikhail, then stumbled over his own feet and reached for the dresser to steady himself. "She'd practically handed over her entire stock. It's not like I could say no, right? Bein' a good angel, an' all."

Severn shifted as though to rest a hip against the dresser, missed, fell against the wall, and then tried again, this time managing it. He fumbled the buttons on his shirt, muttering more nonsense. "... and then I said to her... Wait, no. That was someone else. I think... There were a lot of alleyways and people... so many people. They don't meet many angels, apparently. You lot should get down on their level more." He gave up trying to unbutton his shirt and braced his hands against the edge of the dresser instead, with a sigh. "Where was I?"

"Exceedingly intoxicated?" Mikhail helped with the buttons, trying not to meet Severn's soft eyes and wonder why he was looking up at him with all the awe of the other angels. He'd rather liked that Severn didn't look at him that way, like he was some divine being with all the answers.

Severn's cold, clammy fingers touched Mikhail's cheek, and Mikhail finally met the male's eyes. Their depths were filled with pain, and Mikhail had no idea why. "You loved me... *before?*" Severn slurred.

"I did." He took Severn's hand from his face and clasped it in his, warming it through. "Your recklessness, your penchant for arguing, your defiance, your passion, your poetic way with words."

"Poetic words." He snorted. "Will you always love me?"

Mikhail couldn't imagine not having Severn in his life. He'd been beside Mikhail for a decade. And it had come to mean the world to Mikhail. Their future was an uncertain one, but Severn was his, and he'd find a way to make it work and make *them* work. There was still so much he didn't understand. "Always."

"Even if..." Severn winced and turned his face away. "Fuck, this is messed up."

"You're not thinking clearly." He opened Severn's wet shirt and peeled it off his shoulders, sliding his hands down Severn's back. The male's gaze heated, and when Mikhail eased back and dropped his hands to Severn's trouser fly, Severn's bright eyes narrowed slyly.

"Trying to get in my pants, angel?"

"Trying to get you out of the wet clothes and into bed so you can sleep this off."

Severn's lips parted. He leaned back, eyebrow arched. Mikhail dutifully undid the fly, studiously avoiding brushing against Severn's erection. Once Severn was back in his right mind, Mikhail would make him pay for this behavior, hopefully over the council's table.

Severn caught his hand and planted it against his arousal. "You can't tell me you don't want it. I can *feel* how much you want me." He straightened and tapped his chest. "Right here, around my bleeding heart." He flung his arms over Mikhail's shoulders and bumped foreheads. "The allyanse or whatever... Don't turn me away. I can't lose you. I need this... need you, no strings, no rules, no lies, just you and me, right here, in this crazy moment... We're strangers, did you know? But I don't want to be."

Something had hurt him. Not recently, because Severn had always carried the great weight of sadness where his wings used to be. He covered it with laughter and smiles and wit and covered it well. But Mikhail saw him now. "Who hurt you?" *Was it Konstantin?* He ached to ask but feared the pain he'd see on Severn's face.

Hot and desperate lips sealed against Mikhail's. This kiss was different than all the other times, like one wrong move might shatter Severn. He had never felt fragile in Mikhail's hands until now.

Mikhail kissed him back, trying to slow the pace, tasting spice and gin and warmth on Severn's tentative tongue. He slid his hands down the angel's back and scooped him off the dresser, carrying him across the room to the adjacent shower room. He groped for the shower controls as Severn's mouth turned desperate and his hands slid under Mikhail's shirt. The water came on with a sudden hiss, and Mikhail's plan to slowly undress them both became moot when Severn stepped under the water, still half-clothed, and yanked Mikhail inside with him. Mikhail's elbows struck tiles as he pulled Severn into a hungry embrace. His back hit the wall, and then Severn was holding him still, a hand spread against his navel as he dropped to his knees, freed Mikhail's swollen need, and swallowed him deep. Pleasure was a song both their bodies sang until Mikhail couldn't take the angel's filthy mouth on him any longer and hauled him to his feet. He shoved, driving Severn back, and Severn let him, submitting without a fight. Mikhail's desire stuttered, sensing Severn's hurt, and he kissed him instead of all the other ways he could have penetrated his taut body.

Severn pulled free and tossed his head back. "Will you fuck me, Your Grace?"

There was a wrongness in the way he asked, like his sadness was a lingering storm. "No," Mikhail whispered against his ear. "But I will love you, if you'll let me."

Severn's grip tightened in Mikhail's wet clothes, fists hard against Mikhail's back. Mikhail probed his hole with a finger, teasing before gently easing inside, making Severn pant. Haven, he loved watching his angel lose his mind beneath his touch.

"Tell me what you want."

"*You... in me*," he viciously snarled.

Mikhail pulled free, and Severn turned to face the wall. Hot water streamed down his naked back, and Mikhail ran his hands over where he knew the stumps were, feeling Severn shudder and gasp. He mouthed there next, wishing he could heal all his hurts and destroy all his enemies, but until that day, his touch would have to suffice. His tongue swirling on Severn's shoulder, Mikhail gripped himself and guided his cock down the valley of Severn's ass, gently pushing into his tight hole. Going slow, making Severn grunt and arch his back.

There could be no better place for him in that moment. He fit so snugly inside Severn, as though they were made for one another, as though this was meant to be. Mikhail folded him close, Severn's back against Mikhail's chest, and rolled his hips, stroking the head of his cock over Severn's sweet spot just inside his passage, making the angel spit his deliciously filthy curses. It felt too good, like Severn was a brightness in the dark, like he was a half of Mikhail's whole. The allyanse buzzed and sang between them, the union tying tighter, and he was reminded of Saphia's words of how the allyanse would not be possible if Severn did not feel the same way. Haven, he loved this rough angel, and maybe, just maybe, Severn loved him back.

evern

JUST AFTER DAWN, Severn collected Amii from the church where they'd been locked overnight. They were back in their hot, red-haired nephilim guise, her bird nowhere in sight. Severn woke to the news that the Whitechapel guards had received word from Djall. She wanted proof Mikhail had Konstantin before entertaining any kind of deal. It seemed reasonable enough, but Severn knew his sister. She lied better than he did.

"Ready?" he asked the cambion.

"I was ready before you was born, young one." They eyed him in the same flat, suspicious way as their rayvern. The bird would likely show up eventually.

"You an' that big angel have a connection, eh?" They leered. "What is the word..." They muttered some more as Severn led them down the abandoned street, away from

Whitechapel and toward Tower Bridge. "Ah, the *allyanse*. Bet those emotionally stunted overly feathered pricks told you two males couldn't be mates too, eh? Like sex is a sin." They barked a laugh. "We'd all be better off if more angels were demons."

"Something like that..." His head throbbed and his body ached from the gin abuse, and he had no wish to discuss Mikhail with a cambion who'd suck anyone off for a token. "You'd better get your demon on now." Djall would have spies in the buildings, watching for any inconsistencies in Severn's story. Unless Argothun had told her who he was, she'd think him *Severn the angel*, just like all the rest. Djall had known the same as the others: her brother, Konstantin, vanished, assumed dead.

"They call it an allyanse, thinking it's some special transition, when really, it's the biggest damn lie they've ever told. An allyanse. Pah!" They barked a laugh. "All it is, is them shedding their own lies and becoming true." As they spoke, they shrugged off the pretty-boy exterior and filled out, becoming more demon with every step.

"Why is the allyanse a lie?" Severn kept his gaze ahead on the empty shopping stores, abandoned coffee shop, boutiques, and bars. Most humans had cleared out, sensible enough to know trouble was coming. He preferred to stare at their ghostly dwellings than the ghost beside him. A rayvern sat atop a signpost pointing the way to Tower Bridge.

Amii—now a huge doppelgänger of Severn's true self—snorted, the sound more growl than laugh. "Allyanse ain't nothing but another word for love," they said, voice deeper and gravelly. "Ah, there's Jasper... C'mon, you devil, get down 'ere."

The rayvern stared and hopped along its sign but didn't fly down. Severn clenched his jaw and carried on walking, one foot in front of the other. If the allyanse was just love and not some mystical, unbreakable bond, why then did he feel it twisting inside?

"Stubborn bird," Amii grumbled.

"You're saying the allyanse is what? A myth?"

"An excuse angels tell themselves because they can't stand the fear they all secretly feel things too, just like demons."

If the allyanse was truly just another name for love, then everything he felt for Mikhail, every twitch at his name, every ache at his absence, was real?

"Your voice is all wrong for Konstantin." The words sounded harsher than he'd intended. Everything about this felt *wrong*. He wanted it done and over. Djall would see he had Konstantin, she'd have to agree to a meet, and the angels would kill her—saving thousands of lives from her careless terrorism.

"Don't need to hear me speak, do they?" Amii grumbled.

"No. So stay quiet."

"I just gotta stand there right, looking all incubi?"

"Yup."

"And Tower Bridge is up, right?"

"Right."

"The other side of the river is ours—theirs?"

"*Yes*," he hissed.

Their wings ruffled. *His wings. Fuck.* He should have stayed drunk for this. The only good thing about today had been waking up next to Mikhail, blanketed by feathers as the angel slept soundly. He snored a little. It was fucking adorable. Thinking on Mikhail's peaceful face and the feel of his soft feathers against Severn's naked skin tightened his heart. Love or an allyanse? What difference did a name make? It all felt the same, felt *real*.

"You ain't worried they might try an' kill you?" Konstantin asked. "Being an all-important angel? Being Mikhail's *mate*?"

He was a target, but so was the big-ass demon beside him, and he was betting on Konstantin being more sought-after than Mikhail's so-called mate.

They stopped at the lowered barrier, designed to stop nonexistent traffic from crossing over when the bridge would raise and lower its bed for ships. Mikhail had stopped all Thames traffic, vehicular and water-bound, fearing demons would hide among the humans. It was a good move and meant the Thames was now no-man's-land —neutral territory.

Konstantin huffed and fidgeted. "This skin itches."

"Quiet." He scanned the opposite bank. Empty stores gaped. Roads lay silent and bare. There was no sign of any demons.

"For this, I get to fuck you and your mate together. This shit's draining. I gotta get ether somewhere, and the both of you are lit up like neon signs. Getting a lot of cock, are we?"

He was beginning to lose his patience with the cambion butchering his voice and their blatant disrespect. Where was Djall?

"I gotta admit, though... This body is a mighty fine piece of demon meat. And under these pants... sweet Haven," they whistled, "Imma hung like a horse."

The watching rayvern chittered.

A high-powered gunshot punctured the silence. Severn's heightened senses flashed, twisting him aside. The bullet hissed by and twanged against a wall across the street. He grabbed Amii and shoved them back the way they'd come. "Go!" Amii loped ahead, wings half-exposed like sails, making an enormous target.

Another shot rang out. Severn shoved Amii against a wall. A brick exploded above their heads, raining dust. He grabbed Amii by the arm and dragged them into an alley. "We're taking the back route…"

"I think they saw us," they panted, clambering over trashcans and a fallen fence.

The demons had seen them all right. And they weren't pleased.

WORD CAME AT DUSK: Djall agreed to a temporary truce in exchange for Konstantin's return. The trade would happen on Tower Bridge at dawn. Severn addressed the angels at the table. He knew them all and trusted them implicitly. They trusted him too. He'd never steered them wrong before.

"We will not stand for acts of terrorism," he said, looking at each of them in turn. Solo, among them. Vearn was still missing, and the absence of her sword would be felt keenly, but the rest were efficient killers. Battle-hardened warriors. They would not fail. "The target is Djall and only Djall." Scattered on the table in front of them lay a dozen black-and-white human-sourced photos of Djall. Tall and slim, as demons went, a whip coiled at her hip, horns spiraling. The image was old, but the likeness true.

"Once she falls, the demons will retreat to regroup." The war council nodded, and to Severn's left, Mikhail added his agreement, his presence a blazing fire trying to consume Severn, body and mind. "By killing her and only her, the message is clear. We will not be drawn into a bloody battle in London's streets."

Severn straightened. This was his plan, his initiative, and these angels would follow his word. His position at the head of the table beside Mikhail had never settled quite so easily on his shoulders.

"Aerie has fallen. We have not."

The angels thumped their hands to their chests.

Severn glanced at Mikhail, and the guardian lifted his chin for the final command. "We battle at dawn."

They bowed their heads and strode from the church, taking their chatter with them. The door closed with a loud *thunk* and silence rushed in. Mikhail's stare crackled Severn's skin. He waited a heartbeat and looked up at the guardian beside him. His eyes were full of want, his mouth a halfway smile, his wings slowly unfurling. Colored light spilled through the stained glass windows and touched those wings, making them glitter. Severn's small intake of breath sounded much like a gasp. Mikhail was so fucking beautiful, it hurt to look at him, like he wasn't meant for mundane eyes or liars like Severn.

But his life wasn't a lie.

Not anymore.

All the lies were true now. He was angel, and there was no denying he loved the divine male looking at him with the same awe he felt. Nothing about any of this made sense, but love could not be quantified; it could not be pinned down or tied to rules. The cambion was right. The allyanse was an excuse. Love was just love, all at once simple and complicated. And damn, Severn loved this powerful angel, with his ridiculous naivety and ruthless streak, his restrained power and complete devotion. And the way he looked at Severn now, as though Severn were his whole world.

"We might end this war," Mikhail said, stepping close. "Not tomorrow, but soon. You and I. Together."

His thumb stroked Severn's jaw then tilted his chin up.

It did feel that way, as though side by side, they could achieve the impossible.

The angels wouldn't suffer Severn and Mikhail leading them for long, but it didn't matter, because nobody defied Mikhail. None but Severn.

The guardian's soft lips teased Severn's mouth open. His hard body pressed close and his wings folded in, sealing Severn inside, where the warring world did not exist.

"I am proud of you," Mikhail whispered against Severn's mouth. His hands brushed down his back, leaving no doubt to whom Severn belonged.

Severn tilted his head and sighed as Mikhail's wet tongue and blunt teeth traced and nipped down his neck. He wrapped his arms around Mikhail, soaking himself in warmth and breathing in the tantalizing scent of sunshine and feathers.

Mikhail's hands cupped Severn's ass and lifted, easing him onto the table. The hard nudge of Mikhail's cock brushed Severn's lower waist, a reminder of what was to come.

Severn adjusted his own trousers, wincing at the tightness trapping his erection.

The guardian angel leaned back and purred his pleasure as Severn squirmed. "You tremble for me?" An eyebrow arched, his expression subtly amused.

Severn smiled into Mikhail's neck and brushed the line of his jaw against Mikhail's. There was no need to reply, Mikhail knew the answer. He could never have enough of Mikhail in him, on him, or all over him in all the ways. The need was visceral, like a madness trapped beneath his skin demanding to be sated time and time again.

"I want you... right here on this pretty table," Severn whispered into Mikhail's shoulder. He bit down into warm, soft flesh, punctuating his demand.

Mikhail hissed through his teeth and Severn's alert cock leaked in eagerness. These precious moments when all that existed between them was need and want, Severn lived for them.

Mikhail eased Severn back gently. Severn propped himself against the table on his elbows and admired how Mikhail's dexterous fingers quickly opened his shirt. Mikhail's luscious mouth went to work skimming the ripples of Severn's abs. Fuck, his tongue was divine, like the rest of him. It swirled and teased, flicked over a nipple and summoned a groan from deep within Severn.

Down, Mikhail's mouth roamed. His fingers sank behind Severn's belt and pulled, yanking his trouser waist downward, allowing his sucking mouth access to Severn's hip. When Mikhail's touch roamed achingly close to Severn's poised erection, the member twitched, and Mikhail frustratingly veered away.

Severn plunged a hand into Mikhail's hair. "Ah, fuck." For someone who wasn't sexually experienced, Mikhail was a fucking tease. Severn knotted his fingers in Mikhail's long, silken hair and dragged him back up his body.

Mikhail's eyes glowed with delight and lust. He bowed his head for a kiss, but in punishment for neglecting Severn's cock, Severn pulled his head away and smiled at the angel's darkening gaze. "I want you in me... slowly... so fucking slowly. So slowly you can't stand it. Will you do that for me, Your Grace?"

"Anything." Mikhail's voice held a throaty depth Severn had come to ache for.

Easing Mikhail back with a hand on his chest, Severn straightened, unbelted his own trousers, and kicked them off. Mikhail's gaze dropped to Severn's erect and slick cock. The angel's soft lips parted, and it was all Severn could do not to grab him and smother him beneath his hands and mouth and cock. He turned instead and spread both hands against the table, holding himself up.

Mikhail tore Severn's shirt down his back and arms and fell against Severn's naked back, his hot mouth on Severn's shoulder, his hands everywhere before stroking low. Mikhail's fingers kneaded into Severn's ass, roughly squeezing and parting. A finger gently ringed Severn's hole, soft and quick, like a sudden kiss. Severn lost the air in his lungs, forgetting how to breathe. He shivered, his body demanding to be fucked. But this was too good to be over with quickly. There was a time for quick, raw sex. This was not it. He wanted Mikhail in him, against this smooth table, in this grand place, with the colored light pouring over them and Mikhail's wings a canopy above. No, this moment was too precious to be rushed.

"Enter me." Severn deliberately allowed a growl through, testing Mikhail's patience. Mikhail hated to be ordered but loved when Severn challenged him, and Severn had every intention of challenging him.

Mikhail's hand encircled Severn's throat. The angel's solid chest sizzled against Severn's bare back. "Like this?" Mikhail breathed in Severn's ear.

The hard press of Mikhail's erection probed at Severn's hole before carefully sinking inside. Severn sighed hard, almost groaned, and clenched. "Stop."

Mikhail did stop, his entire body tensing like a coiled spring. "Have I hurt you?"

Severn turned his head, acutely aware of the angel's fingers at his throat, and ran his tongue across his lower lip. "Withdraw—*slowly*."

Mikhail's expression twitched, but the thick pressure filling Severn eased. "Now enter me again, Your Grace, but slower."

Mikhail's gaze scorched through Severn's. "What is this?"

"Sweet anticipation..."

He pushed in, his glare locked with Severn's as the thickness filled Severn again. "Stop." It almost killed him to say it. "Now, slowly withdraw and slide into me again."

A growl rumbled through Mikhail. He trembled now too, his control and restraint straining against the powerful urge to unleash the full demands of raw lust on Severn. It was like teasing a wolf, knowing the wild beast would eventually bite.

Mikhail's grip tightened around Severn's throat. He leaned in, his cock stretching Severn open. His mouth brushed Severn's cheek as he spoke, "You're testing me, Severn."

"That's the"—his cock withdrew, making Severn gulp

—"point"—and eased back in. And now Mikhail had found his perfect rhythm. Easing out and pushing in. Only entering enough to briefly touch the sensitive nub inside Severn's passage. Out and in, tease and withdraw, breathe in and exhale. Severn's heart raced, his skin hot, his balls tight.

Mikhail's fingers tightened at his neck again, choking off much of Severn's ability to breathe. "Fuck, yes," he groaned. "Harder."

"No," Mikhail growled in his ear. "Slower, you said... like this..." His breaths sawed out of him too, in time with the motion of his penetrating cock. He clearly wanted more, he needed to fuck Severn hard, and gods, Severn wanted Mikhail to nail him to the fucking table.

Severn's vision blurred. "Mikhail... please."

Mikhail's shudders rippled through Severn. "Beg again," the angel moaned.

Severn bowed his head and closed his eyes so that every sense became all about Mikhail—the hard grip on Severn's throat, his harder cock easing in and out, too fucking slow, like waves gently lapping on a beach. Severn was going to lose his fucking mind from need any second now. "Harder, *please*!"

Mikhail thrust deeply. His thighs slapped Severn's ass, his cock buried to the hilt.

Pleasure with a twist of pain whipped Severn's spine. He cried out, arched beneath Mikhail, and clutched at the grip on his neck, digging blunt nails into Mikhail's fingers. "*More.*"

Mikhail grunted, thrusting again. And again. His grunts turned rough and ragged, his pounding furious. Severn gasped and groaned with every slamming penetration, his body and mind blurring together until all he knew and all he cared for was Mikhail rooted inside him.

"You're close..." Severn panted. "You feel it? So fucking close to coming."

Mikhail's breaths shortened, his grip dug in, and his rhythm broke apart. He came hard, his pumping stuttering as his cock dispersed his seed.

Severn lifted his head to see Mikhail's wings stretched wide, each feather touched with a fine shimmer of silver. A swell of warmth and comfort held him as close as Mikhail's arms. And gods, Severn buzzed from the sexual high, but it wasn't the end. Nowhere near it. Raging hard and throbbing from Mikhail's touch, he was not done with his angel.

Mikhail placed a soft kiss on the back of Severn's neck. "You ruin me..." he whispered.

Severn grinned over his shoulder, proud to see Mikhail's eyes glassy, pupils full from desire. "I've only just begun."

THEY MADE love through the night inside Mikhail's quaint little house. Hours of bliss, of sensation, power, touch and taste, of angel inside him, all around him, filling him up and breaking him down. He was lost, fallen for Mikhail in all ways, and he never wanted to be found.

Dawn snuck toward London, and Severn crept from the bed to the rooftop to watch the sky bleed red. He stood alone, one hand on the chimney stack looking out over London's patchwork buildings. Some squat, some like spears stabbing at the clouds, and the Thames snaked through them all. The line in the sand.

He'd spent so long hating, he'd blinded himself to all other emotions. Spent so long feeling nothing, he'd forgotten how to love. And now it was here and he was... terrified.

A rayvern flapped to a landing on the ridge tiles on the pitched section of the roof to his left. It squawked and tilted its head one way, then the other, trying to decide how to reclaim the roof from the wingless angel.

"I'm a fraud," he told it, "and he doesn't know."

The rayvern blinked and hopped closer.

He could never tell Mikhail the truth. That was... impossible. And what did it matter? Once the dawn ruse was over, Konstantin would be gone for good. He'd live with the past because he had no choice, but he wouldn't— could never tell Mikhail. There was no one left alive who knew. He'd bury it like the dead were buried. And that would be the end of Konstantin of the Red Manor, Lost Lord of the Incubi, the demon who gave up his heart and soul for vengeance.

"Today is the first day of the rest of my life," he told the rayvern. The bird hopped down onto the flat section of roof and strutted closer. Severn crouched and watched it turn over stones and moss, looking for beetles. "Let's hope it's not also the last."

CHAPTER 24

S evern

SEVERN ORDERED Solo to lower Tower Bridge's enormous section of roadway. The landmark bridge's two spans groaned as they slowly crept downward, eventually sealing together, opening the roadway across the river.

A line of demons waited on the south side, their spiked wings making their numbers look like rows of jagged teeth. The numbers appeared to be few, but more would be hidden among the buildings in the same way Severn had the ranks of angels hidden inside abandoned human buildings on his side of the river.

Angels and demons hovered above, both sides lit by the morning sun's dagger-like rays.

Meeting in the middle of the bridge, where the two spans joined, meant any threats—like sniper shots—could be spotted before they proved damaging. But it also left

Mikhail exposed, and in his battle armor, he was a shining target of all things angel.

Severn's fingers twitched, desperate to reach for the stolen angelblade in its sheath against his back. Instead, as their line crossed onto the bridge's north span, he waved Amii into place between Mikhail and himself.

The cambion wore Severn's true face well. Virtually perfect and disturbing enough that Severn couldn't admire them for long. Amii strode forward, incubi wings tucked closed but held aloft in the proud way of all demons. The gag had been Mikhail's idea.

Across the bridge, demons hissed their disgust, either at having Konstantin trapped or Konstantin himself. These days, it was difficult to know what his kin thought of him.

"*Skree!*" someone shouted.

Severn hid his wince. Amii didn't react at all. They had their chin held high, their face the picture of stubborn lordly arrogance.

Demons didn't wear armor, believing it slowed them down. Their bulks were all shielded by loose chainmail, their choice of weapons—throwing axes, whips, chains— hung at their hips or against their backs. Djall's whip bore a star-like metal tip. Severn had once seen her strangle an angel with it, the tip wedged in his mouth to keep him from screaming.

Djall broke from the demon ranks and started forward. "The skree returns!" She walked like the madam, demanding every gaze land on her, but that's where the resemblance ended. Bigger than the madam, her wings were multijointed and more bat-like than most demons. Glossy black skin shimmered in the early morning light.

Her knee-high, stiletto-heeled, leather boots clipped against the bridge's road surface. In her case, the heels were small blades. She used them for throwing or for cutting throats in a brawl.

"My darling brother…" She stopped in the middle of the roadway. With her hip cocked, she slid her gaze from Konstantin to Severn.

Severn leveled his breathing and his heart. It had been ten years since they'd argued. She'd told him no amount of vengeance could change a war. He'd told her to watch. She hadn't changed at all.

He did not regret what was to come. Djall was kin, but she had also crossed the line.

She sighed and tilted her head in an oddly rayvern-like gesture. "Look at us, a few feet from each other and we ain't fighting. This day truly must be a fucking miracle."

"This demon for a ninety-day truce," Mikhail said.

Her lips turned down at their corners, and while she tapped her fingernail against her chin, her wings flexed slightly. "Hm…"

He'd seen his sister worried, seen her furious, seen her out of her mind on lust. Right now, she was guarded. Severn flicked his gaze behind her to the row of demons, and then beyond them to the empty houses. Any of those hundreds of vacant windows could hide a sniper. Guns were considered virtually useless in battle, but a lucky shot could disable an angel.

"Sixty days," she countered, her upper lip half-raised in a soundless snarl as she addressed Mikhail.

Severn wished he'd stayed beside him. Mikhail didn't need protection, but Severn *needed* to be near him, to see him, to feel him close. He grabbed Amii's bound wrists and pulled them around to his right, stepping beside Mikhail.

Djall peered down her nose. "They say *you* are wingless. Severn the Wingless, we call you. Bets are you're missing other parts too? Gelded and grounded, what a terrible shame."

A growl rumbled from Mikhail, and despite the situation, Severn's heart swelled to hear his angel's protective streak kick in. "Yet here I am, at the guardian's right side."

Her snarl warped into a grin. "They say he's fucking you—"

Mikhail's hand shot out whip-fast. He snatched Djall by the throat faster than Severn could track and yanked her to within an inch of his face, his teeth bared and wings shimmering into sight.

The demons all lurched into motion, swarming forward.

Djall had a dagger in her hand. The blade flashed toward Mikhail's side. Severn batted her strike away and punched both hands between them, jolting Mikhail and Djall apart.

Djall skidded backward and went down onto a knee with a snarl. Mikhail barely moved at all, but with his wings raised and his face fixed in vicious fury, his feelings were clear. This would end in killing.

"Stop!" Severn was between them, hands out, urging both back. "Stop..."

Djall threw up her hand, signaling her horde to pull up short. They obeyed but sneered and growled and jeered, eager to be set free again.

The situation balanced on a blade's edge. Severn stood between both sides, barely holding either back. He could not stop them if they truly wanted to fight, but Mikhail was no fool, and neither was Djall. Many would die, and for what?

Djall straightened, licked her lips, and flicked her wings out—the demon equivalent of cracking her knuckles. "There will be no trade—"

"I'll rip your wings from your carcass—" Mikhail barked.

"Mikhail!" Severn snapped. "Rein it in." Shit. He gently placed a hand on Mikhail's golden breastplate, making the angel glance down. "Stop already." He was beginning to understand why banishing emotional angels was such a good damned idea. There was a time to hurt Djall, but it was not yet. He tried to convey that thought to Mikhail with just his glare.

With a grunt, Mikhail eased back, pulling his wings in, making himself marginally smaller. "Fine. Sixty days."

Djall shook her horned head and pointed at the gagged Amii, casually observing from the sidelines. "There will be no deal because *that* is not my brother."

"What?" Severn spluttered. "Of course they are."

Djall's mouth worked.

Shit.

"You angels think all demons are fools!" She raised her voice, making sure every soul present heard. "Did you really think you could parade a cambion in front of me and lie to *my face*?" Her gaze fell to Severn and fixed on him, drilling deep. "Did you truly believe I wouldn't know my own brother when I saw him, no matter his skin?"

She knew.

She knew everything. She'd known all along...

His heart plummeted, ripping dread through him,

exposing him to the horror of having his entire ruse exposed while Mikhail stood beside him. That could not happen. Severn brought his arm down, signaling, and shouted, *"Now!"*

At first, nothing changed. Djall glared through him, seeing all the lies, and Mikhail turned toward Severn, silently questioning why Severn had signaled the attack too early.

He could feel it all coming undone.

This had to end now. Djall needed to die.

Djall's mouth curved into a sly grin. He'd seen that look on her face a thousand times. She'd won, and they both knew it.

Hundreds of silver arrows screamed down from above and punched into the road behind Djall, sealing her off from her ranks. She whirled and screamed her rage.

Mikhail pulled his blade free.

Severn couldn't allow her to speak. One word and everything he had with Mikhail would be destroyed.

"You liars!" she screeched, but as she saw Mikhail's sword, her screech morphed into a wicked laughter. "He has you all fool—"

Severn tackled her in the middle, drove her backward, and pitched them both over the bridge's iron railing into a fall.

Air rushed. Djall's claws sliced into his face. He stole a gasp, tugged Djall close. Water hit him like a freight train, turning him over and under, ripping air from his lungs. Djall writhed and bucked, but he clung on, and the thick, muddy waters of the Thames consumed them.

CHAPTER 25

$\mathcal{M}$ikhail

MIKHAIL GRABBED the bridge's rail and scanned the churning waters far below. The Thames was never clear. It rushed through London too fast, stirring silt and debris. The river had taken them—*taken Severn.*

Panic shattered reason. "No..."

Could Severn swim? What if Djall cut him with her blades? What if he was drowning while Mikhail stared at the swirling mud-waters?

He had to go in after them—

"Mikhail!"

A voice he never expected to hear again tore him from his panic. He threw a glance behind him, uncertain, torn, seeking the familiar. Demons marched Vearn forward, her hands tied behind her back, her face bruised. But she was alive.

"Mikhail... stop..." Vearn urged, her expression full of pain, but not for herself. "Listen to me."

"Listen? Severn is down there—"

Demons brought a second angel forward. He knew her. He'd ordered her death because Vearn had told him she was a traitor. Severn had killed her. How, then, was she alive and here? And why now?

He bared his teeth at the demons holding them. Anger and fear tried to choke him while blurring his vision. He had no time for this!

Cassandra dropped to a knee and bowed her head. "Your Grace." She lifted her face, and all around, angel and demon watched on, "You are being lied to."

CHAPTER 26

Severn

DJALL GOT her knee between them and kicked. She slipped from Severn's hold, but he snagged something, maybe her wrist or her ankle, he couldn't tell in the rolling waters and racing undercurrents. Then his leg hit something soft, and his hip thumped it next. He broke the surface with a gasp. Djall's fist smashed into his face. Heat bloomed through his nose. He reeled, going under again. His sister twisted the hold he had on her arm and hauled him out of the water, up a muddy bank. He thrashed, gasped and spluttered, spitting blood and mud.

Djall let go and crawled halfway up the bank, battling with the mud. "You were always... the romantic one..." She laughed.

In that moment, he hated her like he never had before. It was a strong hate, the kind that couldn't be ignored.

"You killed... thousands of innocent people." Breathing hard, he steadied his heart. She knew his lies. She crossed a line. She had to die.

Tower Bridge loomed out of the morning mist. It wasn't far, just farther down the river. There was still time to return and make this all right—once Djall was gone.

"Your game is done, brother." She lay on her back with the mud oozing and bubbling around her limbs, trying to slowly suck her down.

A shining thing sticking out of the bank caught his eye—the heel missing from Djall's boot. He still had the angelblade on his back, but its use would be too cumbersome in the slippery mud.

"It's over. Give it up." She panted. "I came to take you home, brother."

He sank his fingers into the mud and pulled the small, thin blade free. He had to get back to Mikhail before the guardian destroyed every demon on that bridge. If that happened, nothing would change. But Mikhail could change. He had. They both had. This day didn't have to end in blood. "And if I don't want to go back?"

She snorted. "Don't be ridiculous."

He pushed to his knees, slipped, and dug his free fingers into the bank, heaving himself toward her. "Things have changed."

"You're damn right they have... we're winning, for the first time in forever. *Demons are fucking winning!*"

"You killed people—humans..." His fingers slipped on the small, mud-soaked handle. He adjusted the weapon against his palm, reaffirming his grip. "Thousands of people lived in the cauldron."

Djall rolled onto her side and swore. Mud sucked on

her wings, pulling her back down. "It was time." She tugged. "And look what it did, *Stantin*. They're running scared." She finally looked at him, gaze flicking down to the blade in his hand. She snorted a humorless laugh. "You *are* skree... I didn't believe it. Argothun said you'd turned... I called him a liar. Not my brother, I told him. Not Konstantin. He hates them too much."

It was true, once. "The angels aren't bad, Djall. They're just misguided. They can change."

She pulled again at her wing, her tugs becoming urgent. "Don't be absurd. Is his cock so mighty a thing you turned angel for it, brother?"

"I love him." It was true. So true, it hurt to say because he did not deserve love. Djall looked at him like he'd lost his mind. "And I won't let you or anyone, demon or angel, ruin what we have."

She laughed gently. "I didn't believe it, even when the captured angels said it about you—who you were, I did not believe it. My brother, so full of fire and vengeance, would not love the enemy, I told them. In that, I suppose we agreed. And we were all wrong."

"Captured angels?"

She swept a hand over her forehead and up her left horn, wiping off the dribbling mud. "They knew all along. They couldn't tell the guardian, not without proof. Because you had everyone fooled, especially Mikhail. So they rather cleverly set you up."

He lowered the dagger. "What?"

"I didn't think angels were so cunning. They proved me wrong."

A slippery sense of unease slithered around him. "What are you talking about? What angels?"

"We caught Vearn when Aerie fell. And when we heard what was happening in angel towers, well, we could hardly kill the two of them."

They had Vearn all this time? But Vearn hadn't known Severn's true identity. "Two?"

Finally plucking her wing free, she pushed up onto a knee. "Did you learn nothing from Mikhail taking your wings?"

He dropped and thrust the blade against her throat. *"What have you done?"*

"Nothing," she grinned. "The angels did it all themselves. Mikhail made a mistake in not killing you, brother. And you have done the same. You should know by now, never leave the enemy alive."

"Who?" He pressed hard, forcing her head back. *"Who did I leave alive? Who knows?!"*

"Cassandra."

But he'd killed Cassandra. Dropped her wingless body off his balcony. "She could not have survived that fall."

"Not alone... but Vearn was waiting to catch her. Saved by an angel, how romantic..." Djall purred. "You're a pretty angel, I'll give you that. I'd fuck you too, if I were Mikhail. What will he do, I wonder, when he learns he's been fucking his nemesis?" She grabbed his wrist. "Tell me this was your plan all along. Tell me it's all a brilliant lie, brother, and I'll believe you. We'll return and rip this skree skin from your bones."

Severn's breath stuttered. His chest tightened, the air suddenly too thin. No... Mikhail could *never* know. "No, I..." He drew back, slipping in the mud, his thoughts churning, unclear and thick, like the river behind him.

He'd told Cassandra his name. He'd thought her dead and his secret dead with her.

Djall sighed and climbed to her feet, flicking her wings free of mud. "Brother dear, tell me you did not fall in love with your own lie?"

He had. He'd fallen for Mikhail, for love, because life without love was no life at all and vengeance wasn't able to sustain him, but love could. And had. He loved Mikhail despite what he was, and Mikhail loved him back.

Cassandra was alive.

Vearn knew.

He'd have to find them, kill them... to keep his secret safe. And kill Djall now too.

She saw the change in him. "Stantin... wait..."

He lunged. Her wings flung out, ready to hike her into the sky, but the mud weighed her down. One flap, two.

She was airborne, and in seconds would be out of his reach.

He grabbed her ankle.

She kicked, connecting sharply with his jaw, but his grip held. He yanked her out of the air, clamped a hand on her shoulder, and thrust the blade into her side. A gasp, she stilled, her big dark eyes disbelieving. Then her forehead struck his already broken nose, and he flailed, landing flat on his back. She loomed, moved in, sharp teeth bared. Severn's heel connected with her knee, crumpling her over him, and then it became a scrabbling of claws and teeth and fists. He shoved her face into the mud, desperate to finish her, to get back to Mikhail, to stop his whole world from collapsing. Djall's wing arch slapped him across the face, momentarily throwing him off-balance. She flipped from under him. Her elbow came down on the back of his neck, igniting a blaze of pain and sending shards of it down his spine. If he could not kill her, he could not go back at all. She'd tell Mikhail, she'd tell the demons every-thing—if she hadn't already.

Cold hands fixed around his neck. She shoved him face-first into the mud. He gasped, swallowing silt and grit. Mud pushed through his lashes into closed eyes. He couldn't see, couldn't breathe. He reached behind him, fingers scraping on Djall. He'd beaten her in combat as demon a hundred times but not as angel. Too small, too weak, his power constrained behind his angel-skin.

His chest heaved, lungs ablaze.

He could not die here. There was too much to do, a war to stop, an angel to love, and he would have worked, he would have made it so!

Djall tore his head from the river's slop. "I should kill you, brother! But unlike the angels you claim to now love, I care." She thumped his head down into the mud one more time, then the weight on his back vanished.

He scooped mud from his eyes and retched up half the river.

"They're telling him now," he heard her say. "Come after me and you'll miss your chance to defend yourself... if there's any defense to give." She spat in the mud. "You are no brother of mine."

When he finally rolled onto his back, he was alone, panting at the quiet as the river gently lapped at the bank near his fingers, washing away vomit and blood.

He could see the bridge still, two great towers rising out of the mist, but it was too far and too foggy to see any demons or angels. Perhaps they'd left, too tired of war to fight?

It seemed unlikely, and as he climbed a low wall, a new sense of dread weighed him down, as heavy as the mud pulling on his loping strides. He had to get back... His body rebelled, Djall's beating making his heart stutter, his chest ache, and his head throb. Mud still blurred his vision and clogged his mouth. But he couldn't stop.

Mikhail would listen.

He always listened to Severn.

Angels lined the roads ahead. On the bridge too, not moving, not attacking the demons opposite, just standing still. *Talking*. He stumbled on, wanting little more than to get to Mikhail, to know it wasn't too late.

Angels he approached turned their faces away.

It was quiet.

So quiet.

Nobody spoke.

Nobody met his gaze.

Severn's heart was the loudest thing in the world. He limped onto the bridge, and the angels parted, revealing Mikhail's back, his glorious silver-tipped wings spread.

It would be okay. There was nobody here. His sister was lying—like she did so well. There was no Cassandra, because she was dead, just like he'd known.

He laughed with relief and almost fell to his knees while hobbling closer. It would be all right. He'd tell them Djall was dead... He'd tell them anything to make them believe in him. To make Mikhail believe...

Mikhail turned. Cassandra knelt on the bridge, Vearn behind her, and behind them, a line of demons.

Cassandra sneered. Vearn glared. And Mikhail...

His proud face was cold. His jaw set. Eyes hard.

Because he was hurting, and when Mikhail was in pain, he wore that look like armor.

Severn slowed, his steps suddenly too heavy, his body left with nothing to give.

"She's lying…" he said, but his voice broke in half. "They're lying!" he said, louder this time, with real force. Angels turned their backs, and Severn's hopeful smile died on his lips. It hurt. It hurt like losing his wings. "Mikhail… wait… Cassandra is the traitor. I did what you ordered of me."

"Yes," Mikhail said, his voice cold. "And you told her the truth before you let her fall." A pause, a fragile moment in which Severn still grasped ahold of hope that Mikhail didn't know, and then the angel said, "*Konstantin.*"

Severn's vision swam. All of the angels had turned their backs now. All but Mikhail. So many. Warriors, like him. He respected each of them, had fought beside them, killed for them—or was that for himself? This didn't feel real. Like he was in a terrible dream, one he couldn't wake from. Like he was in the wrong skin, looking out from wrong eyes.

Another step forward, another, dragging the dead weight of all those lies. "Please… Mikhail, listen, just… listen."

Mikhail drew the sword from his back. Its blade made a long, slow hiss from its sheath. "I've heard enough." He lifted his head, marking each angel beneath his sharp gaze. "*Kill them all.*"

Angels took flight in a deafening burst of wings, and through the storm of feathers, Mikhail started forward.

Severn fumbled for the sword still strapped to his back. The weight of Mikhail's fury pushed ahead of the guardian, stealing the air from Severn's lungs and wrapping invisible white-hot fingers around him. Power crackled from Mikhail. He lifted the sword in both hands. The taste of vengeance twisted his mouth. The sword came down—

Severn swung wildly to block. Blades rang, steel on steel. The force of Mikhail's stroke almost pulled Severn to his knees. He pushed back, staggered, and raised his blade again.

"Isn't this what you want?" Mikhail struck again.

The blow rattled his bones. "No!" The blades screamed. He shoved Mikhail's blade back at him.

Mikhail thrust again. Severn slapped the sword aside with his own.

Again.

Severn parried. Retreating more with every strike.

"Fight me!" the guardian roared.

He wouldn't. Couldn't. He was done fighting. "It wasn't all lies."

Demons howled above. They blackened the skies, and among them, angels glittered. Blades clashed, the war raged, but Severn cared only for the shining angel in front of him. An angel he should never have hated, an angel who was loyal to his cause, to the war, an angel who *could change.*

"Mikhail... stop."

Again, their blades rang. Again, Mikhail swung for him, and steel met steel. Harder, faster. Each blow landed harder and harder. Mikhail would not weaken.

"Mikhail... please..." Severn danced backward, deflecting every blow. "Don't... do this... just listen... *I changed. You changed!*"

Another blow. Severn sensed a wall at his back and

twisted away, slashing downward, pinning Mikhail's blade against the road. Suddenly, he was face-to-face with his enemy. Close, like they'd been close before. And all the time, he'd had Mikhail gasp his name, had the angel look at him with softness and love and all the emotions no angel should ever have. "I love you," he panted. "That is no lie."

It was the wrong thing to say.

Mikhail's wings flew open. He reared back and roared. Power exploded from his body, turning his outline molten gold. Jagged light crackled and danced off every feather's tip. And when Mikhail's blade came down, Severn only narrowly spun away. Power slammed into the earth, shaking the world. Above, dark clouds boiled out of nothing, bringing with them sudden darkness and the terrible electric crackle that made Severn's skin tighten and the small hairs rise.

Mikhail was guardian, and now his power was too much to look upon, too much to even comprehend.

He'd kill Severn, kill them all.

Severn staggered. The air burned with energy and ether. He called to his own power, but it was nothing compared to Mikhail's smothering fury.

Streaks of light stabbed through those boiling clouds. Stars. They slammed into buildings and streets, exploding through concrete, shattering parts of the bridge, pulverizing demons and angels, turning them to raining dust.

Cool tears dried on Severn's mud-and-dust-caked face.

The sight of Mikhail tearing stars from the sky... so terrible, so wrong.

Destruction rained all around. Mikhail's black eyes sparkled with the light from those dying stars. He didn't care. He wasn't made to. His wings shone, and in their brightness, their reaching expanse multiplied. A pair turned to four, turned to six, and Mikhail lifted off the road, the terrible weight of his power pouring off him in golden waves.

He was beyond listening. Beyond anything earthly.

With no other choice, Severn bolted across the bridge. A building exploded to his left, raining stone sideways through the air. Thunder roared, or perhaps it was Mikhail. The ground trembled, and so did his soul. He ran, dodging flying rock. Enormous bridge cables snapped and lashed like wild metal snakes, whipping demons out of the sky and slamming them down.

The bridge buckled.

Severn stumbled and ran on toward the demons. A meteor struck a five-story building ahead. Deadly projectiles flew in every direction. Severn veered, dodging the rocks and dust, running, clambering, falling. Didn't matter where. He just had to get away, to survive, to get away from the world-ending angel before his rage ripped out half of London.

A demon slashed at him out of the falling dust—seeing *angel*. He skipped aside, still running. Wings beat above, bearing down on him. Demon or angel, didn't matter, they all wanted him dead. He sensed an incoming strike and ducked, then glanced behind him and saw the demon pull their sword back for another swing at his head.

A wall tumbled. He stumbled, drew in a breath, and threw himself down, arms over his head as the bricks pounded over him, crushing him tighter, making him small, suffocating him. He drew in breath but tasted only dust and rock. This was no place to die. Yet, wasn't it all he deserved? Shunned by both lives. His love a lie. His life worthless. This was where vengeance had gotten him.

A tawny hand thrust through the stone, grabbed Severn's shoulder, and heaved him clean out of the wreckage. Severn swung the sword wildly enough to make the demon drop him. He fell hard, blinking through brick dust, readying to block what would surely be another killing blow, but the demon crouched, his brow pinched. "You'd better come with me."

The wings, covered in velvety blackness. A face made of inquisitive eyes and two short horns he'd always hated, but Severn had told him they were fine horns when he was Konstantin. But it wasn't possible. It couldn't be. This demon had died long ago.

"You're... not real." He lifted his hand and carefully touched the demon's cheek. Warm, soft. The demon half smiled, showing a hint of sharp teeth, and pressed his hands to Severn's, holding it against his face.

The thudding in Severn's head pounded too hot and heavy. His lungs cinched. And finally, the nightmare drowned him in unconsciousness.

CHAPTER 27

*M*ikhail

MIKHAIL STOOD at the twisted rail on the remains of
Tower Bridge. There was little left of the landmark but a
few defiant steel pillars and limp cables trailing in the river.
Smoke and dust drifted over London, cloaking it in darkness. Bloated bodies drifted with the tidal waters. Demons
and angels, faces down, broken wings sodden. The
carcasses snagged in the trailing cables, collecting like
some gruesome dam.

He should care. But like a house gutted by fire, after
he'd summoned the stars from the skies and his raw power
had burned through him, nothing remained. Just a vacant
shell.

"Your Grace, the bodies..."

Grief, joy, contentedness... *love*.

Gone.

Love. Love was a curse. A weakness. A lie.

Lifting his head, he breathed in the stench of river and dust, fire and blood. London lay mangled and broken, half its skeleton reaching from the mire. Holes had opened in the London skyline where buildings had toppled. He'd brought the fire. Destroyed it all. Demons. Angels. *People.*

And he did. Not. Care.

"Your Grace, shall we collect the fallen?"

The voice was a nuisance, like a fly tapping against a window.

Mikhail let his eyes fall closed. His fingers tightened around the rail.

The missing wings, his cocky swagger, the quick smile, his wicked tongue, so smooth with lies. Mikhail should have seen it.

The soft kisses, his gentle touch, how he threw his head back and sighed whenever Mikhail's lips brushed his skin.

"Would I lie to you, Your Grace?"

Pain stabbed at Mikhail's heart. Hard and sharp, like a shard of glass through the chest. He gasped and curled around the agony, fingers clutched at his chest as though he could tear his own heart out and toss it in the river with the dead.

"Mikhail?"

Throwing open his wings, he launched himself into the sky, beating their great width—back to two wings, no longer six. He climbed higher and higher, leaving the broken city below. Clouds kissed his cheeks and lips. Peace stroked his soul. He broke through the mist into blazing sunlight and made for Aerie's abandoned shell.

When he landed inside Aerie's empty chambers, the

silent city echoed his footfalls. Pulling his wings in, he strode along the cracked walkways, through glass doorways, and finally into his chamber. A relentless wind tore through the space, trying to sweep his presence away.

Plucking a feather from his wings, he approached the wall and presented the silver frond. The wall chinked backward an inch and slid open. Lights flicked on, revealing the long, narrow room beyond. Drapes hung at intervals along the walls, but they didn't cover windows.

The door slammed shut behind him, sealing off the world outside.

He sighed.

A pair of black velvet curtains covered the entire rear wall. He slowly approached until the curtains loomed over him. His heart thudded harder and faster.

He let the spent feather fall from his fingers.

"Would I lie to you, Your Grace?"

Taking the corner of the curtains, he yanked, pulling the entire breadth to the floor. The thick velvet collapsed with a sound like that of wings taking flight.

The revealed display pushed him back a step, then another.

Featherless wings.

Demon wings.

He tracked their span, the multihinged arches, and their grotesque web of veins. They hadn't decayed since the battle in which Mikhail had taken them. They hung as though frozen in time, still somehow proud and enduring in their defiance. And now he knew why.

Will you always love me?

The same thrust of pain through his heart knocked

him to a knee. He breathed around it, trying to hold the broken pieces of himself together before he shattered.

Severn's whispers of a better world as they lay together—those whispers mocked him now. The ghost of Severn's touch burned Mikhail's skin and scorched inside, where he'd penetrated deeper than just the physical. Mikhail had opened himself to the monster, mind, body, and soul, and the beast had feasted.

It was a sin, a terrible, primal sin.

Mikhail had fallen for a lie.

A sob broke from him. He swallowed the rest and pushed the pain down, crushing it to dust. His breathing slowed, his heart too, both falling into a steady rhythm.

Slowly, he raised his head and climbed to his feet in the shadow of those great wings.

He felt nothing.

No, not nothing...

One thing still burned inside, one powerful kernel, so bright, it burned like the stars he'd pulled from the sky.

Vengeance.

evern

HANDS WERE ON HIM, hot hands, rough hands, but Severn was too broken inside to care. He drifted somewhere dark, drowning in grief but never dying. He'd done something terrible, so terrible the pain of it consumed him from the inside out.

A hand gripped his.

Mikhail?

He clutched that hand like it could save him from the agony and blinked into too-bright lights.

Fingers pinched his jaw, forcing open his mouth. A cold hard rod pushed between his teeth, pinning down his tongue.

This wasn't right.

But the pain throbbed and boiled and made him want to die, just so it ended.

He tried to see Mikhail because Mikhail would save him... but that wasn't right either. He'd done something to Mikhail... something that might have broken the world. When he thought on it, the pain doubled, making his body rebel and heave and buck.

"Bite down," a voice said. A voice he knew. But Samiel was dead. He'd died long ago, and Severn had picked up an angelblade in vengeance, selling his soul to destiny to destroy his enemy.

Mikhail.

No, no... that wasn't right either... Mikhail *had* saved him, pulled *him* from the mud, brought him back to life. Made him new. Made him better. His touch had burned like his kisses, full of fire and light and love. He needed him. But another thought tried to chase the others down, a terrible thought... the thought that it was all a lie.

Severn turned his face toward Mikhail to say he was sorry, to beg for forgiveness before this pain killed him.

A demon stared back.

His heart jolted. He tried to pull his hand free, but the demon—Samiel—gripped too tightly. He smiled sadly. "Shhh, Stantin. Everything will be right again soon."

Right? No, no, nothing was right.

He breathed in and smelled demon and regret.

He twisted, tried to turn away, but something had hold of his neck and wrists. His legs were pinned too. The cold lights were too bright, too sharp. He had to get free, get back to Mikhail, to make him see that one thing—one thing hadn't been a lie. Love. He had to see, to know... before it was too late.

"Hold him down," Samiel said, the order firm.

Severn bucked and twisted and thrashed, but the grip on his limbs clamped tighter.

"It's all right..." Samiel leaned over, his face blocking out the light. Twin horns and demon eyes. "It'll be over soon."

Samiel was dead. Was Severn dead too?

He wanted to die.

It seemed only fair.

He'd fucked up everything else. Dying would stop him from fucking up more.

The demon smiled sadly. Lines gathered around his golden eyes. "Begin."

A cold, soft tear escaped Severn's eye.

Begin? Begin what?

Fire lashed down his spine, locking every muscle. He screamed around the wooden rod in his mouth. Fire washed across his skin, ripping it free, inch by agonizing inch. Couldn't breathe. Couldn't think. Vicious agony. Too much. They were tearing him open, killing him.

Mikhail? Where was Mikhail? He needed him now, needed his hand in his, his gentle smile, the way he held Severn, wrapped his wings around him, making him a brighter thing, a better thing. But inside the agony, he saw Mikhail's face, and it was not the face he knew.

The guardian angel's sword blows had landed like lightning strikes. He remembered them again now, slamming into his soul. The memory burned too, and he wished he could give that one up. Why stop there? Could he forget love?

The demons were trying to cut his lies free, and he knew Mikhail would not come to save him. Not this time.

Mikhail *would* come. But not for love.
He'd come for revenge.
And he'd kill them all.

The crone and the rayvern watched from a rooftop as falling stars ripped through the storm of an angel's making. He was powerful, that one, perhaps the most powerful in this time, and dangerous too. Because he had loved a demon with all his heart, and now that love had shattered, taking his bright heart with it.

"Love is a terrible thing," the crone told the rayvern on her shoulder, offering it a piece of meat.

The huge bird cawed its reply, pecked the chunk of meat from the crone's fingers, and swallowed it whole.

"There be dark days ahead, Jasper. Dark, dark days."

To be continued in Eternal Sin, Primal Sin #2 from Ariana Nash. Coming in 2020.
Pre-order today.

~

Did you enjoy Primal Sin? If you did, please leave a review. Every single review really does help.

~

Eternal Sin ~ Excerpt (subject to change)

Mikhail wiped again at the angelblade. The viscous demon blood refused to let go. He'd tried everything to clean it back to its original spotless shine, but the thick, crusted layer of crimson had glued itself to steel.

He threw the blade down onto the desk by the window and waited for his heart to slow—the anger to pass. The filthy sword mocked him. He couldn't scrub the blood off like he couldn't scrub the demons from this earth, of Severn from his mind—*not* Severn. Severn was a lie. *Konstantin.*

He couldn't think on him, or what they'd done, or the things they'd both said and how it had all been a cruel fabrication. Any time those thoughts crept into his head, he lost control, lost all reason and sense and composure. He couldn't function when consumed with all the damned *emotion* Severn had awoken in him.

He swallowed hard and combed his fingers through his long hair, sweeping it back from his face.

Sunlight streamed in through the windows and over the desk, making the sword glow. A desk Severn had fucked him against. The entire house was haunted with memories. Severn sprawled in the beds, his smile a tantalizing question. Severn laughing on the rooftop in the rain. Severn's firm hips, his rounded ass, and the way he threw his head back, his loose golden curls aglow, when Mikhail...

Mikhail turned away with a snarl and soon found himself outside, walking the streets, needing to escape. He was a twitch away from spreading his wings and taking flight, returning to Aerie to stare at the horrid demon wings displayed on his wall. He always returned, especially when his memories tried to convince him not everything about Severn had been a lie.

"I love you. That is no lie."

No, no, no... he could not listen, he could not fall under this insanity trying to bury him. His angels already mistrusted him. He'd... done things. Careless things. Killed angels in his haste to slay demons, killed... people, by accident, but still... it was a sin. He knew it. They all knew it. Vearn had covered up the worst of his mistakes, but it kept happening, because the only way he could function was to turn everything off. All of it. And feel *nothing*. There was peace in nothing. A hollow coldness he welcomed, where only necessity pulled his strings. But it meant he forgot who he was supposed to be.

Whispers spoke of wanting him banished. Angels feared him. And they were right, but he wasn't going anywhere.

The only way for the madness to end would be for

Severn to die. The allyanse remained, and maybe his death would kill Mikhail too, but at this stage, it would be for the best. But the demons had him hidden somewhere. In the two months since Tower Bridge fell, he'd caught demon after demon and wrung answers out of them. But the answers were always the same. Nobody knew where Severn was.

There was one name that the demons spoke of before the torture killed them.

Samiel.

Samiel was Severn's friend, *his lover.* The first time a demon had uttered those words, Mikhail had punched through his ribs and torn out his heart, then crushed that useless organ in his fist. The next time, he'd refrained from instantly killing him to merely breaking each of his wings. And by the third mention of this *Samiel*, his importance as Severn's "lover" could not be ignored. This *Samiel* would know where Severn was.

Mikhail had set about killing every demon until this Samiel stepped forward to stop the slaughter. In two weeks, he'd butchered thirty of the beasts, propped their heads on spikes, and left the gruesome display in the killing fields.

Still, nobody was talking, and Samiel remained elusive.

They should have given him up by now.

But he had a plan.

The demons had infiltrated angels. They'd destroyed Aerie and thousands of human lives in their act of terrorism. Mikhail was done following peace and order and Seraphim's Law. No more rules. No more lines angels did not cross. No more killing fields. Mikhail would take the war to their homes, to their streets.

London would witness the true power of a guardian. And Konstantin would die, watching everything he loved turn to dust.

Pre-order Eternal Sin, Primal Sin #2 today.

Infernal Sin, Primal Sin #3 (coming soon)

Ariana also writes sci-fi and fantasy as Pippa DaCosta. Visit her website at www.pippadacosta.com for more thrilling action, romance and adventure books.

ABOUT THE AUTHOR

Born to wolves, Rainbow Award winner Ariana Nash only ventures from the Cornish moors when the moon is fat and the night alive with myths and legends. She captures those myths in glass jars and returning home, weaves them into stories filled with forbidden desires, fantasy realms, and wicked delights.

Sign up to her newsletter and get a free ebook here: https://www.subscribepage.com/silk-steel